Praise for
Agatha award-winning author
M.D. Lake's
Peggy O'Neill Mysteries

Other Peggy O'Neill Mysteries by
M.D. Lake
from Avon Books

AMENDS FOR MURDER
COLD COMFORT
A GIFT FOR MURDER
MURDER BY MAIL
POISONED IVY

Once Upon a Crime

M.D. LAKE

AVON BOOKS ◆ NEW YORK

ONCE UPON A CRIME is an original publication of Avon Books. This work has never before appeared in book form. This work is a novel. Any similarity to actual persons or events is purely coincidental.

AVON BOOKS
A division of
The Hearst Corporation
1350 Avenue of the Americas
New York, New York 10019

Copyright © 1995 by Allen Simpson
Published by arrangement with the author
Library of Congress Catalog Card Number: 94-94473
ISBN: 0-380-77520-4

First Avon Books Printing: January 1995

AVON TRADEMARK REG. U.S. PAT. OFF. AND IN OTHER COUNTRIES, MARCA REGISTRADA, HECHO EN U.S.A.

Printed in the U.S.A.

RA   10   9   8   7   6   5   4   3   2   1

For Buck Mathison
who has enhanced the quality of my life
and the lives of many others
significantly

Acknowledgments

Thanks to Detective Jo Anne Benson of the University of Minnesota Police Department and Mancel Mitchell, chief of the St. Louis Park, Minnesota, Police Department, who answered all my questions about police work patiently and with good humor; to Dr. Lisa Schneider, who spared Peggy's spleen; and to Karal Ann Marling, professor of pop culture at the University of Minnesota, who listens to me whine, and laughs and laughs.

I am privileged to have friends like these.

One

If you've been paying attention, you'll know that in September I got hit on the head with a pistol and thrown down a flight of stairs. I expected to be burned alive too, but I got away with cracked ribs, a few stitches in my head, and something called "grade-two splenic lacerations." The surgeon, of course, wanted to remove the offending organ—he assured me the spleen serves no useful purpose—but I nixed the idea, pointing out that he'd initially diagnosed a wrist as broken when it was only sprained. Surgeons aren't gods and need to be reminded of it occasionally.

In retaliation, he refused to certify that I was well enough to go back to work until my spleen stopped sending out distress signals—about two months, he pronounced, godlike. I accepted that, since I was in too much pain to be of much use walking a beat anyway.

Two very unpleasant people had been taken off the streets, thanks to my efforts. However, I'd worked on the case against the orders of Lieutenant Bixler, so my request for disability leave with pay was denied. Bixler—who, like the spleen, serves no obviously useful purpose—also refused to find a desk job for me, something that's fairly routine when a cop is temporarily unable to walk a beat. Luckily, I'd accumulated a lot of sick time in the years I'd been a campus cop, and he couldn't deny me permission to use it.

I didn't know what to do with myself. I couldn't play racquetball or ride my bike, and my friends work during the day. My closest friend, Paula Henderson, had quit the campus cops to go to law school, and her fiancé, Lawrence Fitzpatrick, was spending his free time being a house husband while Paula studied, so I didn't see much of them either.

The surgeon wanted me to stay indoors for a month, but I considered that excessively cautious, and after a couple of weeks I started taking walks. I considered flying down to Belize where my old lover, Gary Mallory, had gone in search of the simple life and to write a book—a contradiction in terms, in my opinion, that's typical of men—but before I could make up my mind, he turned up on my doorstep.

"What are you doing here?" I greeted him, still in my bathrobe, holding a cup of coffee. I'd always worked the dog watch, from eleven p.m. until seven a.m., so I was usually sound asleep at that hour of the morning.

"Sandra told me you were badly hurt," he said, trying to take me into his arms.

I spilled coffee down his front as I backed away. "You could have called to make sure."

Sandra Carr, of course, is a very successful author of psychological thrillers, and she'd been Gary's lover before me. I'm very suspicious of old flames who show concern for the well-being of their successors. It's not natural.

"The doctor said no contact sports for at least a month," I added, and watched Gary's face fall. After all, he'd come a long way to comfort me.

"Are you still in pain?" he asked.

"Only when I breathe."

Gary's thirty-five, a little taller than me—I'm five-nine—and lean and wiry. He has a dark complexion, deep-set, dark brown eyes that make him look somber in a kind of haunted way—or vice versa—and a smile that's usually unexpected and always beautiful.

Regarding his two battered suitcases with suspicion as his taxi disappeared around the corner, I invited him in and gave him a cup of coffee. "What happened?" I asked. "Did the screaming of the howler monkeys in the high jungle canopy break the concentration a writer so desperately needs—or don't they have computer repair people in Eden?"

"You've been reading up on Belize," he accused, dodging the harder question.

"Maybe," I replied elusively.

"It wasn't the howler monkeys that drove me away," he said, "it was discovering that Belize has only the second largest continuous reef in the world. I've never been interested in the second best of anything," he added, with heavy emphasis.

I asked him if he planned to return to Belize and the raucous symphony of the jungle.

"Not anytime soon. The *Chronicle*'s offered me a job as a feature writer, at a salary I couldn't turn down." The *Chronicle*'s our largest newspaper. "I was wondering if you'd let me sleep on your couch until I find an apartment."

I thought about it for a long five seconds, then told him I could offer him better accommodations than that if he behaved himself.

Two weeks later Gary was still living at my place and showing no interest in looking for something of his own. But, of course, he was spending a lot of time getting into his new job, and it would have been cruel of me to make him go apartment hunting. That's what he said, at least.

Allowing him to stay temporarily seemed like a nice compromise between throwing him out and letting him move in for good, so I went along with it. Besides, it was nice having help paying the rent, since I was living off my savings. I gave him my spare bedroom—he's always taken pride in living in small spaces—and we agreed to share the living room, bathroom, cooking, and cleaning.

I walked a lot, slowly at first. It was a beautiful fall, one of the loveliest I've seen since I moved here after leaving the navy. Southern California, where I grew up, doesn't have anything to compare to fall, which is one reason I'd never live there again. I hope I never lose my wonder at the way the year dies so gorgeously, in mourning costumes of burgundy, gold, orange, and brown.

About a week after Gary moved in, I took the bus to the University and got off on the road below the Old Campus. I walked stiffly down the stairs to the river and strolled along the bank, watching squirrels getting ready for the winter, racing crews in sculls cutting sharply through the water, and canoes with languid lovers floating downstream.

Around two, I climbed back up to the University, intending to walk across campus to visit with some of my friends at police headquarters. The stairs were steeper than they'd seemed going down and when I reached the top, I sank gratefully into the grass and fallen leaves, to catch my breath and wait for the pain to go away. I rested my back against an old oak and stared up at the almost cloudless, light blue sky.

Another good thing about fall is that there aren't many bugs out and about, and those that are seem to have become, like reformed sinners in the old folks' home, more concerned with their spiritual than with their physical needs.

A loud rustling noise made me raise my head gingerly and peek around the tree. A man burst out of a bank of crimson sumac, laughing as he turned to look over his shoulder. A woman came rushing after him, her long hair flaring out behind her. She caught up with him—he wasn't moving very fast—and grabbed the arm he threw out to fend her off, stuck a foot out in front of him, and tripped him. He fell with a loud whoop, rolled over on his back, and she threw herself onto his stomach and straddled him. They were about five feet from me.

"You *want* me to move out, Christian?" she asked, staring down at him. "You *want* me to?"

"You know I don't," he said, shaking his head from side to side to get her hair out of his face.

"I didn't think so. So what's the problem?"

He clasped his hands behind his head and stared up at

her. "Sometimes I don't think it's fair," he answered. "Not to you and—"

She placed her hand over his mouth. "You don't get to decide what's fair to me, Christian. I love living with you, and being with you. And—I know I'm not supposed to, but I do—I love the way other women look at me when we go places together." She giggled. "They're *totally* green with envy, and the looks on their faces practically scream, 'Why's he dating the ugly duckling?' It just cracks me up sometimes."

The man laughed. "You're not a duck, Pia, you're a swan."

"Quack, quack," she said. "Which means flattery will get you anywhere—in the duck pond, at least." She stood up, still straddling him, jutted out a hip, and primped her hair. Then she stepped away and said, "We'll talk about it again when the season's over, okay?"

He got up too, and took her hands and looked down at her. He was a lot taller than she was, probably a little over six feet, lean and long-legged. His hair was thick and blond and curled around his head like the hair of a young man in a Renaissance painting. She was thin and pale, with delicate features and long, shoulder-length hair of no particular color.

"Okay," he said, like a little boy who's been given a stern talking-to. Then he looked at his watch. "Hey, I'm gonna be late for practice. Gotta run."

"You have a class," she said.

"Coach scheduled an extra practice for this afternoon. 'Bye." He gave her a hug and then took off running with the easy grace that had made him a campus hero.

"You're supposed to be a *scholar*-athlete, Christian," she hollered after him in a despairing voice. "Don't you listen to President Hightower's speeches?"

He called back over his shoulder: "Hey, don't I have a B average, almost?"

"Yeah—almost." And to herself she muttered, "Bringing the team average up to passing—almost."

She hitched her book bag up on her shoulder, turned and came trudging over to the tree I was leaning against.

"You *could* have made some noise, you know," she said, looking down at me sternly. "Like, blown your nose or coughed or something."

"I would have, except I knew you saw me," I replied. "Relationships are strange things, aren't they?"

She gave me a startled look and then burst out laughing. "You don't know the half of it."

Well, I thought I did. "I watched your Christian win Saturday's game about twenty times on television," I told her.

She gave me an incredulous look. "You're a football fan?"

"No, but the guy living with me is—at least, when his team's winning. He was watching the game and I happened to be passing through the room just as they were lining up for that last play. He exhorted me to stay with him and hold his hand. I don't understand how anybody can be that cool under such pressure." I meant Christian Donnelly, the quarterback, not Gary, the fair-weather fan, who'd been biting his nails in anguish.

She shrugged, as if the question didn't interest her much. "I've seen you on television too," she said. "You're that campus cop who almost got burned to a crisp by a couple of seriously defective human beings. You must be sort of cool under pressure yourself."

Cool wasn't exactly the word I'd use for what I'd been—especially as the heat started to melt the soles of my tennis shoes. A television reporter who's had it in for me for years managed to sneak into the hospital with her cameraman and tried to interview me before a nurse charged in and chased them out.

"My name's Pia Austin, by the way, and you're Peggy O'Neill. Professor Silberman, my adviser, told me all about you. She said you were her best student until I came along."

I laughed and said records were meant to be broken.

Edith Silberman had been my adviser when I was an undergraduate at the U. She'd also been my favorite teacher, and after I'd graduated we'd stayed friends. She was proud of me, but thought I should be more than just a campus cop, although she didn't know what. That made two of us.

Pia asked me if it was really true that I always took the night patrol because I wanted it. I admitted it.

" 'Peggy O'Neill, avenger—avengeress?—who stalks evildoers by night,' " she said in a deep, hollow voice. In her own voice, she added, "Don't you get lonely?"

I told her I liked it. I asked her where she was going and she said to the library. I was going that way too.

"But first I have to take care of a little business," she said.

She sat down on a bench, dug into her book bag, and got out a little black case. I winced as she pricked her finger with the glucometer. When she'd checked the results, she returned the case to her bag and we continued on across the campus.

Two

Pia Austin was a senior, a humanities major working on her *summa* thesis. She had a heart-shaped face, a stubborn chin that offset the delicacy of her nose and mouth, and a pale complexion that, in soft light, seemed to glow like porcelain. Holding these contradictions together and giving them a fragile unity were her dark, intelligent eyes. She wasn't conventionally beautiful, but she was beautiful anyway.

I admired Christian Donnelly for his taste in women. As a campus cop, I'd witnessed the abuse varsity athletes are capable of inflicting on women, and I found it remarkable that the football team's quarterback didn't seem to fit the stereotype.

I asked her what her thesis was about.

"I'm translating some of the correspondence between Hans Christian Andersen and a Danish woman named Henriette Wulff into English. You've never heard of her, of course," she added with a sigh. "The only reason she's of interest to anybody now is because she was Andersen's closest friend."

"Lovers?" I asked, because the subject was on my mind. "I thought he had a thing for Jenny Lind, the Swedish Nightingale." I wanted to show Pia that I knew something about the guy. I'd seen the movie.

She laughed. "No! I mean, yes, he had a thing for Jenny Lind, but no, he and Jette Wulff weren't lovers. Jette—that was her nickname—loved Andersen, but I'm not sure she ever thought about sex at all, with him or with anybody else. She loved him like a brother."

Hard to believe, I thought, in this day and age. "What about him?"

"Oh, he thought about sex sometimes. He 'wrestled with erotic thoughts'—that was the way he put it in his diaries—but not with her. They never even called each other by their first names," Pia added sadly. "It just wasn't done for people of the opposite sex to use first names if they weren't related in those days."

"Maybe we should return to that convention," I said. "Think how erotic it would be, when you were finally permitted to speak someone's first name. It's odd," I added, "talking about the sex life of a children's author."

"Oh, Andersen was a lot more than a children's author," she said. "Not that that excuses snooping around in his private life, of course. He wrote plays and novels and travel books too, and his stories were written as much for adults as for children—though you wouldn't know it from most English translations, which stink. In Denmark he's as big as Shakespeare is here. Bigger, probably, since every Dane reads Andersen, but I don't think very many Americans read Shakespeare. You probably haven't heard about the Hans Christian Andersen symposium they're having here next month, have you?"

I told her that, what with one thing and another, I'd missed the news of that one.

"It's called 'Hans Christian Andersen: Yesterday, Today, and Tomorrow,' and it's going to last a whole week. Scholars from all over the world are coming to talk about children's literature, and pick over poor Andersen's bones, literary and otherwise. It's in honor of the new children's library. You've heard about that, haven't you?"

I'd missed that, too.

"That's where I'm going now," she said.

We stopped at the bottom steps of the old library, a sprawling building of gray granite that always reminded me of a ship sinking slowing into a sea of ivy. I said goodbye, intending to continue on to campus police headquarters, where I planned to kill an hour or so catching up on the gossip.

Pia started to turn away and then, hesitantly, turned back and asked, "You want to see something exciting?"

"Nothing *too* exciting, I hope," I said, trying unsuccessfully to hide a grin.

She grinned too, slightly embarrassed. "Okay, not too exciting. Maybe you won't even think it's exciting at all. C'mon."

I figured the kind of excitement you find in a library might be just what I needed.

Pia led the way into the familiar old building. I followed her down the softly lit hall and around a corner to a set of doors that hadn't been there when I'd been a student. Next to them, a brass plaque read: "The Lund-Donnelly Children's Library."

"Gustav Lund is Christian's grandfather," she told me as we walked into the new wing of the library. It still smelled of fresh paint and plaster, and was better lit than the old library. "You probably didn't know that."

"You mean the children's library is named after Christian and his grandfather?" I asked innocently.

"No, of course not!" She turned to see if I was serious. When she realized I wasn't, she gave me the first of what would be several months of stern looks. "The University had been trying to get money for a children's library for years," she told me, "but the legislature wouldn't fund it. They finally did cough up some money, but it wasn't enough. Gus donated the difference, so they named the library after him and his daughter, Denise Donnelly, who's Christian's mom."

"They must be very rich."

"They are. Gus—Gustav Lund—owns Nordic Imports. It's probably the biggest importer of Scandinavian furniture in the country."

Halfway down the hall, she stopped in front of a door

and used a key to open it. A wooden plaque on the wall said it was the Hans Christian Andersen Room.

As she ushered me in, she said, "Christian's grandfather paid for this too—Christian's mom made him do it. If the University wanted his money, they had to stick this room right in the middle of the new children's library. It's appropriate in a way, of course, since Andersen was the start of high-quality children's literature."

"I thought the Grimm brothers were."

"They just collected folk tales. Andersen's stories were original, except for the first few."

It was a large high-ceilinged room panelled in dark oak, its walls cluttered with little pictures, and bookcases filled with leatherbound volumes. A small granite and bronze statuette I recognized as *The Little Mermaid* sat on a table next to the wall as we came in.

Above a chair on the wall opposite the door was a large oil portrait of a man with hooded eyes, dandyish mustache, small pursed mouth, and cleft chin. The high fur collar of his dark coat framed his head.

"That's Andersen," Pia said.

"I thought he was supposed to look kind of like a geek."

"He did. That portrait was painted when he was young and the artist tried to make him look like Romantic poets were supposed to look, but the only thing he got right were the eyes. Andersen's eyelids drooped. By painting him straight on like that, the artist hid his big beak of a nose. Andersen liked this painting a lot. He thought it looked just like him. Or hoped it did, anyway."

"Is it an original?"

"Oh, no, the original's in Denmark," she replied. "This is a copy Christian's mother found in Denmark someplace."

"She must be quite a fan of Andersen's."

"She's a Danophile. She collects almost anything Danish, if it's old or corny enough. But she specializes in Hans Christian Andersen. She named Christian after him."

I wondered what Andersen would make of a football game.

Next to the chair under the Andersen portrait was a bronze stork balanced on one leg. I went over and examined it. "It looks malevolent," I said. I've never liked birds—mostly, I think, because they watch you with only one eye. I expect full attention, even from birds.

"People who knew Andersen said he looked like a stork," Pia explained. "Maybe that's why it was his favorite bird."

I soon learned that Pia's most casual conversation was laced with information about Hans Christian Andersen's or Henriette Wulff's life.

"What are these?" I was standing in front of a wall of framed pictures, silhouettes of scary faces, ballet dancers, birds, a heart with a gallows on top of it and a hanging man.

"Papercuts," she answered, reaching up to straighten one of the pictures, "like those hearts we used to make as kids by folding a piece of paper and cutting out half a heart and unfolding it and getting the whole thing."

"It was the only way mine were ever symmetrical," I said. "I also did really skinny Christmas trees."

She laughed. "Mine were squat, sort of like jagged fire hydrants. Well, Andersen's paper cuts were about a zillion times more complex than that, as you can see. Look at this one." She pointed to one that was a delicate lacy pattern of hearts, swans, storks, and ballet dancers, and a man with a top hat bowing to a woman in a ball gown. "He made them to entertain the kids of his rich and influential friends. He'd cut out dancing figures and set them on tables and tell stories about them as he made them dance." Pia sighed, her eyes moving over the papercuts. "Can you imagine a man doing something like that today, Peggy? Well, maybe with uniformed figures holding guns, of course. Bang, bang!"

"Are these originals?"

She made a face. "Huh-unh. None of them are. Christian's mom copied them from a book of Andersen's art. She taught herself how to do it. She's probably as good at it as Andersen was. Christian says she used to make them for him when he was a little kid."

I looked around the room. "So everything in here is fake," I said.

Pia gave me a conspiratorial smirk. "You think so? Come over here!"

"Do I have to close my eyes?"

"No!" She pulled me over to a glass-enclosed display case in the middle of the room. A poster on the side of it said, in old-fashioned script: "My Dear Sisterly Friend," and under that, in block letters: "The Lost Letters of Hans Christian Andersen to Henriette Wulff."

The inside was lined with dark satin and on it were displayed a small oil portrait of a woman, an old photograph of a man in a stovepipe hat like Abraham Lincoln always seemed to wear, two old books, and some brownish letters and envelopes. I recognized Andersen's name on the covers of the books, the rest was in a foreign language I assumed was Danish.

I took a closer look at the old photograph. "That's Andersen, isn't it?" There was handwriting across the bottom.

"Uh-huh," Pia said. "It's inscribed and autographed to Jette Wulff. That's Jette." She pointed to the oil portrait.

It was of a young woman in a ruffled bonnet and matching collar, staring straight at me, her head cocked slightly to one side. At first all I noticed were the eyes. They were unusually large and beautiful, and seemed to see right through me—which might have been why her wide mouth seemed to hover on the point of smiling.

"She has your eyes," I said to Pia. "Is she a relative?"

She laughed disdainfully at my ignorance. "No, but I wish she was. I think we're related spiritually."

"She's beautiful," I said. "How come Andersen didn't marry her?"

She sighed. "Nobody wanted to marry her. The question

never even came up. You see, Jette Wulff was small and hunchbacked."

I stood there for a minute, digesting that while trying not to smile at Pia's solemnity. "So tell me what's exciting about all this," I said finally.

"Not the portrait of Jette, that's just a copy Mrs. Donnelly had made for the display. The wonderful things are the letters. They're real. They were lost for almost a hundred and fifty years and then, a little over a year ago, Mrs. Donnelly found them in a pile of junk in an antique store. She rescued them just before they were going to go into a landfill."

She pointed to a brass plate on the case that read "The gift of Denise Lund Donnelly."

"They must be quite valuable," I said.

Before she could reply, a frantic tapping made us look up. A large bearded head had appeared in the room's single window, the nose flattened against the pane, an expression of desperation in the eyes, and then it slowly sank out of sight below the sill.

"Oh, Sam!" She went over, unlocked the window, and pushed it up. Leaning out, she said, "I don't suppose it would occur to you to come through the door, like everybody else, would it?"

The head appeared again. "Of course not," it said. "I'm not like everybody else," and dropped out of sight again.

I went over and joined Pia at the window. A man was standing on the lawn below us, breathing hard, his face tilted up, legs wide apart, and hands on his hips. "Besides," he added, "you know how I loathe libraries. I'm allergic to dust, silences, and books that sit primly on shelves with their covers pressed chastely together. Pia, you know I wouldn't bother you, except we're in sore need of an emperor, and you *have* to play the part—just for today, just for an hour or two. Please!"

"Can't Sam. I'm way too busy. What happened to Andy?"

"He called about an hour ago, said he'd come down

with the ague. Sounded like it, too, but you never know with him—he's a good actor and I've heard him do a convincing hacking cough, night after night, playing a dying poet in a lugubrious tragedy. It wasn't his fault the play bombed, I'm sure. In the meantime, we're stuck. The rest of the cast is there, milling about. You know actors, Pia— when they stand around for long periods, without direction, they get moody and mutinous. And what's the good of a moody—My God, is the room on fire?"

"What?" Pia spun around to look. I didn't bother, because he was looking at me.

"He means my hair," I told her.

"I thought it was fire," he said. "Who are you?"

"Not an actor. Who are you?"

"Samuel J. Allen, playwright, director, and—if the part's right and the pay's good—actor too. You are to call me Sam. What am I to call you?"

I told him. He was about thirty, tall and heavyset, but not fat. His eyes were small and round and stared out of the black curly hair that covered his face like some startled animal in a thicket.

"What a lovely name!" he exclaimed. "Peggy O'Neill. Somebody should write a song about it." He hummed a snatch of the one somebody had written. "Be that as it may, I don't need an actor—God forbid, an actor's the *last* thing I need! If you've been paying attention, you'll know I've got an actor, one who's temporarily indisposed, or pretending to be. What I need is somebody to read said actor's lines." He pointed an entire large, long arm up at me and said, "In a word, Uncle Sam wants you."

"Sorry," I said, "I—"

"Oh, do it, Peggy!" Pia exclaimed. "You'll probably be great. You sounded great on television when you were in the hospital."

"Because I thought I was dying," I said. "What do I have to do?" I asked Sam, suspiciously.

"Hospital?" he repeated. "Dying?"

When Pia explained, he said, "Ah! That accounts for

your rather tentative arm movements. I wondered about that, thought you might be partially paralyzed. All you have to do is read the lines—no unusual physical activity required. Your wounds don't preclude reading, do they? So come on, you're holding up the show. I'll lift you out the window."

"Go, Peggy," Pia said.

I was bored with my life anyway, Gary didn't get home until after six and it was his turn to fix dinner, so what did I have to lose?

"Not through the window, though," I said.

Three

It was after three as I followed Sam Allen down the Mall. He explained that he was putting on a Hans Christian Andersen play to satisfy one of the requirements for a Master of Fine Arts in directing. "I'm doing Andersen at Pia's urging," he said. "For the symposium next month, you know. All the actors, set and costume designers are students who'll be getting course credit for the play."

At the end of the Mall, we entered an old building that had once housed the Theater Arts Department, until the University, in a brief period of prosperity, built a new theater building on the New Campus on the other side of the river. The old building became a general classroom building—dingy and poorly lit, suitable only for liberal arts classes in an age of brutality.

Sam led me into the little theater in the middle of it and down one of the aisles to the stage. "Rise and kneel, everybody," he hollered. "We have an emperor for the day!"

The people standing or sitting in little groups on the stage turned and looked at me.

"Looks more like an empress," one of the actresses said, looking me up and down. "You seem a bit confused, darling, and you don't look as though Sam found you through Central Casting."

"I had the misfortune of being in his line of sight when he came looking for an emperor," I said.

"You're not an actor," an actor said accusingly.

"Her name's Peggy O'Neill," Sam said, "and she's a campus cop, so watch yourselves. And don't jostle her, either, she was wounded performing heroic deeds. And now that you know everything you need to know about her, we will move on. If she shows promise, I might create a minor part for her as a reward." Turning to me, he said admonishingly, "But you'll have to be very, very good, Peggy, and there are no guarantees. Places, people! If you're not on now, go sit down!"

Sam shoved a script into my hands. "Just read it the way an emperor would. You'll be fine."

"You mind telling me what the play's about?"

"Ha!" several actors exclaimed.

"Hm!" Sam put a long finger up alongside his nose and looked down at me, considering. "Should I?"

"Sam doesn't believe in telling his actors too much," somebody said. "He thinks it inhibits spontaneity."

"At least tell me if it's a comedy or a tragedy."

"We can but hope the audience thinks it's a comedy," Sam said. "However, *you* aren't to know that. You're an emperor, after all, however *pro tem,* and emperors don't approve of comedy—especially at their own expense. And neither do the people with whom he surrounds himself."

"It's Hans Christian Andersen's 'Emperor's New Clothes,' " somebody called out from the stage, "in an adaptation by Samuel J. Allen, whom you have before you in the flesh."

"Adaptation, hell!" somebody else said. "Sam's stretched a three-page fairy tale into a play that lasts over an hour."

"I've merely realized what's latent in the story," Sam retorted. "I've added nothing that Hans Christian Andersen wouldn't have heartily applauded, had he been here. Indeed, I often feel his sweet presence as I flesh out his ideas, and on several occasions I've even heard him smack his head and exclaim 'I wish I'd thought of that!' "

He looked at his watch. "However, the play'll seem much longer than an hour if we don't rehearse. Peggy, stand in front of the mirror over there behind the throne and preen yourself. You like what you see. Show it. Swell up with self-esteem."

"Study Sam," somebody suggested.

The sets hadn't been built yet, so all we had to work with was furniture and a few props that Sam had scrounged from the Theater Department. In the middle of the stage area was a large, elaborately carved oak chair. Next to it, and slightly behind it, was a floor-length mirror. I went over and stood by it and watched what took place behind me reflected in it, feeling like an idiot and cursing myself for having agreed to this.

Nobody was wearing a costume, of course, but from the context I figured out that some of the actors were court jesters juggling and tumbling and generally carrying on as the emperor—me—postured in front of the mirror.

Two court officials entered at the left and stood to one side of the stage near the front. They looked at me in a disapproving manner and began to talk about how my vanity and great love of finery were having an adverse effect on the entire kingdom.

From the right of the stage came the emperor's wife, who began complaining to her confidante about how her husband was neglecting her. She sighed a great deal and the confidante tsk-ed and offered witty advice.

Two guards came in then and thumped their spears on the floor, which was my cue to turn and ask them what they wanted.

They informed me that two weavers were outside who wanted an audience. I gave the mirror one last look, then sprawled on my throne and ordered the guards to show them in. I tried to speak my lines in a voice at least as low as the average of the male actors in the play. Since most of them were undergraduates, that wasn't hard.

Enter the two swindlers, bowing and scraping and pretending to be weavers. After going through a great deal of pantomime, they came to the point and told me about their wonderful cloth—cloth that was not only exquisitely beautiful, but also had the remarkable quality of being invisible to anyone who was stupid or unfit for his job.

Sam broke into the rehearsal often to direct the actors' movements and placement on the stage, change their way of saying lines, and, sometimes, even revise lines. At one point, he rushed up to the two actors playing the swindlers and, grabbing one of them and shaking him, hollered: "You're not evil enough! Don't you understand, you're playing on the insecurities and self-doubts of people who run a kingdom! You're feeding them the words they'll soon think are their own, filling their minds with lies they'll gradually learn to swear to themselves are true!"

Sam spoke one of the swindler's lines the way he thought the actor should speak it, oily and insinuating: " 'You're a man of great discrimination and experience, my lord, but be honest: When have your eyes ever been so dazzled by patterns as original as these? Where have you ever seen colors so rich, working together in such perfect harmony?'

"The evil," he continued in his own voice, "is that *there's nothing there!* No patterns, no colors—nothing! And you," he went on, swivelling abruptly and aiming a finger at an actor playing one of the ministers, "you must show doubts at first, but little by little must let yourself be convinced—convinced that nothing is something wonderful."

He stalked around the poor actor. "After all," he went on, "if you can't see what the swindlers tell you is there, then you must be unfit for your job, mustn't you? And that's unthinkable!" Panting, he backed off the stage. "Now get on with it!"

It took about two hours to go through the play. I did my best to get into my part, in order to make it as real as possible for the real actors. After a while, I started to enjoy it and, before long, I almost forgot I was only there temporarily.

Sam finally gave us a break and, as the actors drifted

outside, he told me I'd done pretty well. "If I create a role for you, will you play it?"

"Sam, this is so sudden! Why?"

"Because, Peggy, as you were reading the emperor's lines, and starting to enjoy yourself—don't deny it!—it occurred to me that Hans Christian Andersen and I forgot an important character: A cop, a representative of law and order, who also—after a brief struggle—lets himself be gulled by the two swindlers just like everybody else. Will you do it?"

I laughed, and almost surprised myself when I replied, "I guess so, as long as it doesn't call for anything strenuous for a while."

"Good!" He ran his fingers through his beard and stared hard at me, looking a little like Rasputin. "The red hair is going to have to go, I'm afraid."

"Forget it," I said.

He rolled his eyes. "Nobody seems to understand anymore that great art requires great sacrifices! Well, we'll see. Now, rehearsals start every day at three, go until six. The play opens Saturday, November third, and runs four weekends." He gave me a hard look. "This isn't just a whim, is it, Peggy, one you'll regret?"

"I never regret my whims," I told him.

Four

"How'd you manage that?" Gary asked that night, when I told him about it. He was sprawled on the couch, his laptop on his stomach.

"Talent and hard work," I said, "and never losing sight of my dream. Knowing the right people helped too, of course."

"And whom do you know?" he asked dryly.

"Christian Donnelly's girlfriend."

"The quarterback?" He sat up, put aside his laptop. "You're kidding! What's he got to do with theater, and how'd you meet him?"

When I'd told him the whole story, he said, "So the BMOC's girlfriend is the scholarly type, huh? You'd think he'd choose someone who spent more of her time putting on makeup than studying. At least, that was the impression I got of the varsity jocks' girlfriends when I was a student. Of course, jealousy might have warped my judgment."

"The little I saw of him," I said, "he seems like a nice guy. As you know, I distrust handsome men."

"Thanks!"

"For what—trusting or distrusting you?"

"It sounded like they were talking about breaking up, when you eavesdropped on them?"

"I wasn't eavesdropping," I snapped. "I couldn't quite figure out what they were talking about, but it sounded like the subject had come up."

"Maybe, now that he's starting to get national attention,

he's under pressure to find a more appropriate girlfriend. Thank God I'm resisting all calls to greatness."

I went over to reassure him that, even though I was on my way to stardom, he still had a place in my heart.

Later, he asked me if I wanted to go out for dinner. "I forgot to stop at the store on the way home," he said, "and I couldn't think of anything I wanted to fix tonight anyway."

It's strange: Before he went to Belize, Gary insisted on fixing healthy, balanced meals—all four or five food groups, or however many there are—whenever I ate over at his place, and he deplored my devotion to the microwave. Now that we were living together, sort of, he had no more interest in planning and fixing meals than I did.

I went to a cupboard and pulled out a package of ramen noodles—I keep a stack of them, all flavors, for emergencies. "I think there's a red pepper and some scallions in the fridge that aren't too old," I told him. "Bring them over here and I'll show you how to turn ramen noodles into a tasty, possibly nourishing meal. There're mushrooms too. Check 'em for mold."

Reluctantly, he dragged himself into the kitchen.

Sam Allen, true to his word, had added a policeman—his idea of a cop in a fantasy empire—to the play, and given her some good lines. I say "her," but actually the cop was quite androgynous. I wore pantaloons and a wig, but in no other way did I look like any of the male characters. The part called for me to be shrewd, opportunistic, and ambitious: I took my cues from my superiors, who took theirs from the swindlers. I like to think it was a stretch for me.

I discovered there was nothing unusual about Sam adding a new character, since—much to everybody's distress—he showed up at just about every rehearsal with new or revised scenes that forced us to learn new lines and stage directions and forget old ones.

Because of my tender spleen and sore ribs, I had to be careful not to make too many sudden moves at first, and between the times when I was on stage, I stayed off my feet as much as I could. It was challenging and fun, and the month we had for rehearsal passed all too quickly. I figured the doctor would certify that I was able to return to work about midway through the play's run, but I knew I could find somebody to take the dog watch for me the nights the play was being performed.

I discovered that acting is much harder than just lying, which I'm good at. With lying you can usually measure how well you're doing immediately; with acting you have to wait for the reviews. Sam was a good director, who seemed able to bring out the best in the talent he had to work with, including me. There were all kinds of snags— scenery collapsing or not being what Sam had in mind, costumes not ready on time, actors who got sick or forgot their lines—but although Sam hollered and carried on, he never got angry or lost control.

I sometimes dropped in on Pia Austin in the Andersen Room of the new children's library. She told me she was looking forward to the Hans Christian Andersen symposium because her father had been invited to give the keynote speech. He was a professor of Danish literature at the University of Copenhagen and probably the most distinguished Hans Christian Andersen scholar in the world. She hadn't seen him in over three years.

"You come by your interest in Andersen naturally," I said.

She smiled and said she guessed so.

One of the first things I asked her, of course, was how she and Christian had got together. She smiled, activated the screen saver on her computer, and told me about it.

"We met at a summer language camp when we were kids," she said. "Danish camp, naturally. You know how those are, you pretend you're really in Denmark, use Danish money to buy stuff and have to ask for what you want in Danish and sing Danish folk songs and make craftsy Danish things. It's corny but kind of fun when you're a kid. I was born in Denmark, but Mom left my dad when I was seven and she and I moved here—she's from here originally. She never wanted to speak Danish with me, so I had to go to Danish camp to keep from losing it."

Pia had managed to describe a mini-tragedy in two sentences.

She shrugged and watched the fireworks on her computer screen for a moment. "Anyway, Christian and I became friends—we even have the same birthdate, a year apart. He stopped coming to camp after a few years, when he was about fourteen." She made a face. "His dad wanted him to go to football camps instead. But we stayed friends. I even used to go to his high school football games sometimes, even though we didn't go to the same school.

"He was like a dancer, even back then," she said, her face lighting up suddenly. "I once tried to talk him into taking dance—just trying it, you know—but he refused. He said it was sissy stuff." She shook her head disgustedly.

"Naturally he always had lots of girls hanging around in high school, but he invited me to come along too, sometimes, when they went to parties after a game. And we exchanged cards on our birthday. His friends couldn't understand what he saw in me—just like now. I was a year older than him, so maybe they thought he liked me because of my great sophistication." She giggled. "When I came to the U, we kind of lost track of each other for a while. Then last year, on the first day of class, he and a bunch of other football players marched into the Hans Christian Andersen classroom! I was the professor's reader-grader—and I almost fell over with surprise!"

"It's hard to imagine the football team taking a course in Hans Christian Andersen," I said. "Wouldn't that be sissy stuff too?"

"Sure, but every undergraduate has to take a certain number of courses in foreign culture, you know, and the Andersen course, which is taught in English, counts towards that requirement. The athletes have advisers who keep track of courses that are Mickey Mouse enough for them to pass—you know how big President Hightower is on the myth of the 'scholar-athlete'—and the Andersen course is way up on the list. That was the only way Christian could get the other football players to take the course, because it's a Mickey. He took it because he knew it would please his mom, who's a real Danish freak.

"So anyway, all these gigantic guys come thudding into the classroom and Professor Claussen, when he walked in and saw them all squeezed into these little chairs in the back of the classroom, he got this look of horror on his face. It was like his worst nightmare had come true."

Pia laughed, then sat back in her chair and nibbled the skin on a finger thoughtfully for a moment. "About halfway through the course, Christian asked me out—just the two of us, I mean, not with a crowd. Well!" She gave me her stern look. "Since I was the TA for the course—which means I did all the grading—I was a little suspicious, as you can imagine. I told him no—using conflict of interest as my excuse. 'What do I have to do to get a date with you?' he asked me. 'Get an A for the course,' I told him. 'Okay,' he said. And he did."

"Well, since it's a Mickey Mouse . . ."

"Ah, but Peggy, it's easy to get a passing grade—up to a B. That's how Claussen fills the Andersen class, with students who only want a passing grade. But to get an A, you have to do extra work and write a paper. That was my decision, by the way. Claussen couldn't care less, he'd give A's to anybody who asked, if it was up to him.

"Things come easy to Christian," she went on, her face clouding over, "when he wants something." Thoughtful pause. "Anyway, the day after I posted the final grades, he showed up at my office with tickets to a sold-out rock concert that everybody in town would've killed for.

"And that's how we got together. Now, I suppose, it's me who has the ulterior motive for wanting to date *him*, now that he's the big jock hero." She gave me an impish grin. "I'm the envy of half the women on campus—at least. It's sort of like an Andersen fairy tale, isn't it? 'The Little Mermaid,' maybe. Except that I *got* the prince, whereas all the mermaid got was the possibility of an immortal soul after three hundred years—or sooner, depending on how many little children make their parents happy. Shudder, shudder."

"Pia," I said, "you've got Hans Christian Andersen on the brain and frankly, I think it's sickening."

She laughed, only slightly abashed. "Well, Andersen just kind of gets to you after a while. I was the reader-grader for the Andersen course two years in a row, which meant I had to attend every single one of Professor Claussen's classes, even though he never changes his lectures."

"How'd you get to be the reader-grader for the course? You're only a senior."

She made a disgusting noise. "Right, but I've been taking graduate-level courses since I was a junior, my honors thesis is about Andersen, and I read Danish—not that that's so necessary, but it looked good on the application. Besides, there aren't so many graduate students in Scandinavian studies anymore, who would usually be the reader-graders for courses like that. Claussen got permission to hire me by pretending he'd supervise my work very closely. That was a joke. He should have somebody supervising *his!*"

I asked her why she'd spent her summers at Danish camp when she was a kid, instead of in Denmark with her father.

She looked down at the papers on her desk. "Daddy always spends the summers travelling—Spain, Italy, places like that. He never wanted a kid along—especially after I got diabetes. He doesn't like sickness. He's never been sick a day in his life, he says."

"But doesn't he have a family you could've stayed with?" It was none of my business, but I've got a somewhat morbid interest in families.

"Not really. Just an older sister he wasn't close to—she's dead now. For a while, there was his third wife, the one after my mom, but we didn't get along." She shrugged indifferently.

"So you went to Danish camp instead of Denmark."

"Yeah." She glanced away, chewed hair, then glanced back at me with a forced smile. "You going to do the 'dysfunctional family' bit on me?"

"God, no! Are you?"

"God, no!"

"It got you Christian, anyway."

Her cheeks turned a little pink but she smiled and there was mischief in her eyes when she replied. "You sound as though you think that's a little weird, Peggy. You probably think he ought to be hanging out with a pod of top-heavy blond bimbos instead of with me."

"I was also wondering what you see in him," I said. I didn't say so, but I thought Pia had the kind of beauty that only gets greater with age—after men have dumped them for trophy brides thirty years their junior, who go better with their blond furniture, giant screen TVs, and high blood pressure.

"He's a sweet guy," she said. "Maybe, being a cop, you've just got a stereotyped image of male athletes."

"I do. I've had enough experience to know that the stereotype fits at least eighty-five percent of the football players. I'm glad Christian's in the other fifteen percent."

"Me, too," Pia said, and laughed. "Now, suppose you tell me about you, Peggy. You're what—thirty? Thirty-five? And you're not married. Have you ever been?"

"Never."

"Why not? Are you gay?"

"Huh-unh. I don't know why not."

"Ever come close?"

Pia's large eyes and serious, almost solemn face seemed to demand a thoughtful answer and, after all, she'd answered all my nosy questions. "Not really," I told her. "A man wanted me to marry him once a couple of years ago, but he also wanted me to be a mom to his fourteen-year-old son, and I didn't want that. But maybe that was just an excuse not to marry him."

"Well, was it or wasn't it?"

"It wasn't. I didn't want to inherit the problems he took away with him from his first marriage."

Josh—the boy in question—was almost seventeen now, I realized. I saw him occasionally, zipping around Lake Eleanor on his in-line skates, only a few years younger than Christian. He sometimes recognized me and smiled and waved, sometimes didn't. He'd be going off to college soon himself—and if I'd married Al, Josh would have been gone and that objection to marrying his father gone with it. Ah, well, you pays yer money and you takes yer chances, as my mother says on her good days, when recalling the opportunities she's lost.

I saw Al sometimes too. He'd been important in my life for a couple of years and there was still a place in me where he and I lived on, like video memories in a cassette. I didn't think he felt the same thing about me. He'd gone back and married the woman I'd taken him away from in the first place—Dierdre, or Deirdre or however it's spelled—and he always looked a little uncomfortable when we met, not the uncomfortable look of somebody whose heart I'd broken, but of somebody who just didn't know what to say to me anymore.

I felt Pia's large eyes on me, watching me. "So tell me about Gary," she said. "You love him as much as you loved Al?"

"I didn't say I loved Al."

"You loved him," she said flatly. "You just didn't want to become a mother as part of a divorce settlement. Right?"

"Right!"

"Have you had many lovers, Peggy?"

A slightly pleasanter subject. "Not as many as the men who think I've had too many think I've had. How about you?"

"Christian's my first."

"Are you going to marry him?"

She poked a loose strand of hair in her mouth and chewed on it as her eyes roamed around the ceiling. "Someday, maybe," she replied airily. "I sort of like the idea of being married to a professional football player. Of course, he'd be away a lot during the season, but then we'd have half a year when he didn't have to do anything. That's better than being married to somebody who's away from home five days a week just about every week during the best part of the day, isn't it? We'd have lots of money," she went on dreamily, "and travel a lot. I'm going to write books, and I can do that anywhere."

"All this requires that your football player husband become a star," I said. I couldn't help smiling at how she'd planned out hers and Christian's life.

"Oh, Christian's going to be a star, everybody knows that!"

"Aren't football players under a lot of pressure to live wild lives when they're on the road and away from their wives?"

"In a lot of ways," she said, "Christian isn't like other football players." Her eyes danced at me and away and then she laughed. "Now quit always changing the subject back to me. Tell me about you and Gary. How long have you been living together and what are your plans?"

"We aren't living together, exactly. Gary's only staying with me until he gets a place of his own."

"Uh-huh."

Pia was unusually sensitive to tones of voice.

"He's nice to come home to," I went on, slightly irritated. "Besides, he goes out of town a lot on assignment, and I work nights, so it's not like I'm going to be coming home to him every night."

"That would be terrible, wouldn't it?" she said, laughing openly at me.

Five

I didn't see much of Christian, since the football schedule took up most of his time, but I heard a lot about him, and sometimes saw clips of him on sports shows that Gary watched late at night. For once, the University team was winning more than it was losing, and the experts, such as Gary, attributed that in large part to Christian's quarterbacking skills.

Although I liked Christian, I couldn't bring myself to watch him play on television. I've never been able to tell one football game from another, or which team, or player, is which. Although Gary tried to explain to me Christian's athletic genius, the way the ball seemed to float through the air when he threw it—"as though it has wings, and eyes of its own," he gushed—and his ability to dance away from enormous men from the opposing team who seemed bent on killing him, I couldn't work up any enthusiasm for it. I can't get interested in games in which inflicting pain is rewarded.

The team had a good chance to be invited to one or another post-season bowl game for the first time in years, so football mania was gathering steam on campus and in the sports pages of the newspapers. Christian was involved in a lot of the media hype, which contrasted dramatically with what Pia, his girlfriend, was doing in her world, the world of Hans Christian Andersen. According to Pia, professional scouts already had their eyes on Christian, even though he was only a junior.

Sometimes Pia would come across campus to the old theater and she, Sam, and I would walk over to the student union for coffee after rehearsal. Christian joined us occasionally, usually looking a little banged up, with bandages here and there on his elbows and face.

Strangely enough, I enjoyed being around them. I was the oldest of the group, of course, but Pia had adopted me as a friend and that was good enough for Christian. Sam was only a few years younger than I, if that, so he knew something about decrepitude. I enjoyed his sense of humor a lot, and his ironic view of life, something I've always wanted but can never achieve, no matter how hard I try and how many people who don't know me very well I fool.

Christian and Pia acted a lot like a couple who'd been married a long time and whose bickering had become a kind of background music, more important for being there than for what it meant. It annoyed Pia that Christian wasn't working up to what she thought was his ability academically. His attitude was that, since he expected to play football professionally after he graduated, he didn't need to bust his butt studying.

"You could take some business courses," Pia told him, "so some crooked manager won't cheat you out of your outrageous salary."

"I thought you were going to be my manager," he said, giving her his lazy grin.

"Get serious, Christian," she said sternly.

"I'll be your manager, Christian," Sam put in. "I'll get one of those little pocket calculators and I won't let you make a move without consulting it first."

"You're thinking of a Ouija board," Christian said.

"That's it!"

"Jeez, you guys," Pia said in disgust.

Andy Blake joined us sometimes. He was the actor whose illness had given me my big break in show biz. Very little about him was memorable except his voice—

which I guess is not unusual among actors. His clothes must have come from Goodwill, the jeans with patches and tears that looked honestly come by, the jacket too short in the arms, and a dirty cap that he always wore backwards. Although he was skinny and not very tall, his voice was rich and deep, and when he put on his costume, appropriately padded, he became the emperor in manner as well as voice.

He was in love with Pia. I sometimes caught him looking at her with what I recognized as all the signs. I asked Pia about it once and she shrugged and laughed. "I know," she said. "You wouldn't think it to look at me, would you, but I break hearts right and left."

One day, she invited Sam and me over to her and Christian's apartment for dinner. They lived in a neighborhood a couple of miles from campus, where new apartment buildings that had the personality of processed cheese had gradually replaced the old homes that had once been there.

While Sam had made a beeline for the most comfortable chair in the living room, Pia showed me around. She was proud of the apartment, since it was the first place she'd lived after leaving home. It was quite large, by student standards.

"I don't suppose the Athletic Department is paying for this," I said. Getting caught doing anything as blatant as subsidizing an athlete's off-campus apartment would bring down the wrath of the swindlers who weave the fiction that college football is strictly for amateurs.

"Oh, no," Pia said. "Christian's parents pay the rent. Most of the jocks live in dorms, but once we got together, Christian wanted a place of his own."

There was a master bedroom, with a giant unmade waterbed in it. I looked at Pia in mock disbelief and she blushed.

"I get seasick," I said.

The room was decorated with Christian's trophies and photographs of him in the costumes of a variety of sports.

"Christian could've done just as well in baseball or tennis as he's doing in football," Pia told me proudly.

The floor was littered with his stuff. "I *told* him you were coming over," she said, as she kicked a pair of shorts under the bed.

Down the hall was a smaller bedroom. "This is my study," Pia said. It was a much tidier room than the other bedroom, with shelves of books and magazines and a cluttered desk. A twin bed in a corner was neatly made up, and on the walls were pictures of people I didn't know.

Pia picked up a studio portrait of a man and a woman smiling happily, their heads touching. "My mom and stepdad," she told me. She looked a lot like her mother.

"And this is my father." She picked up a small snapshot that was stuck in the mirror and handed it to me. It showed a somewhat younger Pia standing next to a tall, lean man in a garden. She was staring up at him, smiling, her mouth open as if trying to tell him something. He was wearing sunglasses and faced the camera without expression.

"He doesn't like having his picture taken," Pia said, as if apologizing for him. "He thinks he's old and doesn't like to be reminded of it. That picture was taken the last time I visited him, three years ago."

We went back out to the living room, where Sam was watching cartoons on a color TV, frowning in concentration. Pia said she didn't expect Christian home until later. During the football season, he usually ate with the rest of the team after practice—for purposes of solidarity.

"Bonding," Sam said, still staring at the TV.

Just as she was about to start dinner, Christian walked in, followed by two giant men. Christian was carrying a huge package wrapped in white butcher paper and the giants were each carrying a six-pack of beer, barely visible in their meaty hands.

"Steaks!" Christian hollered, and pretended to be throwing a pass. Sam, surprisingly quick, caught the package before it flew past his head.

Pia seemed to know the other men, whom Christian introduced to me as Darrell Howitzer and Lance Danielli. "They're on the offensive line," he said. "They keep me alive and looking good, so be nice to them."

They chuckled, hollow, volcanic rumbles emanating from deep within their chests. In spite of the chilly weather, they were wearing shirts with the sleeves torn out that showed their massive arms, which they held out from their barrel-like torsos. Their necks flowed smoothly up into wedge-shaped heads, or the other way around.

They gave me easy grins, dismissed me quickly. I was a woman in her thirties and therefore something beyond their comprehension: not a mom, not a man, not a chick—something else, they didn't care what.

I'd met their kind before in the line of duty—I may even have met them. They were all as alike as sides of beef in a packing plant and unless they were very lucky and got pro-football contracts, these were going to be the best years of their lives. "Scholar athletes," President Hightower liked to call them, trivializing two noble human activities in one breath.

They regarded Sam much as they regarded me. I hadn't been sure Sam was gay until they walked in with Christian, but then he began to exaggerate his normally theatrical flair into a caricature of gay flamboyance, as if taunting them. Whenever he spoke, they watched him with carefully blank faces, and made comments they thought were subtle. Sam obviously enjoyed the effect he was having on them.

Pia was annoyed that Christian had brought his teammates home with him unannounced, but she limited herself to giving him the exasperated look I'd seen on her face more than once, usually when he told her he didn't have time to go to class, or when I teased her about Hans Chris-

tian Andersen and Henriette Wulff. Then she resigned
herself to the situation and tried to make the best of it.

Christian barbecued the steaks on a grill on a little bal-
cony off the living room while Pia baked potatoes in the
microwave and made a salad. It all tasted great—and a
nice change from Gary's cuisine—but I almost lost my
appetite watching the two offensive linesmen putting
away three or four times what I ate with a minimum of
chewing.

"You a prof, man?" Howitzer asked me tentatively, wip-
ing grease from his lips with the back of his hand.

"A campus cop," I said.

"Yeah? A campus cop, huh?" He knocked down a slug
of beer from a can, thought about what to say on this subject. I suspected that the variety of things his mind could
come up with would be small and simple, but difficult for
him to put into words nevertheless. "The guys like havin'
you around?"

"I've never asked them," I said.

"Bein' a campus cop ain't like bein' a regular cop,
man," the other football player, Danielli, stated. "You
don't have to worry much about the rough stuff. You carry
iron?"

"Plastic," I replied.

His voice took on a slight edge, as though he suspected
I might be making fun of him. "Whaddaya mean, 'plastic'?"

"Our pistols are made of plastic," I said. "They're
Glocks."

"Whadda they shoot, man, rubber bands?" Howitzer
asked.

Both jocks laughed, the one choking on steak, the other
on beer. They exchanged high fives—honest!

"Boom-Boom is just kidding, man," Danielli explained,
when he'd brought himself under control.

"*I* picked up on that," Sam put in mildly. "I hope you
did too, Peggy. 'Boom-Boom'?"

"Howitzer's nickname is 'Boom-Boom,'" Christian said, grinning at Sam.

"Let's take a moment to think why," Sam said, scratching his beard thoughtfully.

"I saw you once, man," Howitzer said to me, "when things got a little out of hand at a party at the frat house."

"Like a riot, he means, man," Danielli supplemented.

"Yeah. You was there, swinging a club or somethin'." Boom-Boom named the fraternity, hoping I'd remember, proud of it.

I said that was probably me all right, I swung a mean club. I've never actually swung a club at a drunk frat boy, just wanted to a couple of times.

"Police brutality, man," Boom-Boom said and laughed uproariously, to reinforce the already-established fact that he was a great kidder and I wasn't to be afraid. More high fives. "I recognized your red hair," he added. "You remember that night, Danielli?" He jammed an elbow into his colleague who, apparently, didn't have a nickname. Hitting me like that would have put me back in the hospital. "You was really wasted, man."

"You was the one who was hammered, man, not me!"

"We was both blasted, man."

"It's so *nice* that you boys have so much to talk about," Sam said, "and a vocabulary capable of capturing its every nuance." He reached out and patted each of them tentatively on a massive knee. They both scowled at him, then glanced up to see if Christian was watching.

They had nothing to say to Pia, rarely looked at her when they spoke, but treated her with a certain wary respect, the way they might treat an unattractive daughter of one of their mother's friends—if their mother was present.

Neither of them offered to help clear the table, just drank beer and watched in exaggerated disbelief as Christian turned down Sam's and my offers to help and started doing it himself. While both he and Pia were out in the kitchen, Howitzer turned to Danielli and said, in what he probably thought was a quiet whisper, "Pussy-whipped, man."

Danielli grinned, then glanced over to see how I would take that.

"Nothin' more contrary to nature than a pussy-whupped man," Sam drawled, suddenly affecting a country-western accent, "or more natural than a dick-thumped gal." He somehow managed to switch a nonexistent chaw of tobacco from one cheek to the other, then looked around for a place to spit.

"Sam," I said, getting up fast and trying to keep both laughter and panic out of my voice, "I wonder if you'd mind taking me home now. My spleen's starting to act up."

"Sure, Peggy," he said, his round eyes glittering dangerously. "I was thinking of leaving about now, myself."

We went out into the kitchen and thanked Pia and Christian for dinner and then got out of there without saying good-bye to Christian's offensive linemen. For some reason we didn't think they'd mind.

"How badly does it hurt?" Sam asked me as we walked down the stairs to the street.

"What?"

"Your spleen."

"Mine doesn't hurt at all," I answered. "It was yours I was worried about."

He laughed, then shook his head. "I should have guessed."

We didn't say much until we were almost at my place. Then he said, "Wasn't it Alfred de Musset who exclaimed: 'How glorious it is, but how painful too, to be exceptional in a world like this!'?"

"Gee, Sam, I dunno," I answered, laughing.

"Contrary to what you might think, Peggy, I'm referring to Christian, who has so much natural ability and so much dedication to his sorry craft, yet he needs the good will of cretins like those two, to make it work for him."

"Isn't it kind of like being an actor?" I said. "You can't

afford to alienate the scene changers or you're likely to have a wall collapse on you."

"I suppose so," he said mournfully, "but for the actor the cause is so much worthier."

Six

One day around noon, I dropped by the Hans Christian Andersen Room to see Pia. The door was open and a woman was standing at the display case, staring in with a half-smile on her face. She looked like she was daydreaming. Pia introduced her to me as Denise Donnelly, Christian's mother. She was a small woman with bright blue eyes and blond hair that was turning gray. It was hard to imagine someone so plain being Christian's mom.

"Christian and Pia have been singing your praises for weeks," she said, giving my hand a firm squeeze. "You've made such a big impression on both of them—and on Sam too. Sam tells me you're quite the trooper."

Christian and Sam came in then. "Don't listen to her, Peggy," Sam said as he swept Mrs. Donnelly dramatically into his arms, almost lifting her off her feet. She turned her cheek and let him kiss her, her eyes sparkling, then freed herself and went up on tiptoes to give her son a kiss.

"I'm taking Christian and Pia to lunch," she told me. "I see so little of my son during the football season, you know. Of course, you and Sam can come along too if you'd like."

"Peggy and I have an important luncheon engagement of our own," Sam replied tactfully.

We walked across campus to a little student cafe. When we'd ordered, I asked him about his background—his accent told me he'd probably lived a long time in the East. He said he'd grown up in Massachusetts, but as soon as he'd graduated from college, he'd moved to New York to try to break into theater. He'd written a few plays and directed and acted in off- and off-off-Broadway productions.

"I have a knack for bittersweet comedy," he said, making a rueful face. "But after a while, I got tired of living hand to mouth, working menial jobs to support myself between shows." He decided finally to return to school and get a Ph.D. in theater. He applied to a lot of schools, chose ours because they offered him the chance to teach beginning classes in acting, to support himself while he worked on his degree.

"How'd you get to know Christian and Pia?"

"They were friends long before I knew either of them, of course," he said. "Last year, when Christian had to declare a major—even football players have to have majors, isn't that bizarre?—he took a notion he might want to try theater arts, so he enrolled in my acting class." He sighed. "It didn't work out. Football began occupying so much of his time, he didn't have the time to commit to performing. He could be a wonderful actor—and he still might, someday, if he ever gets football out of his system before it kills or cripples him. I'm not entirely without hope."

"They're an unlikely couple, Pia and Christian."

He gave me a startled look, as though he'd never considered it himself. "You think so?"

"Of course I do, Sam!" I laughed. "Pia's small and delicate and scholarly—and Christian's not."

"But surely you must've noticed that Christian isn't your average, run-of-the-mill campus hero, Peggy."

"True, I suppose. And you're an unlikely friend for a big football star too, if you don't mind my saying so."

"Me? *Quelle* surprise! Luckily, not every football player has just emerged from a cooling lava flow, like those two specimens you met the other evening."

"Still, your being a friend of Christian's certainly caused them to furrow their brows."

Sam smiled. "Was that what those washboard-like surfaces were above their eyes? Well, Christian's the best quarterback the University's had in about twenty years, and the only chance Boom-Boom and his colleagues have of getting into a bowl game. And that enhances their chances of getting professional contracts—which is the only hope they have of not ending their lives on highway construction gangs, with or without balls and chains attached to their legs. So they aren't going to complain much about whom Christian hangs out with."

"There were a few times there, Sam, when you could've got yourself killed," I remarked.

"I know." He scratched his beard, narrowed his eyes in annoyance at the memory. "Sometimes I can't help it. I used to try to convince through sweet reason and good works, but it just doesn't work with the walking dead. The first thing they think of when they encounter gays is sex—so it's only natural that they think we see them solely in terms of sex too. What a pathetic absence of imagination they have!"

"That sounds like the source of the conflict between men and women," I said.

He nodded. "I'm sure it's the same thing. But there's something else, when it comes to us—gay men, I mean." He dumped a packet of sugar in his coffee, stirred it, took a sip. "I think we threaten the straight man's hold on power—which is always being threatened from all sides anyway. They wonder who in our relationships *has* the power, and the thought that nobody does—that power's a funny, slippery thing that passes back and forth between two equals like a bar of wet soap—is terrifying to them—and to a lot of straight women too, unfortunately."

"But apparently not to Christian's mother," I said. "You seem to have a really nice relationship with her. I was a little surprised. My mother thinks homosexuality is a Jewish invention to weaken Christianity."

Sam laughed. "Mrs. Donnelly's quite the ordinary little woman, isn't she—on the surface? But don't underestimate her, Peggy. She's a tough cookie, when she wants something. She pretty much forced her dad to cough up the money for the children's library—and she'd kill for Christian. Any friend of his is a friend of hers. Which means me, among a few other chosen. Besides," he added with a mischievous grin, "I'm not sure she really believes in homosexuality. She may think I'm just playing a part in a play that's a little over her head. But for whatever reason, she likes me and accepts me the way I am—and I extend the same courtesy to her."

"I've never quite understood what rich women do with their time," I said. "Does she work for her father in the furniture business?"

"No, she leaves all that to her husband, Clay. I think, now that Christian's moved out—he's an only child—she's pretty lonely, since Clay doesn't share any of her interests. She's on the board of a lot of worthwhile organizations, of course, but mostly she spends her time collecting Danish antiques, a lot of which she's donated to an immigrant museum somewhere. She's a Danophile—don't get her on that subject or she'll bore you to tears. Apparently she had a wonderful time in Denmark as an exchange student, and it marked her for life. Christian, her student year in Denmark, and finding those lost letters from Andersen to Jette Wulff are the high points of her life."

"But what'll she do for an encore, I wonder," I said, "now that she's given her Andersen collection to the children's library."

"She'll find something. Christian says she's thinking of putting together some kind of memorial to Hans Christian Andersen's mother."

"What about Christian's dad? Gary tells me he's the president of the Sports Boosters. I had to ask him what that meant."

Sam's face darkened. "The only reason Clay Donnelly's not like those two linesmen you met the other day is because he failed to make the team twenty-five years ago—which meant he had to think seriously about his future. That seems to have involved marrying the boss's daughter.

Now he's vice president of Gus Lund's Scandinavian import company. Mr. Donnelly, needless to say, treats me like I'm something the cat dragged in."

I asked Sam about his love live. I'd never seen him with anybody other than Christian and Pia and some of the members of the cast.

Instead of answering, he looked at his watch, said, "I've got to run," and signalled for the check. While we were waiting for it, he turned back to me and said, "That's another reason I left New York. Too many things there reminded me of someone I was together with for almost five years—four years, eleven months, and twenty-nine days, to be exact. We missed our five-year anniversary by two days."

I didn't ask what happened, just waited to see if he wanted to tell me about it. I didn't think he would, but as we crossed College Avenue and entered the campus, he said the word that didn't surprise me: AIDS.

"It's easier for me to remember the good times we had together here," he went on, "where I'm not always stumbling across things that remind me of the last year we had together there— the bad times, and the horrible times that came after the bad times. Jim was a nurse. He had a lot of experience in auxiliary parts before he took center stage himself."

He broke off, cleared his throat, then turned and gave me a little smile. "Now suppose you tell me about you, Peggy. I can't believe you just sponge up the details of other people's lives, in lieu of having one of your own."

Sam probably didn't mean it to sound as awful as it did.

Seven

A few days before the play was to open and the symposium was to begin, I walked over to the Hans Christian Andersen Room because Pia wanted me to meet her father.

When I'd asked her why, since they hadn't seen each other in three years, she looked embarrassed and said it was because she was nervous and didn't want to be alone with him until they'd had a chance to get reacquainted. She asked me if I'd pretend I didn't know they were meeting for lunch, and then she'd be able to invite me along too.

Pia was standing at the window by her desk, staring out. She turned as I walked in and told me her father hadn't arrived yet. As always, her desk was a clutter of paper surrounding the desktop computer. Propped up next to the computer was a big faded blue book that I knew was one volume of the correspondence between Andersen and Jette Wulff that she was translating for her *summa* thesis.

I went over and looked into the display case in the middle of the room. "You've never finished telling me how Jette Wulff's letters and stuff ended up here," I reminded her. "Sam popped up at the window and changed the direction of my life, remember?"

She came over and stood next to me. "Jette spent a lot of her life travelling around, trying to find a place where she could feel at home. So did Andersen—they were a lot alike in that respect. They didn't feel comfortable among the Danes. He came from the poorest of the poor in Denmark and the upper-class people who helped him never let him forget it. They couldn't," she added, "because they didn't know any better. I mean, they were nice to him and all, and helpful, but they put constant pressure on him to be more like them. They even tried to make him write the way the 'best' writers of the time wrote, guys who are forgotten now, such as—"

I clamped my hands over my ears.

She went on, only slightly shamefaced: "Jette came from the upper class, but she was a physical outsider, the way he was a social one. She was tiny and hunchbacked—in fact, she was the model for Andersen's 'Thumbelina'—I'll bet you didn't know that, did you?"

"No, I didn't," I agreed.

"Anyway, Jette couldn't do what was expected of a woman in those days, which was get married and have children. So being different was what made both Andersen and her human, I think."

"You're babbling again," I said.

"What was the question?" she asked. "Oh yeah, how'd the letters get here? Well, Jette really liked this country, you see. She had friends here, and I think that, like so many other people, she thought her strangeness would be more acceptable here—or, at least, she could hide more easily here than in Denmark. Ha! And then her brother died, in South Carolina. So she decided to emigrate, to be close to where he was buried. She was also interested in women's education, and America was a leader in that at the time. She said she wanted to—Stop that, Peggy!"

"She wanted to stop that, Peggy?"

"You know what I mean. Stop whistling that song. It's horrible. The movie was horrible too."

I'd begun whistling a song from a movie about Hans Christian Andersen that starred Danny Kaye. For some reason, Pia clapped her hands to her ears.

"Okay," she said, when she'd calmed down a little.

"When Jette went on board the ship to America, she had those letters from Andersen with her—there are seven of them—and that autographed photograph."

She laughed, staring down at the display, forgetting the story again. "Once she wrote to Andersen that the only passport a Dane needed was a photo of him. And that wasn't really such an exaggeration, either. By that time—1858—he was famous all over the world."

"So she sets off for America with his letters and his photograph," I said, to nudge her along. "What then?"

"Then the ship caught on fire and she burned to death. That's what." She gave me an accusing glare, as if I'd started the fire myself, and she looked as though she were about to cry, as if Henriette Wulff's ship had only burned up the day before. "It happened when the ship was about five days from New York." She swallowed hard and said, "Everybody thought her luggage burned up too, but then the letters and photograph turned up here."

"Christian's mom found them?"

She nodded, looked at her watch. "After surviving the fire and the ship sinking and everything, they ended up in a bunch of old books and crap that an antique dealer was about to toss out, can you believe it? Luckily, Mrs. Donnelly decided to rummage through the stuff first, and found them."

"How valuable are they?"

"You can't put a price on things like this," she said. "There was a big fuss in Denmark when they heard the news. They wanted her to sell or donate them to the Hans Christian Andersen museum in Odense, Andersen's birthplace. A wealthy Dane even offered her a lot of money for them. But she said no, she wanted them as the centerpiece of this room."

I glanced around. "I don't see any alarm system connected to the case."

"The library keeps promising to put one in," she said. "They haven't done it yet, but I guess there's no hurry.

The biggest threat might be some of the Danes coming to the symposium who are outraged that the letters are here instead of in Denmark. Some of them are pretty fanatical when it comes to Andersen."

"Unlike you," I said.

"Puh!" She stared down at the display in the case for a few moments longer, then went over to the desk against the wall under the window where she worked on her thesis. "Mrs. Donnelly made the library let me work in here. Otherwise I'd have to work at home, since I'm only an undergraduate. I know you don't believe it, Peggy, but I feel Jette's presence in this room, inspiring me."

Behind us, somebody cleared his throat. A man was standing in the open door. He was very tall, and thin, with long, carefully trimmed hair that, in the dim light, looked like pewter. He looked older than he had in the snapshot I'd seen of him.

"Daddy!" Pia ran across the room to him and threw her arms around him, looking up into his face. He gave her a smile and a hug, then stared over her head at the room, finally landing indifferently on me.

They spoke together for a minute in what I assumed was Danish and then she pulled him into the room by the hand and introduced us. His name was Jens Aage Lindemann. The "Jens," like "Jette," was pronounced with a y-sound, and "Aage" sounded like "ogre" without the "r."

"You seem tired," she said, when the formalities were over. "You're not still suffering from jet lag, are you?"

"Not at all." He looked around the room. "What is this place?"

"You know what it is," Pia said, laughing. "It's the Hans Christian Andersen Room. I've written to you about it."

"So you have, and so it is. It's really quite ghastly, isn't it?" He picked up the bronze replica of *The Little Mermaid,* examined it briefly, and put it back down, then went over and stood in front of the painting of Andersen above the high-backed chair. "He didn't think he was going to be immortal for his children's stories when he posed for this one, did he?" he said, smiling. "He thought he was going to be the next Heine." Lindemann's eyes were hooded, like Andersen's in the portrait, but unlike Andersen's, his lacked warmth and curiosity.

He moved along the wall to the papercuts that Mrs. Donnelly had made. "You Americans haven't raided the Andersen museum in Odense, have you, Pia?"

"They're just copies, Daddy, you know that!"

"Copies!" He shook his head. "What a strange and foolish thing to want to do."

"Oh, Daddy!" Some of the enthusiasm had drained out of Pia's voice. "Come over here," she tried again, "if you want to see something genuine!" She pulled him over to the display case.

He studied the contents for a while, his hands clasped behind his back. I found myself holding my breath, waiting for his reaction. "Andersen's letters to his 'Dear sisterly friend," he said finally, as if speaking to himself. "It was so very important in those days to put a safe label on a friendship between two people of the opposite sex."

He turned to his daughter. "They belong in Denmark, of course—not that it matters a great deal. I'd hoped they'd contain passionate declarations on Andersen's part, since he would never see her again, but there's nothing new in them at all, just his usual complaints about his physical problems—boils under his armpits, wasn't it, this time?— and the usual gossip that characterized their entire correspondence. They seemed completely unaware that anything was going on in the world around them other than what they experienced themselves. Have you read the correspondence between Flaubert and George Sand, Pia? Now that's a correspondence worth reading."

He spoke so easily, so humorously, that if you weren't

paying close attention, you might not notice he was trashing something his daughter cherished.

Pia's thin lips almost disappeared. "Andersen and Jette weren't *French intellectuals,*" she said, making the term sound like something the unwary might step in in a dog owner's backyard. "You've spent your whole life writing about Hans Christian Andersen, Daddy, and yet you can't appreciate something as wonderful as this!"

Lindemann found it hard to meet her stare, which was something in his favor, at least. He gave a little laugh. "I suppose you're right, Pia—a lifetime of reading and writing about Hans Christian Andersen seems foolish to me now, so perhaps I'm a bit unfair to him. Let's go get something to eat and you can tell me all about yourself."

She asked him if I could come too. He looked me up and down without much interest and said, "Of course."

I started to say I'd just remembered another engagement but caught Pia's look of entreaty and changed my mind.

We walked across campus to the student union cafeteria.

I asked Lindemann if he'd just arrived.

"I arrived yesterday," he answered. "I had a meeting with the editor of your University Press this morning, to discuss the details of a book I'm going to write for them."

"On Andersen?"

"Yes, certainly." He remembered that he'd just admitted he was tired of Andersen, and added, "It's something I should be able to write in my sleep. And last night I had to give a talk to an organization of local Danish-American patriots called 'The Sons of Denmark.' " He made a face. "I tried to give them some idea of what's going on in Denmark today, but all they wanted to do was drink Danish beer and talk about Denmark the way their grandparents and great-grandparents remembered it. I'm afraid I disappointed them greatly—I'd forgotten the old songs, and couldn't tell them what was good about the good old days."

Once we were seated with our trays of food, Pia dug into her purse, brought out her glucometer, and tested her blood. I'd seen her do it several times already, so I could tell that, this time, she did it with forced casualness. Her father winced when she pricked her finger, and concentrated on his salad. Her face was a little pink—she had one of those complexions that show every nuance of feeling— but her mouth was fixed in a determined line, as though she'd begun a series of tests on her father, and he wasn't doing very well.

"I didn't realize you were going to write an Andersen book for Americans, Daddy," she said when she'd finished. "Is it going to be a biography?"

He shrugged. "More than that. I'm going to explain to Americans what Andersen grew out of—and what he wasn't able to grow out of—as well as what's unique about his stories."

"I think Professor Claussen's writing a book like that," she said.

Lindemann laughed contemptuously. "Eric Claussen's been writing *the* book on Andersen for Americans for as long as I've known him, my dear. If he hasn't finished it by now, he never will."

It wasn't the pleasantest lunch I've ever sat through. I thought Pia's cheerful, rapid-fire conversation was to keep the knowledge of her father's indifference from herself. Watching them, listening to them, they reminded me of a happy tune bouncing frantically over a heavy, bloodless bass.

"Where's this boyfriend of yours, Pia?" Lindemann asked. "Or are you saving him to show me at dinner tonight?"

"He's either at practice or in class," she told him. "And you won't be able to see him tonight, either, I'm afraid. A television station is taping an interview with him and his father."

"A television interview!" Lindemann exclaimed. "Your Christian must be very famous indeed."

"Around here he is," Pia said.

Eight

On the Thursday before we opened, Sam interrupted the rehearsal to lecture us. "Remember, we're not playing it for laughs," he said, stalking around among us. "Your careers depend on the strength of your performance before the emperor. You have to convince him that you don't believe he's naked and you have to convince yourselves too, because you don't want to have to confront the possibility that you are stupid or unfit for your jobs, do you?

"And even more than you, the emperor has to deceive himself, because if *he* can't see the clothes he's wearing, *he's* not fit to be emperor. You have to deny the testimony of your eyes and repeat—and believe—the lines the swindlers feed you. You do it so well, finally, that you lose all integrity, becoming one with the parts you're playing. Think of yourselves as university administrators."

"Sam," an actress asked, "is all this really in Andersen's story, or is it just you?"

"*Just* me? I regret your choice of words, Molly—but let it pass! It's in the story. Read it, if you don't believe me. It's the most universal story ever written."

"You told us not to read it," Molly reminded him. "You said knowing too much would constipate us."

"I suppose," I said, "that when the child speaks up and says the emperor's naked, Sam, he could have had her killed."

"I flirted briefly with the idea of having you arrest her," Sam replied. "After all, people who see too clearly are a danger to society. But in the end I decided to leave it the

54

way Andersen wrote it—unclear how the emperor's going to deal with his terrible humiliation. Besides, I'm not sure you could bring it off, Peggy, at this stage in your career as an actress."

He sighed. "I do wish I could have done the play with full nudity. You'd have done it, Andy, wouldn't you?"

Sam had settled for long johns, with the flap in back half-open, revealing a patch of Andy Blake's butt.

"Had the part called for nudity," Andy declared piously, "I would have done it—for my art! Isn't that what starlets always say in interviews?"

"Who's your Art?" somebody asked.

"Isn't it strange that art never seems to call for frontal male nudity?" Molly observed dryly.

"Don't *you* start seeing too clearly!" Sam warned her.

That night, I was lying on the couch, my feet in Gary's lap, reading Jared Diamond's *The Third Chimpanzee* in an effort to find out how much longer the human race has, if it continues on the way it's going. The news wasn't encouraging. Gary was using the remote to look for something interesting to watch on television. I hate it when somebody other than me holds the remote, so I told him to put it on mute.

Every now and then I looked up and watched him for a few moments, wondered what, if anything, I'd gained by having him living with me. It was hard to think of anything specific, but I liked it anyway. Maybe people who keep cats feel the same way, but I'm allergic to cats.

"Hey," Gary said suddenly, "here's Christian Donnelly. Highlights from last week's game and an interview with him and his dad coming up."

"Turn on the sound," I told him. This must be the interview Pia had mentioned to her father yesterday afternoon.

Christian was backpedalling for all he was worth—fading back, the announcer called it—about to throw a pass. I recognized him even through his masked face. His golden hair flared out around his shoulders from beneath his helmet.

Ignoring the huge men converging on him, intent on doing as much damage to him as they could, Christian threw a long pass. It looked effortless, almost as though he were shaking something off his fingers, but the ball seemed to take on a life of its own as it flew downfield. It came down precisely in time to meet the outstretched hands of a thin black man who'd jumped up out of a crowd of bodies, twisted around to catch it, and then, clutching the ball to his belly, fallen into the end zone on his back, laughing.

The camera returned to Christian, at the other end of the field, getting up off the grass and laughing too. As he turned to walk to the sidelines, he slapped one of the opposing players on the helmet. The man didn't seem to notice, either because the helmet was too thick and padded, or because he had no feeling in his head.

In other clips, Christian was shown holding onto the ball and dodging the opposing players as he worked his way upfield. It was beautiful to watch and the crowd and the sportscaster loved it. Even I held my breath as, just as he was about to get hit by some anonymous behemoth, he'd slip away or, at the last moment, sink to the ground.

"He flirts with death, doesn't he?" I said.

"I haven't seen too many college quarterbacks with his field presence," Gary replied. "I haven't seen too many professionals with his presence, either."

Then Christian, in street clothes, appeared on the screen with two other men, seated in comfortable-looking chairs in a television studio. Gary told me that one of the men was a well-known local sports columnist. He spoke through a nose that must have been enormous before somebody or something had flattened it.

The other man was introduced as Christian's father, Clay Donnelly, a stocky man with a wide mouth turned down at the corners like a predatory fish, and tight, curly black hair receding at the temples.

The sports columnist and Donnelly did most of the talking, with Christian playing the role of the modest college athlete, giving polite answers to inane questions. I'd heard him do parodies of these kinds of interviews, with Sam playing the interviewer.

"The team that puts the most points on the board is going to win," Christian said, absolutely deadpan, in answer to a question, and I wondered if I was the only viewer who noticed the mockery in his eyes.

I remembered Sam, pretending to hold a microphone, asking Christian one day if he could rephrase that in language the average fan could understand. Christian had flipped a piece of pumpkin pie into Sam's beard.

The columnist asked Clay Donnelly what he thought the team's chances were of getting into a post-season bowl game, and Donnelly, treating the question as worthy of serious thought, replied, "Good, Syd, very good," more ponderously, probably, than Einstein had proclaimed that E equals mc^2.

"And what's the key to this year's success, Clay?" the columnist asked, giving the television camera a broad wink.

"Football's a team sport, winning's a team effort," Donnelly replied gruffly, "but I guess I'd have to say that Christian's gotta be a key factor." A jagged smile, like a crack in the highway, opened on his face, and was quickly smothered as he glanced at his son, almost shyly, and then away.

"Thanks, Dad," Christian said. He threw an arm around his father's shoulders.

"And what do you think of Christian's chances of landing a pro contract, Clay?"

"I'll let Christian answer that one for himself," Donnelly replied.

Christian turned and gazed calmly into the camera. "I'm going to wear a Super Bowl ring someday," he said.

When the program was over, I asked Gary if that's how

real men treat their sons: Short, Hemingwayesque sentences, small, humorless smiles.

"How else do you make a man out of a boy?" Gary replied gruffly, giving me a smile so tight it must have hurt.

Nine

The next night was the banquet to open the Hans Christian Andersen symposium and Pia had asked me if I'd go as her guest. Christian couldn't go, of course—the football team was playing the next day in a neighboring state and had already flown there—and Sam refused. "He said he might go if he thought he was going to live forever," Pia said. "He also lied and said he had nothing to wear."

"But aren't you going to sit at the head table with your father?" Her father was the keynote speaker.

She shook her head, and, without any particular expression, said, "The people who arranged the conference didn't realize Daddy had a daughter here." She added quickly, as if reading my mind, "It's okay. I'd feel like everybody was staring at me if I was up there at the head table and I don't like people watching me eat. I'd probably poke a forkful of food through my cheek or something equally stupid."

She picked me up at my place in her car and we drove downtown to get her father at his hotel. I asked her how dinner had gone with him Wednesday night.

She shrugged, stared straight ahead. "Okay, I guess."

"Your father still hasn't seen Christian?"

"Nope. But it's probably for the best. Daddy went on and on about how dumb professional athletes are. I tried to tell him about Christian—about how nice he is—but he didn't want to hear." She glanced over at me and quickly away as the car veered towards the curb. "He thinks Christian'll end up causing me pain, and that I'm infatuated with him because he's a campus hero. That's not very flattering, is it?"

"No, it's not," I replied.

Her father was waiting for us outside his hotel. Pia told him to fasten his seatbelt but he just laughed and said something in Danish. She snapped something back at him. I couldn't understand the words, but I understood anyway: We weren't going anyplace until he fastened his seatbelt, which, with an irritated expression on his face, he did.

We made small talk for the first few minutes and then he looked at Pia and said, "Well, Pia, that's quite a fellow you have for a boyfriend!"

Pia turned and gave him a startled look. "That's what I was trying to tell you Wednesday night! What's changed your mind?"

"I saw him on television last night," Lindemann said. "And today your University newspaper seemed to devote itself mostly to Christian Donnelly and his family. Even you were mentioned, Pia, as the hero's girlfriend."

She glanced over at him in surprise. "You watched Christian on television, Daddy?"

"Not exactly by design, my dear!" he said with a fruity chuckle. "But last night, after I returned to my hotel room from a dreary evening with your Danish professor, Eric Claussen, I couldn't sleep, so I lay in bed and decided to sample American television. As I switched channels, I happened to hear an announcer say they were about to show an interview with your Christian. I assumed it was the interview that kept me from enjoying the young man's company Wednesday night, so I decided to watch, to find out just who this boy is who has won my daughter's heart."

He described the program Gary and I had watched the night before too.

"First they showed what they called 'highlights' of last week's football game that consisted largely of your Christian throwing that funny ball long distances and, occasionally, running for his life, and then some not very intelligent fellow interviewed him and his father."

Pia glanced at him quickly, then back to the street. "What did you think, Daddy?"

Lindemann was silent for a moment or two. "That he's quite a charming lad," he said finally. "And that he has a great deal of intelligence under the mask of what he's pretending to be."

"What do you mean by that?" Pia demanded, turning to stare at him, the car again veering towards the curb. At her best she wasn't a very attentive driver.

Lindemann turned to his daughter. "There's more to your Christian than meets the eye. I wonder if he lets you see it?"

"Of course there's more to Christian than he shows to the assholes who watch sports shows!" she said angrily. "Do you think I'd be living with him, if there wasn't?"

"I'm sure I don't know the answer to that," her father said quietly, "but it's a pity he wants to waste himself on a brutal and stupid game. You should use whatever influence you have over him to encourage him to do something more with his life."

"He's doing what he loves!" she replied.

"That's too bad."

The banquet was in the Faculty Club, which overlooks the river that divides the University in half. As we stood in the doorway of the lounge outside the dining room, surveying the crowd, two scholarly-looking men, one totally bald and one with long white hair, rushed over and began speaking to Lindemann in German.

Pia was craning her head, searching the room for Christian's parents. When she spotted them, she tugged on her father to get his attention.

He glanced to where she was pointing, nodded, and said, "I'll join you later, Pia," and turned back to his colleagues.

When we finally reached her, Mrs. Donnelly gave Pia a

big hug, shook my hand, and told me how nice it was to see me again. I almost didn't recognize her without her glasses. Her gray-blond hair was piled loosely on her head and she was wearing a neat navy suit with a little matching hat and high heels. She looked more refined and middle-aged than when I'd last seen her. I assumed this was the image she wanted to project tonight, one worthy of the brass plaque on the wall that said "Lund-Donnelly Children's Library," and as the woman responsible for the Hans Christian Andersen Room and the discovery of the long-lost letters.

She introduced me to her husband. Seated in the television studio, Clay Donnelly had looked shorter than his five-ten or eleven. He still had the robustness of the locker room about him, but heavy jowls pulled his lips down into a perpetual frown and his belly strained at the button on his dark blazer.

"Nice to meet you," he said, more or less, glancing up at me from his wine glass and back down again.

Mrs. Donnelly said, "Peggy's a campus policewoman on disability, Clay, that Sam was kind enough to put in his play." She made me sound like a human reclamation project.

Donnelly looked up at me again, said, "Yeah?" and then reached out and stopped a waiter passing by with a carafe of wine and a tray of cheese with toothpicks in them. I could see I was beginning to grow on him.

"I'll bet you're nervous about tomorrow night, Peggy," Mrs. Donnelly chattered on happily.

"A little," I lied. Whenever I remembered that I was about to appear on a lighted stage in front of an audience, I felt like throwing up.

"You shouldn't be. Sam tells me you're a natural actress. How I wish I'd been born with talent!"

"But you must have been," I said, trying to set an example for social grace. "From what Pia's told me, we might not be here tonight, if it weren't for you."

She gave me a conspiratorial smile. "You're right, of

course. I did have a little something to do with Dad's decision to help fund the children's library."

"And the Hans Christian Andersen Room," Pia stuck in.

Mrs. Donnelly glanced at Pia and laughed. "That too. You know, Peggy, the University didn't want to build that room! But when I realized how sterile the library was going to look, I said to myself, 'I'm not putting my Andersen collection in anything that looks as cold and antiseptic as that!' So I discussed it with Dad and he talked to the right people at the University about it. They had no choice, naturally, since Dad's money was making the library possible. They were not pleased," she added, "but it serves them right for building a children's library that looks like a laboratory, don't you think?"

I remembered Sam telling me that she was a tough cookie when she wanted something. I glimpsed some of that now, under the sugar glaze.

Pia's father joined us then.

"Oh, Daddy!" she exclaimed. She took his arm and introduced him to the Donnellys.

"Nice to meet you, Professor," Clay Donnelly said, his enunciation no better than when he'd said the same words to me.

"Thank you," Lindemann said, smiling down at Donnelly. "It is also nice for me to finally meet the parents of my daughter's lover. Pia has gotten herself involved with quite an impressive family, I must say! A grandfather who builds libraries, a mother who collects Anderseniana, a father who is president of something called, I believe, the 'Sports Boosters,' and a son who is a local sports hero! Are all American families so richly gifted, I wonder?" He was laying the sarcasm on a little thick, I thought.

"Clay and I are very fond of your daughter, Professor Lindemann," Mrs. Donnelly said quietly.

A voice behind me rasped, "There you are, Denise!"

A tall, elderly man was pushing his way towards us through the crowd as though being pursued, which he was. The man behind him—like a teapot, short and stout—

looked as though he was about to have a stroke as he struggled to keep up. A large woman with him was clinging to his arm, apparently trying to restrain him.

The tall man kissed Mrs. Donnelly on the cheek, nodded to Clay Donnelly, and turned to Pia with a big grin. "Hello, sweetheart," he said, giving her a big hug. "I suppose Christian's off somewhere, getting ready for tomorrow's game. I wish I could be with him—instead of here." He gazed around the roomful of well-dressed, well-behaved people with contempt.

"Hi, Gus," Pia said, giving him a big smile.

"This is my father, Gustav Lund," Mrs. Donnelly said, and introduced him to Professor Lindemann and me. Lund was wearing a double-breasted suit in a loud maroon plaid that must have been fifty years out of style, and his eyes were bright blue under brows that looked like snowy hedges.

Still keeping his arm around Pia, he said to Lindemann, "You've got a mighty fine daughter here, Professor. She's gonna make a fine addition to the Lund family someday, if I do say so myself."

"Oh, Gus!" Pia said, snuggling into his loud suitcoat and blushing. She'd got more warmth and affection from Christian's grandfather in thirty seconds than she'd got from her father in the hour or so I'd spent with them.

Lund pointed a gnarled thumb at the angry man standing next to him, simmering, and said, "And this is Carl Vedel, Grand Poohbah of the Sons of Denmark, and his daughter, Mary. Carl's still upset about those Andersen letters you found, Denise. He thinks we stole 'em from him and Mary."

"If I was to get a good lawyer—" the other man began, in a high, querulous voice.

"Now, Father!" his daughter said.

"Why don't you, Carl?" Lund retorted. "Good lawyers are a dime a dozen. I call a bunch of 'em by their first names or worse—and they call me 'mister.' Hell, I'll even loan you a couple of mine—just so we'll be on an even playing field in the courtroom."

Vedel looked to be somewhere around sixty-five. He wore a grizzled fringe of hair, a pot belly, and a shiny dark suit.

"Oh, Father," Mary Vedel said. "Mr. Lund and Denise didn't *steal* the letters. They aren't that kind of people!" Her tone of voice, which belied her words, and the glitter in her eyes, made me look at her more closely.

She was about forty, tall—close to six feet—with a dark complexion and eyes squeezed small by high cheekbones. Her dark hair, streaked with gray, hung straight to her shoulders. She wore a look of suffering like a fashion statement, a loose-fitting ankle-length dress of some drab color, and a gold crucifix on a chain.

She looked at Clay Donnelly. "Hello, Clay," she said. "It's been a long time."

"How's life been treatin' ya, Mary?" Donnelly replied mechanically.

"Not too bad, thank you." Her eyes remained steady on his face for a long time, forcing him to stare down into his empty glass.

"Mary's right, Carl," Gus Lund cut in. "If you're too ignorant to know what you've got, you don't deserve to have it." He seemed to enjoy the results achieved by pouring gasoline on fire. "You could've looked through that crap more carefully before you unloaded it on us, y'know."

"They're talking about Henriette Wulff's letters," Pia explained to her father in a whisper, as the two old men continued to quarrel. "Mrs. Donnelly found them in Mr. Vedel's basement."

"Stole 'em, she means," Vedel said, overhearing.

Lindemann looked down at Denise Donnelly and said, "You created quite a stir in Denmark with your little discovery, Mrs. Donnelly."

She looked up into his face and replied dryly, "Yes— with my 'little discovery.' "

He laughed. Then his eyes narrowed. "We've met before, I think."

"I suppose it's possible," she replied. "Denmark is such a small country, after all, isn't it? And I visit there often."

"Denise and I took a course in Danish life and culture," Mary Vedel broke in, "when we were exchange students in Copenhagen. You came in and spoke on Hans Christian Andersen, Professor Lindemann. Twice. We didn't care much for your lectures, they were dry as dust. Don't you remember, Denise?"

"Mary!" Mrs. Donnelly said in a shocked voice. "That's not a very nice thing to say! No, I certainly don't remember that!" She made a tsk-ing noise, shaking her head. Then she continued, "Would you excuse me, please? I think we're about to be called in to dinner." She turned and threaded her way quickly through the crowd in the direction of the restrooms.

Lindemann followed Mrs. Donnelly with his eyes for a moment, then turned back to Mary Vedel. "That must have been a long time ago indeed. I had to do such things when I was just starting out in the academic world—help teach survey classes to eager young American exchange students, sometimes even act as chaperone for them on little outings in the countryside." He gave a mock shudder and turned to Clay Donnelly. "You were an exchange student in Copenhagen too, Mr. Donnelly?"

"Yeah, right," Donnelly replied.

"In a uniquely American way, then, you seem to have followed in Hans Christian Andersen's footsteps," Lindemann said with a laugh.

"I don't get what ya mean, Professor."

"Oh, you must know the story, Mr. Donnelly."

Mary Vedel broke in. "He means the story of when Andersen decided to leave home and go to Copenhagen, Clay," she said harshly. "His mother asked him what he was going to do there and he replied, 'Become famous. First you suffer terribly and then you become famous.' "

"Exactly," Lindemann said. "You've become famous

twice-over, haven't you? Once as president of something called the Sports Boosters and once as the father of Christian Donnelly. Did you have to suffer terribly in Copenhagen first, Mr. Donnelly?"

Donnelly chuckled nervously. "I didn't get much out of it one way or the other," he said. "Not like Denise, anyway." His brow was wrinkled, as if he were trying to figure out what he'd done to deserve all this attention.

"But you got the fairy tale ending, Clay, didn't you?" Mary Vedel persisted, her voice edged with spite. "You got the princess and half the kingdom."

"I got the princess, all right, I guess."

"Indeed you did!" Lindemann said. "Indeed you did! But didn't you get half the kingdom as well?" Turning to Gustav Lund, he asked, "Didn't you give your son-in-law half the kingdom, Mr. Lund?"

"Clay doesn't have anything to complain about," Lund answered, glaring at Lindemann.

"Of course not," Lindemann said, his voice strangely harsh. "I didn't mean to suggest he had. Besides, we don't live in a fairy tale world, do we?"

And on that odd note, the doors to the banquet hall opened and we filed in to dinner.

Ten

Lindemann, the Donnellys, and Gustav Lund were all sitting at the head table, along with the University president, Bennett Hightower, Hightower's wife, and other officials of the University and the library.

"Who's that man who looks like a silver toothpick with hair?" I whispered to Pia.

"The Danish consul general," she whispered back. "He's kind of like an ambassador, except on a smaller scale. There's a big Danish population here, you know."

The tables were decorated with little Danish flags and we were served by blond waitresses dressed in ethnic costumes who all looked alike—pert and toothy and thrilled to be sliding plates of grotesque banquet food in front of us. I was afraid they might suddenly break out into some kind of Danish folk song and dance, maybe with yodels or whatever joyful noises they make in Denmark, but they restrained themselves nicely. As I always do on occasions like this, I quickly shook pepper on the sauce on my chicken, hoping that would make it look less like snot.

Pia and I shared a table with Professor Claussen, the Danish professor who taught the Hans Christian Andersen course Pia had been the reader-grader for, and his wife. Pia attempted to discuss her *summa* thesis with Claussen—he was one of the readers for it, along with Edith Silberman—but he didn't show much interest.

Claussen was tall and loose-limbed and dressed in what I call the 'professor costume,' the kind of clothes you see professors wearing on television and in the movies: a jacket with leather patches at the elbows, a yellow cotton v-neck sweater underneath, and a bow tie. All very new and expensive, unlike the reality being caricatured. He wore a neatly trimmed white mustache and goatee, and an expression of mild disdain at all times.

His wife reminded me of somebody but at first I couldn't figure out who. She was about fifty, still beautiful, with high cheekbones, sharply defined features, and large gray eyes. She wore her dark hair short, in the kind of bob I associated with the twenties.

"Greta Garbo," Pia whispered into my ear, reading my mind.

I turned and smiled at her, nodded.

Mrs. Claussen toyed with her food, as if not quite sure what you were supposed to do with it. I asked her what she did for a living and she glanced up at me, surprised: At professional gatherings made up mostly of men, it's easy to overlook the possibility that the wives might do something other than stand or sit by their husbands, pretending to listen intently.

"I'm a painter," she replied.

I gave her a questioning look because, after all, she might have meant "house painter." You can't be sure anymore.

"As an artist, I use my maiden name," she said. "Julie Land."

I'd heard the name, even recalled seeing some of her work. She did colorful abstractions.

"We had your father over for dinner last night, Pia," Eric Claussen said, overriding whatever might have come of that conversation. "I hadn't seen him in ages. We had a very nice time, didn't we, Julie?"

"So you're Christian Donnelly's girlfriend," Julie Land said to Pia, unable to hide her surprise.

"That's right," Pia said, a little defiantly. "I am."

Julie Land laughed. "Good for you. But your father doesn't approve, I'm afraid. He made it clear last night that he doesn't think a football player's an appropriate boyfriend for his daughter."

Pia looked surprised, but didn't say anything. I'd got pretty good at reading her mind too, so I guessed she was thinking the same thing I was: It would be surprising if Lindemann had enough fatherly instincts to care who his daughter's boyfriend was.

"We've met before," Julie Land went on, "but you wouldn't remember it. We spent a rainy midsummer eve weekend together in Denmark twenty-some years ago, Eric and I and your parents. You were just a baby."

Pia laughed and said she was sorry she couldn't remember the occasion.

"Mrs. Donnelly named her son Christian after Hans Christian Andersen," Professor Claussen told his wife. "She collects little stork and mermaid figurines, and ashtrays with 'Greetings from Odense, the birthplace of Hans Christian Andersen' on them. She's unloaded much of it on the children's library. That's what the Hans Christian Andersen Room's for."

"It also contains Andersen's letters to Henriette Wulff," Pia said icily, "and she also donated a valuable collection of translations of Andersen's tales to the library. Don't forget that, Professor Claussen."

"Yes, yes, of course." Claussen waved all that away with his fork. "The letters, of course, belong in a respectable research library in Denmark, or the Andersen Museum in Odense."

Pia turned red and her mouth thinned away into nothing in her pale face. "Typescripts are good enough for libraries," she said. "Mrs. Donnelly has put the letters where people who love Hans Christian Andersen can see them."

After dinner, the director of the children's library, a tall, stooped man with a bald dome that glittered, a fringe of gray hair combed into a ducktail, and buck teeth, spoke. He assured us the library would be a magnet that would attract scholars from all over the world—assuming the University fulfilled its promise to allocate funds for books, he added with a quick toothy smile at the University president, Bennett Hightower, who didn't seem to notice. Hightower had carved a successful career out of not hearing unpleasant things until it was too late to do anything about them.

The director also thanked Gustav Lund and his daughter Denise Lund Donnelly for making the children's library a reality. Gustav Lund stood up then and reluctantly moved to the microphone. He said he wouldn't have done what he'd done without the nagging of his daughter, who should really be up there at the microphone in his place except that she was too shy.

He glared at his daughter, who smiled painfully out at the audience and seemed to want to disappear beneath the table.

It was also Denise Lund Donnelly, Lund added, stressing the "Lund," who had saved the letters of Hans Christian Andersen to Henriette Wulff from destruction. And he insisted that she stand up and that we give her a round of applause too. She gave her father an angry look, as if he'd broken a promise, then stood up quickly, her face beet red, and just as quickly sat down again.

Then, much to the annoyance of the director of the children's library, Lund said he wanted to introduce the president of the local chapter of the Sons of Denmark, Carl Vedel. "Where are you, Carl?" he hollered out at the dinner guests. "You're out there somewhere, I know that. Stand up!"

Across the room, Carl Vedel stood up—short, rotund, his face a mask of suppressed fury. He glared around the room and sat down again. His daughter reached over and patted his hand.

The director of the children's library introduced Bennett Hightower, called by some the "Compleat University President," since he has neither vision nor courage, only a burning desire never to enter a classroom again. He's an affable man who looks as though he'd been cut out to be a butler, but taken a wrong turn somewhere and ended up in academic administration. He gave his set speech on the function of a university in a materialistic age and then shook Gustav Lund's hand and the hands of both Denise and Clay Donnelly.

The Danish consul general, the thin sliver of a man with the shock of gray hair, spoke next. He listed Denmark's achievements through the ages and then introduced Jens Aage Lindemann, whose talk would officially open the Hans Christian Andersen symposium. Describing Lindemann's publications, titles, and honors took a while. Among other things, he mentioned that Lindemann had been knighted by the Danish queen for his contribution to Danish cultural life. I wondered if that made Pia a lady, or dame. I glanced at her, sitting next to me, thin and pale, her long blond hair framing her delicate face. There was a smile on her mouth and she had eyes only for her father.

Lindemann seemed to come to life when standing in front of an audience of his peers. According to him, Andersen had been some kind of "natural" genius whose greatness lay in the fact that he didn't have the adult's ability to make fine distinctions between what was real and what he wanted to be real. "In the argot of your American teenagers, Hans Christian Andersen just didn't 'get it,' " Lindemann said, eliciting a bloodless laugh from the audience.

I'd known any number of people who didn't 'get it,' and a few who couldn't distinguish between fantasy and reality, but none of them was ever going to be the subject of a week-long symposium two hundreds years later, except possibly of criminologists.

All his life, Lindemann continued, Andersen felt like a child who had been given the run of the toy store, and he behaved like a child too. Just as the child takes malicious pleasure in sticking out his tongue at the adults who care for him, so Andersen delighted in exposing, in his tales, the absurdities of the upper-class society upon which he was so dependent.

"But he stuck out his tongue carefully," Lindemann

went on, "so that he would not give offense and lose his hard-won place as a kind of permanent houseguest in that society. He saw with the clear-sightedness of the child the evils of his times, but profited too much from the status quo to want to do anything about them." Today we must treasure Andersen for what he was, Lindemann said, a natural genius who could live himself into animals and inanimate objects as well as into a variety of human types, and tell stories that children and many adults still find entertaining. But we also must not turn a blind eye to his weaknesses, the greatest of which—in Lindemann's opinion—was his failure to confront the social injustices of his times, preferring the more comfortable, and convenient, childlike belief in God's love and a happy life for everybody after death.

Lindemann was sure, he said with a smile, the symposium would address these issues in great detail. Pia growled something I didn't catch. I glanced at her. The smile was gone from her mouth, the light from her eyes.

Her father's speech seemed to be designed to end there, and Lindemann put his notes aside. After taking a sip of water, he went on, more quietly: "Tomorrow night we are going to see a stage adaptation of Andersen's 'The Emperor's New Clothes.' Andersen, as many of you know, got the idea for his story from an old Spanish tale. In Andersen's version, the swindlers claim that their remarkable cloth is invisible to anyone who is stupid or unfit for his job. In the Spanish original, the cloth is invisible to anybody who is not the son of his alleged father."

He paused, then went on, almost whispering: "Paternity, of course, is a much stronger motive for pretending not to notice that you are naked than simple incompetence, or stupidity. Imagine what it would have meant to the emperor, who owed his right to rule to his royal blood, if people came to believe he was not his father's son! And think what it would have meant to his ministers if they could not see the clothes the emperor was wearing, since, after all, they too owed their positions of power to their fathers."

He leaned on the lectern and let his gaze sweep around the room, his face suddenly glistening with sweat. "But also," he continued, "in those days—if not in today's more relaxed moral climate—about the worst thing that could happen to a man would be if his wife had been unfaithful to him—it would make him a laughingstock, wouldn't it? So you see, the Spanish version offers a much stronger motive for silence and self-deception than Andersen's simple tale does since, after all, haven't incompetence and stupidity been almost *de rigueur* for civil servants from time immemorial?"

After the audience's anemic titters had subsided, Lindemann went on more seriously: "Why did Andersen change the story? Because the age in which he lived—the Victorian Age—was one of prudery and hypocrisy and, as I have said, Andersen thrived by being a man of his times, for being so brought him fame and honor beyond the imagination of most people. He knew how to tweak the people of his age—but he knew better than to upset them. In short, Hans Christian Andersen could create a child who could say, 'The emperor is naked,' but he did not have the courage to say it himself."

It was a strange way to end a speech inaugurating a symposium devoted to Hans Christian Andersen. I recalled that Pia had mentioned that her father had been married three times. I wondered what his experience of cuckoldry had been. Idly and unforgivably curious, I glanced at Pia to see if she looked at all like her father. I thought she had his mouth.

"A strange and rather disappointing speech," pronounced Professor Claussen, trying without much success to sound disappointed. "It opened no new vistas, and I don't understand the point he was trying to make at the end—everybody knows the Spanish origin of 'The Emperor's New Clothes.' "

"Perhaps he was putting in a plug for the play," his wife suggested indifferently.

Pia seemed to agree with Claussen about her father's speech. "Daddy's spent too much of his life studying Hans Christian Andersen," she muttered, disgustedly. "He's lost all perspective. It's obvious that the reason Andersen changed the story from being a question of paternity to being a question of being unfit for your job is because no child could understand the idea of paternity, but every child knows what it means to be unfit and stupid and to have to pretend you're not! It's only adults who need to be reminded of how it feels!" She shook her head and added, "I think it's horrible that he's going to write a book on Andersen for Americans. What could he possibly have to say?" She looked like she wanted to cry.

Later, as we drove him back to his hotel, Lindemann seemed elated by his speech and how it had been received. Pia didn't say anything, just stared straight ahead through the windshield. Apparently noticing her silence, he asked her what she thought about his remarks at the end of his speech on the origin of "The Emperor's New Clothes."

She told him, not mincing her words. He listened intently to what she said, his hooded gray eyes boring into the side of her face, his mouth twitching in what might have been a smile. Then, turning away from her, he said in a strange voice, "Perhaps you're right, Pia. No child can understand the importance of paternity. You have to be old to do that."

Eleven

Sam scheduled a final run-through of the play in the afternoon on Saturday—we just went through our lines, but didn't have to wear our costumes or move around.

I drove to the University that night. The doctor hadn't said I could drive yet, but we hadn't really been speaking much in the past month anyway. Gary had offered to drive me, but I didn't see any reason why he should have to get there early and hang around waiting for the play to start, especially since he was working against a deadline on a feature article for his paper. I found a parking place close to the bar where we were going to hold the cast party after the play, and walked onto the campus, threading my way among the Old Campus buildings and down the Mall to the theater.

It was a cold fall night, the quarter-moon almost invisible behind a thin layer of cloud. With a pang of regret, I remembered how much I enjoyed patrolling the campus on nights like that. This isn't me, I thought. I'm supposed to be in a uniform, not a costume.

I glanced at my watch nervously. It was almost seventhirty, plenty of time to get into my costume and makeup. Some of the more experienced actors had advised me not to get to the theater too early, since standing around waiting for the curtain to go up would just intensify my firstnight jitters.

A dark shape suddenly emerged in front of me from the path between the library and the building next to it, heading in the same direction I was. I recognized the jaunty gait and the beard. It was Sam Allen. I called his name and he stopped and turned.

He flashed a big grin. "Going my way?"

"I thought I might," I said.

He looked closely at me, asked if I was nervous, and I admitted it.

"I'd be worried about you if you weren't," he said.

It was noisy and full of purposeful chaos backstage as the actors scrambled into their makeup and costumes, the laughter too loud even for theater people, the joking a little forced. I wasn't the only one trying to cover up first-night jitters. I changed into my costume, Sam's idea of a cop in a fantasy kingdom—bright blue pantaloons, a vest with a garish yellow ruffle at the throat, matching yellow stockings, and a blue cocked hat with a long yellow feather in it. I put on a monstrous fire-engine-red wig and an oversized badge that said "Police."

Sam burst into the room. "All right, you mothers," he roared, "pregnant with roles that will be born tonight, let's see how you look."

"Hey, that's good," somebody said. "Is it yours, Sam?"

"The credit's usually given to Stanislavski," he replied. "Anybody besides Peggy O'Neill admit to butterflies? Excellent—just keep them flying in formation, that's all. Remember, *you're* the reality, what's out there's the illusion!" He made a disdainful flapping gesture in the direction of the audience.

A few minutes before the play began, I embarrassed myself in front of my fellow actors by peeking through a hole in the old curtain to see how many people were in the audience, something you're not supposed to do. It wasn't standing room only, but there weren't many empty seats either. I saw Gary, sitting down near the front with Lawrence Fitzpatrick, Paula Henderson, and Ginny Raines, my closest friends on the campus cops. I was going to have to try to forget they were there. Ginny, especially: we get together every couple of weeks to watch old musicals on VCR, so I know what a merciless drama critic she can be.

Farther back, in the middle, Pia was sitting with Mrs. Donnelly and her father Gus Lund. The seat next to Pia was unoccupied. Her father wasn't with her.

And then the curtain went up and the play began. Waiting for my cue to step out on stage was probably the longest twenty minutes of my life, and I'm sure my first lines sounded as horrible to the audience as they did to me, but after a few minutes I seemed to discover—I can't explain how—my fictional voice, and when I did, all the fear went away. I think I caught a glimpse of what's thrilling about being on stage: being somebody you're not in a small, well-lit, fictional reality, surrounded by a watchful darkness, and watching yourself too, using yourself the way a musician uses her instrument.

At the end, when the little girl—the little sister of one of the actors—pointed to the emperor and shouted, "But he's not wearing clothes!" it felt real to me and, at the same time, felt right aesthetically too.

When the emperor, realizing the truth of the child's words, stiffened, hesitated a moment, and then continued his dignified march across the stage, forcing his toadies—me among them—to do the same, I couldn't decide whether I thought the play was comedy or tragedy, although the audience had laughed in all the right places.

When the curtain fell, the sudden burst of applause felt like a jarring intrusion into something that had been better than real for a time, but now I was going to have to adjust to a new reality that was less intense and, somehow, less true.

Backstage after the curtain calls, we all stood around hugging one another and laughing, the tension suddenly released. It was one of the happiest moments of my life.

"Where's the emperor?" Sam hollered.

Andy Blake called "I'm coming!" from the hall outside and a few moments later he came rushing in, in the long rather flesh-colored underwear Sam had designed for him for the final scene, his makeup slightly smeared. We gave him a round of applause.

Sam went around hugging all of us and telling us how well we'd done, and then we retreated to the dressing rooms and cleaned off our makeup, changed into our street clothes, and the magic was over for the night.

Gary, Paula, Lawrence, and Ginny were waiting for me in front of the theater when we came outside. Gary thrust a bouquet of red carnations into my hands and gave me a kiss, and they all told me how great I'd been. I thought so too, but it was nice to hear it confirmed by knowledgeable and unbiased critics, and I may have blushed.

After they'd left, I walked with the rest of the cast across campus to Harold's Pub, where we were holding the cast party.

Sam had allowed Pia to join us and she was walking between me and Andy Blake. After she'd told me how wonderful I was and that I hadn't looked or sounded nervous at all, she said, "Daddy wasn't there. He was going to have dinner with some friends and then come to the theater with them." She shrugged doubtfully. "He looked tired when I saw him this afternoon, so maybe he just took a taxi back to his hotel and went to bed. I know he doesn't like plays adapted from Andersen's stories."

Typical, I thought.

A minute later, as we were passing the library, she exclaimed, "Oh, damn it! He forgot to turn off the light."

"Who?" I followed her glance and saw light glittering through the almost-naked branches of the oak tree outside the window in the Andersen Room.

"Daddy," she replied. "I'm going to do it. You all go on, I'll catch up."

"Forget it," Sam told her. "It's probably just a custodian. The light'll be out before you get there."

"I'll only be a minute," she said, and hurried off.

I'd caught the note of worry in her voice and set off after her. The others continued on to Harold's.

"He's probably not still in there," Pia said when I caught up with her. "He just forgot to turn off the light, or else the custodian's in there."

The library stayed open until midnight. We went down the dimly lit hall of the old library and through the door into the new children's library, well lit but empty. At the Hans Christian Andersen room, Pia tried the door.

"It's locked," she said. She used her key to open it, stepped inside. Behind her, I heard her sudden intake of breath and then she screamed, "Daddy!" and rushed into the room.

Her father was sprawled facedown on the carpet in the middle of the room. Pia knelt and clutched his shoulder and tried to turn him over. From where I was standing, still holding the bouquet of carnations Gary had given me, I could see that his head and face were bloody. The statuette of the Little Mermaid lay next to his body.

"Help him!" Pia screamed, turning to me, her eyes wide with horror.

Incongruously, I noticed in the bright light of the room that she had a smear of purple greasepaint on her pale cheek that made her look like a terrified clown. I dropped the flowers outside the door and went inside, glanced around to make sure nobody else was in there, then knelt beside Pia and pushed her out of the way. I felt for Lindemann's carotid artery. Pia's eyes were on me, her hands to her mouth, her lips moving in silent prayer or supplication.

"He's dead, Pia," I said, and reached for her. She jerked away and threw herself on her father's body. The scene brought back, like a brightly lit tableau on the stage, myself when I was eighteen and I'd just discovered my own father, dead on the rug in his study.

I looked at my watch: It was ten-twenty. I stood up and looked around the room. Hans Christian Andersen's hooded eyes and the malevolent eye of the statue of the stork stared back at the scene. Cold night air was blowing into the room from the window next to Pia's desk. The pane was broken, pieces of glass littered the desk and the floor around it. The glass in the display case that had held the Andersen materials was smashed too.

I asked Pia if there was a phone in the room. She stared at me a moment, then stood up and shook her head.

"We have to leave the room now," I told her. "Come on." I put my arm around her waist and gently guided her back towards the door through which we'd entered.

She stopped in the doorway and looked back into the room. "Poor Daddy," she said, speaking in a soft but clear and strong voice, "he just couldn't learn to fly properly, that was his problem." Then she turned and led the way down the hall.

Twelve

A couple of campus cops were the first to arrive, Jesse Porter and Floyd Hazard, the latter in civilian clothes and nicotine reek that added a lot to the quality of the scene.

"So who's the stiff?" Hazard asked, trying to take charge. He'd just been made a detective—the job I'd applied for but didn't get. He was wearing a trenchcoat that looked new. I didn't realize they still made them.

"Her father," I said coldly, indicating Pia. Pia and I were sitting together on a couch covered with hideous green plastic. I told Hazard and Jesse to secure the building and try to find anybody in the children's library who might have heard or seen anything out of the ordinary.

"I'll check out the scene of the murder," Hazard said, practicing media-speak. "You didn't touch nothin', did you, O'Neill?"

I gave him a withering look and warned him to stay out of the room until the crime scene unit got there. As he strode masterfully out the door, I noticed he was wearing Korfam shoes, somewhat spoiling the effect he was apparently trying to achieve with the trenchcoat.

Buck Hansen arrived with his homicide team a few minutes later. Buck paused in the doorway of the lounge and took a long second look when he saw me, then nodded and continued on down the hall. Buck and I go back a long way.

I didn't want to be there, I wanted to go home. It had been a long day, a physically and emotionally strenuous evening, and now a terrible night. I gave Buck a few min-

utes to get his people to work, then went down the hall after him and stood outside until he noticed me and told me
to come in. Trying to avoid looking at Lindemann's corpse
and the technicians kneeling around it, I went to the
smashed display case. The letters from Andersen to
Henriette Wulff were missing, leaving only the autographed photograph of Andersen, the old editions of his
tales, and the poster headed "My Dear Sisterly Friend."

I told Buck what had been in the case and who the
dead man was. Floyd Hazard, Detective, was standing
over by the body, glowering at me, his hands in his
trenchcoat pockets. Bonnie Winkler, an assistant medical
examiner, asked him to move out of her light. I could appreciate that.

"Do you know anything about those flowers?" Buck
asked me. One of the crime scene people had picked them
up and bagged them.

I explained them, then returned to the staff lounge and
told Pia that Andersen's letters were gone—sooner hear it
from me than from Buck.

"It doesn't make any sense!" she whispered in an astonished voice.

Murder always makes sense, to somebody. I sat down
next to her, absently took out a Kleenex, licked a finger,
and wiped the greasepaint off her cheek. She paid no attention, just stared straight out in front of her.

Buck and his assistant, Sergeant Burke, came in a few
minutes later and I told them how we'd happened to find
the body.

Pia told Buck she'd last seen her father around five-
thirty. She'd been working as usual in the Andersen room
when he came in, around four-thirty, she guessed. He told
her he was tired, and bored with the symposium which
was winding down for the day anyway. He wanted to rest
someplace where he wouldn't be disturbed, but he didn't
want to go back to his hotel, since he was meeting some
friends for dinner at a restaurant near campus and then re

turning with them to see the play. Before she left the room, she gave him the ticket she'd gotten for him.

When she left, he was in the chair under the Andersen portrait, his eyes closed. She reminded him to turn off the lights when he left.

"And what were you doing in there?" Floyd ("Philip Marlowe") Hazard demanded.

Pia told him. He licked his pencil and made a note in his notebook. His lips moved. I'd seen Hazard's lips move when he looked at his watch.

Andy Blake stuck his head in the door, looking worried. Pia saw him, said "Excuse me" to Buck, and got up and went over to him.

I told Buck who he was. Pia spoke to him for a few minutes, Andy gave her a long look, tragicomic under his backwards cap, squeezed her hand, turned, and left.

"Your father just knocked and came in?" Buck asked her when she returned.

"Uh-huh." She chewed hair. "I always leave the door open, so people can come in and look around. It doesn't bother me, and I like to hear what they say about the room and the display and all the other stuff."

"But you locked it behind you when you left?"

"Uh-huh." She looked puzzled. "But the murderer came through the window, didn't he?"

"That's what it looks like," Buck agreed. "But I'm wondering what your father was doing—or where he was—while that was happening. Even if he'd fallen asleep, he'd have heard the window breaking."

"I didn't think of that," she said.

"Maybe it was somebody he knew," Hazard stuck in shrewdly, his eyes narrowed in thought.

We all turned and looked at him.

Buck asked her for the names of the men he'd told her he was going to have dinner with. She gnawed at a fingernail, tried to remember, then shook her head and said she didn't think he'd mentioned their names.

"Did you see anybody you recognized in the hallway outside the room?"

"Sure, lots of people. The symposium was over for the day and everybody was leaving. Nobody asked me about my father, though, or seemed to be hovering suspiciously around the Andersen room or anything. I didn't hang around very long, either."

"As far as you know, nobody knew he was alone in there."

"Huh-unh."

Buck asked her about the missing letters. "Why would anybody want to steal them?" she asked. "You couldn't sell them, or show them off or anything, 'cause everybody would know they were stolen. It just doesn't make sense, unless—"

"Unless what?" Buck asked.

"Well, there was a big fuss in Denmark when Mrs. Donnelly found the letters. It was in all the papers and stuff, and some rich Dane offered Mrs. Donnelly a lot of money for them. The Danish government did too, I think. But she wouldn't sell them, she wanted them here, for the Andersen Room."

Sergeant Burke, taking notes, asked her who Denise Donnelly was. She told him.

"I've heard a lot of nasty comments from Danish scholars who come in and look around," she went on. "They think it's just too phony for words and they're mad that the letters are in there. They call it 'Andersenland,' and one of them asked me where the rides were."

Buck asked her if she knew anybody specifically who might feel strongly enough about the letters to want to steal them.

She frowned. Thinking about what had happened to Jette Wulff's possessions seemed to have taken her mind off her father's murder. She named a few people, said there were lots more she didn't know. Sergeant Burke wrote down the names and had to ask her to spell most of them. "You can search their luggage, can't you?" she asked Buck.

He shook his head. "I'm afraid not. Not without grounds."

I reminded her of the old man I'd met with her grandfather at the banquet the night before.

Pia's eyes widened in horror. "Carl Vedel!"

Pia spelled the name for Burke and I told Buck about our encounter with the man and his daughter at the banquet.

It was midnight before we left the library. I drove Pia home and followed her up to her apartment, neither of us saying much. All the lights were on inside.

Christian met us at the door and took Pia in his arms and hugged her tightly. Sam was in the overstuffed chair, a book open on his lap. Christian looked as though he'd been in a war, with a bandage above one eye and another on his arm. In the excitement of the evening, I'd forgotten that the football team had won that day. He was unshaven and his hair uncombed, as though he'd just pulled off his helmet. He looked older than usual, like a gladiator after a hard-fought battle.

Pia suddenly burst into tears, tore herself away from him, and ran out of the room. Christian hesitated a moment, then followed her.

Sam asked me to tell him what had happened.

I told him and then I went home and told Gary, and that's when I remembered why it's nice having somebody waiting for you sometimes, when you come home at night.

Thirteen

Jens Aage Lindemann's death was a critical success with the media: A distinguished professor from Denmark, murdered not on the mean streets—that could happen to anybody, anywhere—but at the University, in the Hans Christian Andersen Room, in the heart of the children's library! And, piling horror upon horror, the murder weapon had been the little mermaid! If you believed the television anchorwoman, just before she switched on her happy face to report a bake sale for an old people's home, the murder of Jens Aage Lindemann and the theft of Hans Christian Andersen's letters were blows to innocence itself.

President Hightower, flanked by his handlers, deplored the violence that had so cruelly invaded what, mixing metaphors, he called "the olive groves of Academe, those hallowed halls of ivy which stand as Reason's bulwark and our last great hope against the mindless Unreason that threatens our world today."

"Hightower could put you to sleep with a declaration of war," I muttered to Gary.

"The University," the man droned on, "will cooperate in every way with the police in their efforts to bring to justice the culprit or culprits responsible for the murder of Jens Aage Lindemann—not just a Danish knight, but a true knight in the service of world peace through international understanding."

"I didn't know they had knights in Denmark," Gary said.

"Well, Hamlet was a prince, so I suppose Laertes and those other guys must have been knights," I replied.

The review of "The Emperor's New Clothes" in the paper was good, except that I wasn't mentioned.

I followed the investigation on television on Sunday and in Monday morning's newspaper. Buck Hansen was quoted as saying that the police were following a number of leads, but he wouldn't say that an arrest was imminent. On the television news Sunday night, he'd looked as though he hadn't slept since I'd seen him at the crime scene the night before.

I had no intention of offering to help, even though, in the past, I'd gotten involved in trying to solve murders where I knew less about the people involved than I did in this case. Maybe I was growing up, I told myself, or maybe I was still too sore from the last time I'd stuck my nose in where it didn't belong.

Or maybe I identified too closely with Pia, since I'd lost my own father to violence. One middle-aged, white-haired man lying facedown in a pool of blood looks a lot like another, in my experience.

Besides, I'd been passed over for reassignment to detective in favor of Floyd Hazard, who'd prepared for his new role by purchasing a new trenchcoat and switching to unfiltered cigarettes. Let him solve Jens Aage Lindemann's murder.

I called Pia on Sunday, to see how she was doing. Sam answered the phone and told me she was bearing up well. She was spending the day at her mother's place.

I remembered that, just before the play Saturday night, I'd met Sam coming from the path between the library and the building next to it. That must have been at least an hour after Lindemann had been killed, if what I'd read in the papers had been correct, but I asked him if he'd noticed anything suspicious around the library anyway.

"Until I got to the Mall and you hailed me, I didn't

see a soul," he replied. "But I wasn't near the children's library anyway—I'd had to park my car in that faculty lot behind the old library and took my chances on getting ticketed by one of your flatfooted colleagues."

"And did you?"

"Fortunately not. It was a cold night, and the catchpoles and beagles were no doubt huddled in shelters, warming their frozen mitts over portable stoves."

"You were lucky I wasn't patrolling the Old Campus that night, Sam," I told him, and we hung up.

Pia called Monday morning as I was wondering what my corn flakes were coated with that resisted penetration by milk. The medical examiner had finished with Lindemann's body, she told me, and released it for disposal. She said her mother, Nancy Austin, had offered to help her with the details, but she'd refused. She was twenty-three years old, after all, and could handle things like that on her own, she said, and her father was no longer her mother's business. Lindemann had had an older sister, but she was dead, and neither Pia nor her mother knew the addresses in Denmark of any other surviving relatives.

Lindemann had had two other ex-wives, one who'd come before and one after Pia's mom. All Pia knew about wife number three was that she'd remarried and had been living in Germany the last time her father had mentioned her. Nancy Austin gave the police the name of wife number one—a doctor in Copenhagen. Pia had called her on Sunday. She'd been very kind, expressed her sympathy to Pia—whom she'd never met—on the loss of her father, and couldn't give her the whereabouts of any members of Lindemann's family in Denmark, which was understandable, since she and Lindemann had been divorced for over twenty-five years.

"I don't have time to take Daddy's body to Denmark right now," Pia said. "I'm way behind on my thesis."

"I'm sure Edith would give you an extension," I told

her. "But from the little I saw of him, I don't think your father would want you to put sentiment above scholarship." The words came out a little drier than I'd meant them to.

"You're quick, aren't you, Peggy? My poor dad—father—wasn't a warm-hearted man. I'm going to bury him here—it's as good a place as any."

It was ironic that a man who hated this country would meet a violent death here on his first visit, then end up being buried here by a daughter he hardly knew and didn't seem to care much about.

"And this way," Pia said, reading my mind again, "I'll get to visit him sometimes."

"Is his body still at the morgue?"

"No, he's right here in our apartment, in a jar. It gives Christian the creeps, but it doesn't bother me. Christian says he'd pay for a locker at the bus station, but I told him not to be so squeamish. Daddy's gone, these are just ashes. I considered taking them to the memorial service," she added with a laugh, "but decided it would give his colleagues too much satisfaction."

The University had scheduled a memorial service for her father on Wednesday night at the Campus Club.

"And by the way, congratulations," she added, as we were about to hang up.

"For what?"

"The play got a great review in the *Daily*—and you were even mentioned!"

"I was?"

"Yep. The scene where you keep repeating 'I see' was singled out as one of the funniest."

"Huh!" I said modestly. "Save me a copy of the *Daily*, will you?"

It was the only scene in which I had very many lines. The emperor calls me in and he and his counsellors want my opinion of the cloth the swindlers are weaving. They keep feeding me my lines, though, so all I can say is, "I see." Sam coached me a long time on it, to get the right tone of voice between "I see" meaning "I see," and "I see" meaning "I understand what you're telling me to think." It's not as easy as it sounds.

"If you ever decide to change occupations, Peggy," Pia said, "you've got a future in theater."

"I see," I said.

Early Tuesday morning, as I was on my way out of the house, intending to go for a walk, the phone rang. It was Ginny Raines. She told me Captain DiPrima wanted to see me in his office at ten o'clock. DiPrima was campus police chief.

"I'm on leave," I reminded her. "Doesn't he know?"

"Your friend Buck Hansen'll be there too," she replied.

I laughed. I was pretty sure I knew what it was going to be about.

Giving my bike a longing glance, I took my car and arrived at campus police headquarters a few minutes late. As I passed her office, Ginny whistled a snatch of Schumann's "Important Event," which was appropriate, I guess, since Schumann and Hans Christian Andersen were friends, according to Pia.

Captain DiPrima's door was open and he was chatting with Buck when I walked in. Buck grinned and gave me a wink. Lieutenant Bixler, my nemesis, was leaning against a bookcase over by the window, scowling.

I took a chair across the room from Buck and turned my attention to DiPrima, feeling I was going to enjoy this session.

One reason I've always preferred to work nights is to avoid administrators, so I hadn't seen much of DiPrima. He'd been chief less than a year, but I'd heard he was reasonably competent, and benign as long as things were going well. He's a slight man of medium height with dark, close-set eyes and crewcut, graying hair.

"I think you know Lieutenant Hansen," he said. "He wants your help in the investigation of Jens Aage Lindemann's murder."

Bixler's scowl deepened and he made a quiet, but still awful noise, kind of like a stump grinder.

I switched my bright-eyed look to Buck.

He gave me a slightly embarrassed grin. "I'm a little surprised you haven't offered to help before now, Peggy. It's been two whole days."

Buck had never come right out and asked me to help him before, although, in a few cases, I'd suspected he was grateful for my help even as he was urging me to keep away.

I turned to Captain DiPrima. "I thought Floyd Hazard was on the case. Didn't somebody tell me he'd bought a deer stalker cap and a magnifying glass?"

Bixler bounced to attention off the wall. "Knock off the wisecracks, O'Neill. What Hansen means is, you're some kind of friend of the victim's daughter, you met the victim, and you found the body." He ticked off these facts on sausagelike fingers. "Usually it don't take that much to get you sticking your nose in where it don't belong."

I gave him a gentle smile. "I'm growing up, Lieutenant Bixler," I told him. "I've finally begun to realize that, as you've so often reminded me, I'm just a simple beat cop. I don't have any business playing detective."

"Or maybe you're scared," he jeered. "Maybe you learned your lesson the last time you didn't mind your own business."

That was pretty clever, for Bixler. "You're probably right," I replied.

When Bixler's face gets red, as it was now, it looks like a half-empty hot water bottle—or half-full, if you're an optimist. "If you've got anything that can help solve this murder, O'Neill," he blustered, "you're obligated to share it with the cops working the case."

"Right!" I turned to Buck. "Jens Aage Lindemann was killed by the stork general because he couldn't learn to fly properly."

Buck didn't seem particularly surprised to hear that. "That's a new one," he said. "Where'd you get it?"

"From his daughter. There's a story by Hans Christian Andersen in which the baby storks are warned by their mothers that if they don't learn to fly properly, the stork general will stab them to death with his beak."

Buck laughed. "Whoever killed Lindemann must not have known the story, since it wasn't a stork that killed him. It was a mermaid."

Captain DiPrima was looking a little confused. "I hope that before you're through with this case, Officer O'Neill, you'll come up with something better than that."

I turned to him and said, "I want to be a detective."

"You gotta be kidding!" That was Bixler.

"Didn't you interview for the last detective vacancy?" DiPrima asked.

"Yes, I did, and I got turned down. Apparently I didn't do as well on the oral interview as Floyd Hazard. You'll have to ask Lieutenant Bixler why."

DiPrima chose not to do that. "I don't think we have a detective vacancy at the moment," he said. "Do we, Lieutenant."

"No." Bixler.

"That's too bad," I said, and started to get up. "I'm on leave—doctor's orders."

DiPrima started to turn a little pink himself, although he was no match for Bixler in that department, perhaps because he hadn't dealt with me before. "But helping your friend Lieutenant Hansen wouldn't involve anything physically taxing," he said. "No more taxing than sitting at a desk, surely. And, of course, we'd put you back on active duty"—he gave me a gracious smile—"effective, shall we say, two weeks ago?"

I do believe I'm being bribed, I thought, amazed. I liked the feel of it. I sat back down.

"I've been a patrolman long enough, Captain," I said. "I need a change. I'd make a good detective."

DiPrima frowned. "Blackmail doesn't work with me, Officer O'Neill."

I clutched the side where my spleen is. "I'm on leave, Captain, and living off my savings because Lieutenant Bixler wouldn't authorize a medical leave. The doctor said he thought I'd be able to return to duty in about a week."

I got up and marched to the door. DiPrima waited until I got there and then said, "If you agree to help Lieutenant Hansen, we'll talk again when the case is over."

I turned and looked back at him. "When this case is over," I told him, "I want the department to send me to the detective training course at the State Bureau of Criminal Apprehension." It's an eighty-hour course in all the latest investigative techniques.

"*If* you're helpful in apprehending the perp," Bixler stuck in.

"No. Regardless of how this case turns out," I said, still looking at DiPrima.

"You know something you're not telling us, don't you?" Bixler whined.

When I continued to ignore him, DiPrima said, "That's enough, Lieutenant. Clearly, Officer O'Neill has us over a barrel, and she knows it." He tapped his teeth with a pencil for a moment, then nodded. "All right, I agree to both of your demands."

I thought of asking for it in writing, but decided to take him at his word. DiPrima seemed like the kind of man who believed in honor among men, and that would include women too, at least with a witness as strong as Buck present.

"Okay," I said.

Buck got up and thanked DiPrima and shook hands with both men. I stayed at the door, watching. Bixler looked as though he wanted to cry—not a pretty sight.

Fourteen

"I'm not sure I can stand being a detective," I said, as soon as Buck and I were outside the building. "One of the advantages of working the dog watch is you don't see much of people like DiPrima and Bixler. Rapists, murderers, drunks, yes—but with those you pretty much know where you are. With administrators, you don't."

"I thought you handled those two birds pretty well."

"I would've helped you anyway, Buck," I told him, "even if DiPrima had turned me down. I'm surprised he agreed to my terms, though."

"I'm not," he said with a grin. "Lindemann's murder has given the University a black eye—especially since the media discovered that nobody considered installing a burglar alarm in the Andersen Room a very high priority. So the president has personally demanded that your chief cooperate with us in every way in solving the case."

"Hightower always takes bold initiatives after the barn's burned down," I said.

"The Danes have begun identifying Lindemann with Hans Christian Andersen himself," Buck went on, "and they seem to be holding the University responsible too—even though the killer could just as easily have been one of the visiting Danish scholars."

We crossed College Avenue to the espresso bar in the little strip mall that's sprung up opposite campus police headquarters. I ordered a double *macchiato,* Buck a tall *latte* that he gunked up with cinnamon and chocolate and then we found a table next to the big plate glass window where we could watch cars and students playing dodge-em, and he filled me in on what he'd got so far.

Bonnie Winkler, the medical examiner, had estimated that the latest Lindemann could have died was around six-thirty. I already knew that from reading the newspaper. Pia had last seen her father at five-thirty, and Buck hadn't been able to turn up anybody who'd seen him alive after that, or would admit it if they had.

I asked about the men Pia had said he was having dinner with.

"A Norwegian and a German," Buck told me. "They wanted to talk about a conference on Andersen in Berlin next year and they expected him at the restaurant at six-thirty. He never showed up."

"Weren't they concerned?"

"Nope. They thought it would be just like him to take a better—or more interesting—offer, if one turned up."

Whoever had broken into the Andersen Room, presumably, had carefully picked the pieces of glass out of the bottom of the frame in order to climb through without getting cut, and the frame itself had been wiped clean of fingerprints. The crime scene crew, however, had found a trace of fresh blood on a piece of splintered wood in the window frame, and it wasn't Lindemann's.

"If we get a strong suspect," Buck said, "we can do DNA testing."

The pattern of blood splashes on the carpet around the body indicated Lindemann had been struck while standing, then struck again—two, possibly three times—while falling or partially down. The murder weapon had been the bronze statuette of the little mermaid, wielded as a hammer. The killer had wiped it clean of prints, but traces of Lindemann's blood, and his hair, had been found on the rock on which the mermaid was reclining, a piece of white granite.

With a little shudder, I remembered how Lindemann had picked up the mermaid statue and examined it when he'd first entered the room. There should have been ominous music.

Most of the symposium participants—over a hundred—had visited the room, and they'd left plenty of evidence of their comings and goings, further complicating the police's job.

"In fact," Buck said, "the only objects in the room without fingerprints on them were *The Little Mermaid* and the table it was sitting on."

I remembered Sam Allen's head slowly rising in the Andersen Room window, like a bearded sun, the first time we'd met. Anybody over about five-nine could have reached it, broken the glass, and crawled through, if they'd been strong and agile enough.

"But the killer couldn't have come through the window with Lindemann in the room," I said, "so Lindemann must have stepped out—probably to go to the bathroom. When he returned, he surprised somebody in the act of breaking into the display case. Maybe Lindemann tried to capture the thief, or recognized somebody who couldn't afford to be recognized."

"We've learned that a lot of Danes are angry that the letters managed to survive for a hundred and fifty years, only to end up in a room in America that's mostly full of what they think of as junk. The trouble is, we don't have enough evidence against anybody to get search warrants, or warrants to take samples of their blood."

"How about the man Pia told you about, the one who thinks the letters belong to him?"

Buck made a face. "Carl Vedel. He has a little antique shop a couple of miles out of town. He and Gustav Lund have known each other a long time—they're both interested in Danish immigrant furniture, which Vedel also restores and sells. Vedel thinks Lund and his daughter somehow tricked him out of the letters. He admits quite frankly that he's angry about it."

"Lindemann met both Vedels at the banquet," I said, "so

he'd have recognized them if he'd caught one of them in the act."

"The trouble is, Vedel's too short to have reached that window without a ladder and there aren't any ladder marks in the ground. Also, you can't reach the window from the tree."

"Vedel's daughter, Mary, is tall enough. What kind of alibis do they have?"

"They live together. Mary has a part-time job at the University, and helps her father some at the antique shop. They claim they were in the shop all day Saturday until they closed. They stayed home that night, watching television."

"Not the strongest of alibis," I said.

"I asked both of them if they'd give blood samples voluntarily, to help us exclude suspects. They were outraged and refused. Maybe, if I get really desperate, I'll hunt up a judge who'll sign a warrant on so little evidence—I know one or two like that. Of course, the Vedels could get a lawyer and it might take months before we could serve the warrants on them, if ever."

Buck scraped the dregs of his *latte* onto a finger, contemplated it a moment, and then licked it off. "And then there are the Danish-Americans," he went on, shaking his head. "God knows how many of them may have coveted those Andersen letters, or thought they deserved a better home than the Andersen Room. And there's also the possibility that somebody might have stolen the letters with the intention of selling them to a rich Dane for his private collection. Apparently Mrs. Donnelly received some pretty substantial offers for them from Danish collectors, when they first turned up."

"You'd expect a professional thief to break in much later at night, though, wouldn't you?"

"True, but it was dark and there's that big oak tree. Once all the scholars left the symposium, the children's library was nearly deserted."

After we'd sat there a few moments in silence, I said, "It seems a little pat, though, doesn't it?"

"How so?"

"Almost choreographed. Lindemann exits stage left. The thief's head pops up at the window. He peers around, sees the coast is clear. He breaks the window and crawls into the room, tiptoes over to the display case and breaks the glass, and he's in the process of pocketing the letters when Lindemann reenters the room. Lindemann does a double take, recognizes the thief. The thief grabs the statuette of the mermaid and kills him with it. Or she does, of course."

"I see you're thinking in terms of theater these days, Peggy. I hope I get time to come and see you. You must be quite an actress, to be able to play a cop who sees only what's best for her career."

"The world's full of role models for that," I told him.

"I don't suppose it was a woman," he said. "Lindemann wouldn't have fled from a woman."

"You don't think so? You must not have talked to Mary Vedel personally, Buck. It's far likelier Lindemann would run from her than from her father."

"I'll take your word for it." He gave me a curious look. "What's the matter, Peggy? You look unhappy."

"You know me," I replied, "I like people to somehow earn their deaths. I don't like it when innocent people get killed just because they're in the wrong place at the wrong time."

"It happens all the time."

"But it shouldn't. Have you considered the possibility that Lindemann's murder was the intended crime, the Andersen stuff was taken to throw you off the trail?"

"Of course. But the problem with that is, there were a lot of better places to murder Lindemann, if that's what the intended crime was, than the Andersen Room. And better weapons too. Usually, if you come to kill, you bring your weapon with you, you don't expect to find something handy to use. Also, how would the killer know Lindemann would leave the room long enough for him to break in like that? Surely he would just have knocked on the door and, when Lindemann let him in, gone in, killed him, and left."

"You're probably right, but just in case you're not, I wonder if you've turned up anybody who might have profited from Lindemann's death."

"Well, he wasn't very popular among his colleagues— we've managed to pick up that bit of information—but nobody's been willing to point to anyone specifically."

"According to Pia, he'd never been in the US before."

Buck nodded. "I guess not—although we're checking to make sure. Apparently he despised this country and had refused invitations to come here in the past. Even his daughter told us she'd begged him for years to come. We don't know what made him change his mind and decide to come this time—as far as I can gather, the Hans Christian Andersen conference wasn't any more important than other conferences he refused to come here to attend."

"Ah, but had he ever been invited to be the keynote speaker at a Hans Christian Andersen symposium before? Also, it's not uncommon that when professors start to get old, and the juices aren't flowing the way they used to, they begin to hustle to collect all the awards and honors they can get, no matter how silly, to prove to themselves and the world that they've still got what it takes."

Buck laughed. "Maybe you're right. However, he spent last Monday afternoon discussing with the University Press the details of a book he was going to write on Hans Christian Andersen."

"I know. He mentioned it to Pia and me at lunch last week. But he didn't need to be here in person to do that."

"I've talked to the editor at the press. He said Lindemann insisted on complete control over the layout of the book, number, size, and quality of the illustrations. He thought it was the kind of negotiations that could best be done in person."

Buck sighed, leaned back in his chair. He had a mustache of cinnamon and chocolate that gave a kind of swashbuckling cast to his face. "Lindemann flies six thousand miles, to a country he's never been in before, to give a speech at a symposium to open a children's literature library, and gets murdered. Was it just an accident? Or did somebody follow him here with the intent to kill him? Or was somebody already here, waiting for him, who wanted him dead?"

I sat up. "What do you mean, 'somebody already here'?"

"You usually look close to home for a murderer," he reminded me. "His second wife's an American who lives here in town—Pia's mother."

"I've met her," I said. "She's really nice. She probably never even saw Lindemann while he was here."

"When we questioned Mrs. Austin," Buck said, grimacing, "she denied she'd had any contact with him since their divorce. Unfortunately for her, the hotel he was staying at keeps a record of phone calls made from their customer's rooms. Lindemann called his ex-wife Saturday morning and they talked for about three minutes."

Oh, hell! "How'd she handle that?"

"Told us she'd lied because she hadn't wanted to get involved and the call wasn't relevant to Lindemann's murder. Said he'd wanted to get together with her for dinner—probably to talk about old times. Said she hung up on him."

"People lie to cops," I said. "That's standard. It doesn't have to mean anything."

"I know." He sighed at the lies people tell cops, especially when the topic of conversation is murder.

I'd had lunch with Nancy Austin and Pia. She didn't seem like the kind of person who would waste energy holding a grudge against anybody.

"They've been divorced fifteen years and Nancy's got a great life now," I said. "She doesn't have a motive."

Buck shrugged. "Who knows? Apparently Lindemann's parents were well off and left their money to him and his sister, who never married and died a few years ago. We don't know how much money he had—but maybe he called Mrs. Austin to tell her he was cutting Pia out of his will."

"Oh, come on, Buck!"

"It doesn't only happen in Agatha Christie, Peggy. We're not excluding any possibility, no matter how farfetched, at this stage of the investigation. Besides, I thought you said you wanted us to look for a personal motive—so Lindemann could 'deserve' his death."

I hate it when people throw my own words back at me.

I remembered the strange way Lindemann had ended his talk on Hans Christian Andersen at the banquet Friday night, with an account of the Spanish version of "The Emperor's New Clothes," where the point of the satire was a man's fear of being illegitimate. I told Buck about it. "He might have been projecting," I added. "I wonder if he left any illegitimate kids around."

"If he did, Interpol will probably find out for us. Or we'll discover he left his money to an illegitimate child somewhere, and the child has a passport with a US stamp in it for last week. Sometimes it's just that easy."

But Buck didn't believe it was going to be that easy this time.

When we'd finished our coffee, he said, "Since you're officially a part of the case, Peggy, you ought to take a look through the evidence we have. Nothing in it seems particularly enlightening, but you have to start somewhere. You want to do that now?"

I said sure, and started to dig into my purse for my share of the bill.

"It's on me," he said, "in honor of your new status as a real detective."

"Okay," I said, laughing. "But it's not official yet."

"No, but at least you're officially assigned to a murder case. That's worth celebrating."

I said I supposed so.

* * *

As we crossed back across College Avenue to our cars, Buck asked me what Pia Austin was like.

I told him it was hard to say: Although she was twenty-three, she could change from child to adult to crone faster than any woman I'd ever known.

"What was her relationship with her father?"

I shot him a quick glance. "She loved him, but he didn't seem to know she was alive. Are you asking me if I think she might have murdered her own father?"

"It happens."

I shook my head. "No. She knew his limitations, and I think she accepted them. Besides, she had a key to the Andersen Room, she wouldn't have needed to come through the window. And she's too short to reach it anyway."

"You really like her a lot, don't you?"

"Yes. She's kind of got under my skin."

I was trying to drown out the memory of something Pia had said about her father after his speech at the banquet. She'd been really angry at him for his attitude towards Andersen, and said she thought it was horrible that he was going to write a book on him for Americans.

Nobody would kill their own father for something like that, would they? Of course not!

I followed him downtown in my car, sliding behind him down the ramp into the official parking area beneath the police building. I'd been down there before, when bringing somebody to jail. I never enjoyed being down there.

The nameplate on Buck's door says "Mansell Hansen," his real name. Nobody calls him "Mansell" more than once, however. I once asked him if the stress is on the first or second syllable, but he pretended he didn't hear me. It's quite possible he doesn't know himself anymore.

He went behind his cluttered desk and I took the old leather chair in front of it.

I asked him who else Lindemann had called during his stay here besides his ex-wife.

He opened his notebook and thumbed through it. "Pia several times at her apartment. Professor Eric Claussen, once at home and twice at his office. Claussen told us the calls concerned the details of the symposium and the banquet. Also, he and his wife had Lindemann over to dinner Thursday night, and one call was about that, he said. Lindemann also called Carl Vedel."

"Why?"

"Vedel's the president of the Sons of Denmark. He said Lindemann called him to get directions to their meeting place—he gave a talk there Tuesday night. That's all. Of course, we have no record of how many people called him."

"Okay," I said. "So where's the evidence you want me to look at?"

He took me down the hall to the Property Room where a sleepy cop reluctantly fetched two large cardboard boxes. He put them on a long table and shambled back where he'd come from.

"This is everything we found in Lindemann's hotel room," Buck said. "The clothes he was wearing are still at the crime lab. Here's an inventory list. I'll be in my office if you need me."

It's depressing, going through a dead person's belongings. It's not as bad as going through the belongings of somebody you knew and loved, but it's bad enough. Fortunately, Lindemann seemed to have been an experienced traveller, and he hadn't brought very much with him. It only took me five minutes to go carefully through everything.

His plane ticket explained why he hadn't packed much. He'd intended to stay less than a week, returning to Denmark on Sunday morning. He'd only come here to discuss his book contract, talk to the Sons of Denmark, see Pia briefly, and give the keynote speech at the banquet Friday night. He'd planned to spend only one day at the symposium, Saturday—probably to remind the world's Andersen scholars, or himself, that he was still king of the hill—and then fly back home.

Murder had kept him here longer than he'd meant to stay. It was going to keep him here forever.

The only other item of interest was a copy of Friday's *Daily,* the University newspaper, the one that contained an article on Christian Donnelly and his family. At the banquet Friday night Lindemann had mentioned to Pia that he'd read it. I looked through it carefully, searching for cryptic scrawls, but there wasn't anything, just a picture of Christian staring out at me with his sleepy eyes full of some secret amusement. He was holding a football.

I returned the boxes to the property clerk and went back to Buck's office.

"Okay," I said, "now I've wasted twenty minutes doing what real detectives do. Amateur sleuths don't waste their time on stuff like that. So what do you want me to do?"

He looked up from something he was reading. "I want you to attend the symposium, circulate, and pick up clues as they drop from the scholars' lips. But tread softly, Peggy. A lot of those people think they're too good to be involved in a murder investigation—murderers and murder suspects don't have Ph.D.'s from ancient European universities, I guess—and they're way too important to be harrassed by flatfeet. You've always been good at that kind of thing, because of your ingratiating personality and ability to blend in. You ought to be even better at it when you're doing it legitimately."

"It'll be a change, anyway."

Fifteen

By the time I got to the University, I was starving, so I bought a hamburger and fries from a Cholesterol-R-Us place near the Old Campus and ate them while considering where to begin.

Shortly after Pia and I became friends, we'd had lunch with her mother, Nancy Austin. I'd liked her. It worried me that she'd lied to Buck, and I try not to live with worry any longer than I have to. Besides, Nancy—she'd asked me to call her that right away—had probably known Lindemann better than anybody else I could talk to, even though she hadn't lived with him in fifteen years. So I decided to start with her.

She was director of the University's Study Abroad Program, housed in one of the oldest and most beautiful buildings on the Old Campus, a construction of brick, ivy, functionless turrets, and leaded glass. I walked into the main office, gave the receptionist my name, and asked if I could speak to Mrs. Austin. He disappeared around a corner and returned a moment later to tell me I could go on back to Nancy's office.

She watched me come in with a questioning look on her face, but didn't ask me what I wanted until I'd sat down and she'd offered me a cup of coffee.

Nancy Austin looked a lot like her daughter—the same dark and intelligent eyes, the same determined chin and pale complexion. The vulnerability on Pia's face was missing, but not the mobility. And, of course, her face looked a lot more lived-in than Pia's.

I told her I'd been assigned to help the city homicide police with the investigation into her ex-husband's murder. It was the first time I'd ever said that, although on a couple of past occasions I'd allowed people to think I was talking to them officially—but the moment wasn't marked with trumpets.

"I spent quite a lot of time on Sunday talking to policemen," she said. She smiled faintly. "You must know they even caught me in a lie."

I nodded. "Why?"

She shrugged. "It seemed like a good idea at the time. I didn't realize hotels keep records of outgoing phone calls. Jens Aage's call wasn't relevant to his murder, so I just thought it might give the police wrong ideas, and cause me grief. When I left him fifteen years ago, I swore he wouldn't do that to me anymore. I should have known better."

"But didn't he tell you why he wanted to have dinner with you?"

She shook her head impatiently. "I already told the police he didn't! He just sounded—he sounded like he used to when we were married, when we'd go out to dinner on Sunday night, and he'd try to pretend we were lovers, meeting clandestinely. That's how he liked it—he couldn't stand the fact that we were married. Marriage is just repetition, he'd say, and he was always thinking up ways to try to make it more—"

She broke off suddenly. "Sorry, Peggy! I haven't thought about our marriage in a lot of years. I didn't realize it was still somewhere inside me, just as new and awful as it was at the time." She got up and walked to the window, stared out at the naked trees in the overcast afternoon, then turned back to me.

"Anyway, when he called me Saturday morning and asked me if I'd have dinner with him—'How about Sunday night,' he said, 'Just like old times'—I lost it. I told him to go to hell and hung up. If he'd actually been there, and I'd had something to hit him with—'The Little Mermaid,' say—I'd have done it. But he wasn't, and I didn't."

After a few moments, she continued, "It's amazing how something evil you think is dead can suddenly rise up and bite, isn't it? Pia told me her father was looking old and tired. He'd probably got a whiff of mortality and was turning soft and sentimental—men like Jens Aage sometimes do when they start to grow old, and they don't have as many ways to keep life itself from seeming repetitious."

I thought back to my few encounters with Lindemann. I supposed it was possible he was going soft and sentimental—but certainly not where Pia was concerned. Maybe he did just want to relive the good old days with somebody who'd been there. He didn't seem to have anybody else.

"Pia tells me you don't like Denmark very much," I said. "And yet here you are, in charge of sending students there."

The walls of her large office were decorated with bright posters of places in the world where University students could go to study. Most of them featured buildings, bridges, and bodies of water I thought looked vaguely famous, with obscenely healthy-looking people in various kinds of native costume doing ethnic things as they laughed into the camera with mouths full of large, white, and perfectly straight teeth. I prefer teeth with character, like mine.

Nancy shrugged impatiently, came back to her desk, and sat down. "I send students lots of places, Peggy, not only to Denmark. Denmark's a lovely country, I just made a bad decision while I was there—several bad decisions— and that ruined the place for me."

"You probably don't have a lot to talk to Christian's mother about," I said.

She smiled, shook her head. "No—nothing, in fact. My husband and I hardly ever see Christian's parents, I'm afraid. Hank doesn't share Clay Donnelly's interest in sports and Donnelly doesn't share Hank's interest in politics. Denise is something of a blue-eyed idealist when it comes to Denmark, so we don't socialize."

I asked her how she and Lindemann had got together in the first place.

She stared at me for a minute, considering, then said, "Sure, why not?—though it's not going to help you solve Jens Aage's murder. I went to Denmark on an exchange program when I was nineteen—over twenty-five years ago." She looked around her office. "I can still recall coming in here, to pick up the application forms from the man who had my job then. I was a small-town kid—they called women students 'coeds' then, to make sure we knew we were curiosities who didn't quite belong in college. I didn't particularly care which country I went to, but we've always had close ties to Denmark here on account of our large Danish-American population so I let myself be talked into going there for the year. Denmark came as quite a cultural shock. It was the late sixties—you remember the sixties?"

"I lost a brother to them," I told her. "A half-brother, actually, but I loved him anyway."

"Then you know what I'm talking about—the 'Age of Aquarius,' raise your consciousness through music, drugs, sex, and dirty feet. I steered clear of all that very fastidiously—and ended up in bed with my teacher! I had no idea what Jens Aage found attractive about me, I was just flattered by his attention. He was young, but seemed very sophisticated to me, very European, with a blend of cynicism and sentimentality I'd never encountered before and found irresistible." Nancy shook her head in amazement at the person she'd been then.

"His wife had just left him and he seemed deeply saddened about it. He said she was a medical student who had no time to work on their marriage. Poor man! I had nothing but time for the marriage, since I had no particular career goals at all. By the time I left him, I was the same shallow American girl who'd arrived in Denmark eleven years before. I'd just grown older. You don't look as though you know what it's like to be a 'girl' pushing thirty, Peggy."

"Thanks," I said.

"No, Jens Aage wasn't a part of the drug scene of the sixties, but he did think of himself as a part of the 'sexual revolution.' He just didn't bother to let me in on all that entailed. He didn't remain faithful to me for long, I discovered later, but I didn't suspect anything for a long time."

"He must have been very good at sneaking around," I said.

"If academics had to be good at it, they'd be the most faithful husbands in the world, but they don't. They keep irregular working hours, as I'm sure you know, and aren't accountable for their whereabouts to anybody, day or night. Jens Aage stayed late at the University sometimes— and sometimes took mornings or afternoons off for his extracurricular activities too. 'He was at the library, he was at a meeting,' if anybody asked. But who would ask? He also travelled regularly to other universities in the Scandinavian countries and Europe, for conferences and meetings and to give guest lectures."

She swallowed coffee, then made a face, either at the coffee, which must have been cold, or at what was coming.

"Finally, he returned home late one Sunday afternoon and it was obvious that he'd been with a woman—I could smell her. I confronted him with it and he said we'd discuss it over dinner that night—over a nice dinner, with candles and wine, at our favorite restaurant. When we'd eaten, and were sitting there with our cognac—God, how sophisticated we were!—he told me he believed monogamy cheats people, men and women both, out of nine-tenths of their sex lives.

"He wanted me to have affairs too, so we could meet afterwards, as we were doing then, and talk about them— compare notes, relive the adventure with cognac and candlelight, he said. I think Jens Aage liked reliving the experience of sex more than sex itself. He said it would keep the life in our marriage. And then we would stroll home and . . ."

"What'd you do?"

"Threw up." She laughed, sounding pleased. "I was pregnant with Pia, so morning sickness might have been a contributing factor, but mainly it was disgust, I think. I stuck it out eight more years. Why? Now, I don't know, Peggy. I guess I wanted to make my marriage work—my parents had been opposed to it, and I didn't want to prove them right.

"But it was more than that. It was also that I felt I was to blame. Jens Aage made his way of life sound so reasonable, so natural. 'Sex is the great synthesis of mind and body, spirit and flesh, reason and emotion. We only live once, so why limit ourselves to knowing just one other person so completely? Sex is as natural as drinking water, so why regulate it?' It was me who was unnatural, I was still living in the Victorian Age.

"And I stayed with him because I was afraid of the unknown too. I had a baby and was far from home and didn't know how to do anything useful—just speak Danish! For Christ's sake, poodle clippers in Copenhagen could do that better than I could, no matter how long I lived there!

"I left Jens Aage on my thirtieth birthday. It wasn't because I felt he was going to dump me for a younger edition of myself. Oh, no, he was quite content to have Pia and me hanging around his apartment, for him to come home to. We gave him some kind of anchor, appealed to some residual need he had for the trappings of a conventional life."

"The other women probably wouldn't have been the thrill they were," I said, "if he didn't have married life to contrast them to."

She shrugged. "Who knows? I just woke up one morning with a clear head. I bought plane tickets for Pia and me, packed, and flew back here. I had nothing. I could probably have got a Danish court to force him to pay child support, but I didn't have the money to hire a lawyer, and I was afraid he might fight for custody, or somehow use Pia to punish me for leaving him."

"You must have hated him."

Nancy gave me a surprised look and then laughed. "Of course I hated him, Peggy—he'd stolen eleven years of my life! But I didn't kill him, if that's what you're getting at. Of course, when you finally do meet his killer, he'll tell you that too, won't he—or she?"

"That's been my experience," I admitted.

"If I was the murderous type, I would have done it twenty years ago."

Unless something new had come up in the meantime that he wanted to talk to her about. I assumed Buck's detectives were trying to find out if she and Lindemann had been seen together, at his hotel or a restaurant.

"Until he called Saturday morning, you hadn't seen or spoken to him since the divorce?"

"That's right. He occasionally wrote to me, trying to make me feel guilty for leaving him, but that stopped fairly soon. And when Pia was a child, we exchanged letters concerning visitation, but she's dealt with that herself for the past seven or eight years."

I asked her if she could think of anybody who might have hated Lindemann enough to murder him.

"Well, for starters, I suppose you'd have to look among his lovers—going back at least thirty-five years . . . and his lovers' husbands too, or boyfriends. And his colleagues at the Danish universities." She shrugged. "I once knew the names of some of them, but I've forgotten them all now. Nobody stands out in my memory as having hated him, but nobody had any real friends in the academic world there either—it was too cutthroat. And, of course, there are his other wives."

"You haven't seen any of his colleagues, or their wives, who've come here for the symposium?"

"Me?" She laughed, as though I were nuts. "When I left

Denmark, Peggy, I left all of that behind. I didn't make Lot's wife's mistake."

"And so," I said, "here you sit now, the director of the U's Study Abroad Program."

"When I got back here, I needed a job and I had the kind of experience they were looking for. I started out as one of the advisers in the program. I did that for ten years before getting the director's job."

"You send young women to Denmark to study too, don't you?"

She laughed. "You make it sound like lambs to the slaughter! Denmark's a pleasant enough country, and the Danes are good people, just like people anywhere. But I always make the women come into my office for an interview before they fly off to Denmark—or anywhere else, for that matter—and lecture them about the dangers of homesickness and being in a foreign country where you are exotic to the inhabitants and they're exotic to you—but neither of you is at all exotic in reality. It's not as necessary now as it was when I went off to study abroad—young women are much more sophisticated than I was."

Nancy Austin leaned across her desk suddenly and looked into my eyes. "Peggy," she blurted out, "Jens Aage Lindemann was an awful man. He had the morality of a mink. He looked like somebody you wanted to take care of—he had a needy smile—and he could be incredibly charming. But inside he was as cold and gray as the afternoon out there. He was incapable of love and he left the world a little poorer than it was when he came into it. Not on any grand scale, of course, but on the little scale on which he operated—the scale of people like Pia and me, whose lives he touched—he was just as devastating."

"We can't let somebody get away with murder," I reminded her, "just because the victim's a rat—or a mink."

"Why not?" she blazed. "Look what he's done to Pia!"

"What's he done to her?"

"You haven't noticed? How much she loved the son of

a bitch and how much she wanted him to love her—in spite of a lifetime of neglect!"

"Civilization as we know it would crumble," I said, "if there was open season on fathers who neglected their kids."

"For a long time," she went on, waving that aside, "I wanted them to have a good relationship—it's supposed to be healthy for a child, isn't it, to have a good relationship with her father?"

"It doesn't hurt, anyway."

"So I didn't tell her any of the things he did when we were married—how could I tell a child things like that? Besides, I was afraid she'd think I was just being vindictive. So I never told her anything negative about him, and she went on loving him and missing him. But he was never, ever there for her, Peggy!

"When she was still a child—twelve, thirteen—she'd beg to be allowed to go to Denmark in the summer, to be with him. And so I'd let her call him—long distance, at my expense—and ask if he wanted her. Usually he made some excuse—he was writing a book or travelling in Europe. Sometimes he said she could come, even sent her plane fare, and then would dump her on his sister and she'd hardly ever see him.

"I thought that, sooner or later, she'd see through him and dump him the way he'd dumped her, but it didn't happen."

"Oh, I'm not so sure she was all that blind to his faults," I said.

"Maybe you're right—now. She doesn't seem as upset over his death as I would have expected her to be."

"Maybe," I said, smiling, "that delicate face of hers fooled even her mother."

"I hope you're right."

I asked her how Pia got along with her stepfather.

"Poor Hank," she replied. "He'd never been married before, when we met. We decided not to have children, you know—it's my family that has diabetes in it, not her fa-

ther's, and I didn't want to risk putting another child
through what Pia's had to go through—and myself either,
to be honest. So Pia's the only child Hank's got. She was
thirteen when we married and he's the father she should
have had. He's done all the things a father's supposed to
do—taken her to dance classes, taken her and her friends
to the amusement parks—I've never enjoyed amusement
parks, I'm afraid. Gone to endless parent-teacher conferences.

"But she's always treated him as a pal, not a father.
Hank's never complained. We no longer see all that much
of Pia," she added and took another swallow of cold coffee. "So what's so urgent about finding out who killed
him, Peggy?"

"What would happen if every woman who was betrayed
by a man like Lindemann turned around and killed him?"

She thought about it for a few seconds. "The world
would be a better place?" she asked, laughter and rage
fighting for the high ground on her face.

Sixteen

On the phone the day before, Pia had told me the crime scene people were through with the Hans Christian Andersen Room and she was back working there.

Startled at the news, I said, "You don't believe in ghosts, do you?"

"No—except maybe Jette's," she replied. "I've sometimes felt her presence flitting around the place." She paused, to let her rational side get a word in: "But that might be just because I get so involved in her words as I translate them."

When I left Pia's mother, I walked across the Mall to the library. The door to the Andersen room was open, but the woman inside looked too solid to be a ghost— especially a tiny ghost, the kind that Jette Wulff would have been. She was staring down into the display case, her back to me.

Pia's desk was empty. In the wall next to it, a piece of plywood had replaced the glass in the broken window.

The murder weapon, the statuette of the Little Mermaid, was gone, of course. I glanced at the place where Lindemann's body had lain, could still see the slightly darker stain of Pia's father's blood.

The woman turned when she heard me enter. It was Mary Vedel, Carl Vedel's daughter, whom I'd met at the banquet Friday night. She looked much the same as she had then: a dark, ankle-length dress; dark, gray-streaked hair that framed a white, pudgy face; tiny features; a crucifix dangling from a chain around her neck.

I asked her where Pia was.

"Miss Austin went off to the symposium for a while," she said, "to attend somebody's talk on Andersen—although I can't imagine why. The talks I attended this morning were deadly dull."

She glanced over at Pia's desk, shaking her head. "It was her father who was killed in this room, you know, just three nights ago, and yet she's back in here working. I find that strange."

I did too, actually—admirable, too—but I didn't say anything, I just smiled and shrugged.

"She obviously must not have loved him," Mary Vedel went on. "Look there! That must be his blood."

I kept my eyes on her, since I'd already seen the bloodstains. Besides, she was more interesting to me, since it was possible she'd been there, stealing the Andersen letters, when the blood had spilled.

"Miss Austin allowed me to be in here while she's gone," she went on. "After all, there's nothing left that needs watching over now, is there?—not that the University did such a good job of guarding the room when it did contain something of value. You were with the Donnellys at the banquet. I recognize you."

I told her I was a friend of Pia's.

She nodded, as if she already knew that. "And how is Mrs. Donnelly taking the loss of her precious letters?"

"I haven't heard."

"It must have been a terrible blow to her." The poorly disguised pleasure in Mary Vedel's voice didn't go well with the crucifix. "Finding those letters in my father's basement was, I'm sure, the high point of her life. Poor Denise! Not everything's turned out well for the rich man's daughter, has it?"

"What do you mean by that?"

She smirked, apparently pleased to have hooked me with the line. "Losing the letters, of course!" She gestured at the display case. The old books were still in there, and the poster for the Henriette Wulff exhibit: "My Dear Sisterly Friend," but without glass now, it looked abandoned.

"I'm sure she'll get over it," I said.

"Oh, certainly. Nothing troubles Denise for long, I'm sure."

"I thought you were a friend of hers," I said.

"Did you?" She chuckled. "We were friends, of course, before we went to Denmark as exchange students. But our friendship couldn't survive the class difference between us, I suppose. However," she added, "I did play a rather large role in Denise Lund Donnelly's life." Her lips twitched with amusement at some private joke.

I raised my eyebrows—waggled them, actually, since I'm not very good at arching them.

"You see," she went on, "it was I who told Clay Donnelly that Denise was Gus Lund's daughter—and I told him who Gus Lund was too!" She stared down at me—she was a couple of inches taller. "I regretted telling him that afterwards—I had a schoolgirl's crush on Clay myself." She smiled again, perhaps at the same private joke. "That was the last I saw of Clay—or the last time Clay paid any attention to me, I should say."

She stared down at me for a long moment, fingering her crucifix, then continued, as if speaking to herself: "Denise knew he was there, of course, knew he was watching her, following her around, but—"

"Excuse me," I interrupted, "I'm a little confused here. She knew who was where? Clay?"

"Denise knew Clay was in Copenhagen," Mary Vedel said impatiently, "following her around like a puppy, after I told him who she was. But Denise had no time for him— Denise chased the blond Danish boys."

She snickered. "They thought she was interesting—at first. That was because her Danish was so poor. She insisted on speaking Danish to them—to learn the language, she told them." Her face lit up at the memory. "Oh, and she did learn it—too well for her own good, I'm sorry to say! Because within six months, she'd learned Danish so well that she could no longer hide from the Danish boys how essentially dull she is!"

As she stood there, still fiddling with the gold cross hanging from her neck, I thought that the entrance to hell might resemble Mary Vedel's little mouth buried in her doughy face.

She turned and stared into the empty display case for a minute, brooding, looking puzzled. "I was surprised when I read their wedding announcement in the paper. Denise must have grown tired of chasing the blond Danish boys. She must have decided to settle on what was there on her own front stoop—Clay Donnelly."

Turning suddenly and looking at me, she said: "I wasn't invited to the wedding, of course, although I'd known Denise since we were at Sunday School together. I didn't really expect to be, either. It was a fancy wedding—although Clay's family was no better off than mine! You'd suppose *he* would have invited me, wouldn't you, since I was the one who put him on to her."

"At the banquet Friday night," I said, "you mentioned you'd taken a class in Denmark, and Lindemann came in a couple of times and talked about Andersen."

She nodded. "A very uninspiring teacher. I could tell he resented having to be there at all, among a bunch of American exchange students, and undergraduates at that. He stared out the window the whole time as he lectured. *He* certainly couldn't have kindled anybody's interest in Hans Christian Andersen!"

"Did you ever meet him again?"

She looked at me for a moment, her little round eyes, like raisins in a pudding, alive with amusement. "You mean, do I have a motive for wanting to murder him? No, I never saw him again until Friday night. The police think my father and I killed him to steal back the letters Denise and her father found in my father's basement." She looked over at the boarded-up window. "I suppose it would have had to be me, wouldn't it? My father couldn't have come in that way, whereas I think I could." She gave me a tiny

arc of a smile in her heavy white face. "But I had no motive. I don't think Denise and her father stole the letters
from us. Besides, in the antique business, it's every man
for himself."

She turned slowly, looking around the room with grim
satisfaction on her face. "What a terrible place for a man
like that to die! Now that the letters are gone, everything
in here is just pretend!"

Her eyes returned to me. "At the banquet, after dinner,
I asked Denise what she's collecting now that she's emp-
tied her home into this room. Do you know what she told
me?"

I shook my head. Mary Vedel's malice was numbing.

"She's putting together an exhibit on Hans Christian
Andersen's mother! Don't you think that's strange?"

I shrugged. "Why?"

"She was an uneducated woman," she replied, as if I
should have known. "She came from the dregs of Danish
society and she died a hopeless drunk! She had an illegitimate daughter by a married man who abandoned her, and
Hans Christian was born less than two months after her
wedding!" Mary Vedel broke out laughing. "Why create a
memorial to a woman like that!"

"What right do *you* have to judge her?"

Mary and I both spun around as Pia burst into the room,
her eyes blazing like cannons. "You think you would've
been so much better if you'd been in her shoes?"

"I'm sure I can't answer that, Miss Austin," Mary Vedel
said, looking down her nose at Pia, "but I'm sure I
wouldn't expect a memorial, just because I managed to
spawn a genius! You seem to have adopted some of the
enthusiasms of your lover's mother."

"That's right," Pia snapped, "I have."

"I'm sure she's pleased. When we were young, it was
always important that Denise be pleased. I don't suppose
that has changed much over the years." She looked at the
tiny watch embedded in her wrist. "Well, I have a class in

a few minutes." She turned to me and bowed slightly. "It's been nice talking to you," she said, and strode to the door—careful to step over the bloodstains of Jens Aage Lindemann.

Seventeen

"She's creepy," Pia said, probably loud enough for Mary Vedel to hear. "She came in, wandered around, and then stood in front of that table over there where the statuette of the Little Mermaid was—as if she'd known that's where it had been. She didn't say anything to me. Then she looked at the dark spot on the carpet over there, and finally she came over to the display case and stood staring in, as though there was something fascinating inside, but I knew she was really staring at me. When I started to get goose-bumps all over, I decided I'd better go take in a lecture, and left."

"She said she had a class now. Isn't she a little old to be a student?"

"She's not a student, she teaches advanced Danish in the Scandinavian Department. I guess she's been doing it forever. She's a teaching specialist; that's a nonstudent position for people who have some skill or something the University wants taught."

"I can't imagine she'd be a very good teacher."

Pia shrugged. "I think the U's just about to phase out Danish language teaching anyway. The Danish-American kids don't have any interest in learning it anymore, and nobody else wants to. She's only got four or five students."

"Do you know anything about her?"

"Huh-unh. I almost never saw her when I was assisting Claussen with his Andersen class. To her I was just another unwashed undergraduate, and she's old enough to be my mother, God forbid! Denise—Mrs. Donnelly—once told me she'd known her when they were students in Denmark. Mary Vedel couldn't get along with the Danish family she was living with and didn't make friends with the other Americans, so she came home early. But I guess she must've learned Danish pretty well, since she's teaching it."

"She gave me the impression there'd been something between her and Christian's father in Denmark."

Pia shrugged, stared at the door. "Probably all in her mind." She shuddered. "She looks to me like the crucifix-carrying type who'd murder somebody and not turn a hair. And her father, at least, was really pissed off about those letters—especially when he learned Denise was offered a lot of money for them."

I asked her how she felt, being back in the room where her father had been murdered.

She glanced around. "It's a little spooky, I guess. I'd like to say I feel my father's presence in this room with me the way I feel Jette's, but I don't."

"Even though his blood's still on the carpeting?"

"That dark spot's mostly because it's wet. I got up most of the blood this morning with paper towels."

"Pia!" I exclaimed, open-mouthed.

"I'm an unnatural daughter, right?" She tried to smile, started to cry. I put an arm around her. She buried her face in my blouse and gave it a good, fairly noisy soaking. Somebody poked his head in the door, saw us, and disappeared.

After a while, she stepped back. "There!" she said, sniffed and dug into her jeans for a Kleenex. She wiped her eyes and blew her nose and then looked at me. "What are you doing here anyway?"

I told her I'd been assigned to help with the investigation of her father's murder. She went over to her desk, sat down, and asked me how I'd managed that. I pulled up a chair and told her.

"Good," she said, and sniffed loudly.

"I'm supposed to start by circulating among the people at the symposium, see if I can pick up any gossip they might not want to tell the police."

"Or overhear the villains chuckling over their perfect crime," she said, blowing her nose again.

"That would be the ideal scenario," I agreed.

"Good luck!"

"I just came from talking to your mom," I said. "I—"

"She didn't kill him, I hope you know that."

"I hope I do too," I said, smiling.

"What'd she tell you?"

"She didn't confess, Pia—or I probably wouldn't be here."

She gave me a sideways glance and said, "Mom told me the cops caught her telling a lie. I suppose you asked her about that?" When I nodded, she said, "Well, who wouldn't lie? I mean, my father's wanting to have dinner with her didn't have anything to do with his murder—did it?"

I said probably not, but you never know what might turn out to be important. It's better to tell the truth, I added virtuously. Now that I was officially on the case, I wanted nothing but the truth from everybody.

"Your mother spent a lot of time with him," I said, "a lot of wasted years."

"She blames herself as much as she blames him, Peggy. And also, she's got a wonderful life now. Her marriage to Daddy—to my father—didn't ruin her life, it was just a temporary setback. And besides, it wasn't all wasted. She got me out of it, you know. How else could she have done that?" While waiting for my response, she gnawed on a thumbnail that already looked pretty well chewed.

I decided to pass on trying to answer one of the hard questions.

"Why do the cops care about a phone call anyway?" she asked after a while. "Whatever nut wanted those letters killed my father. Maybe we were just talking to the nut who did it," she added, scowling at the door through which Mary Vedel had disappeared.

I told her the police had to consider every possibility. "The letters might have been taken just to throw attention away from the real reason for the murder."

"That's terrible!" she said, her eyes blazing with indignation. "Stealing Jette's possessions just to confuse the police!" She saw the look on my face. "What're you laughing at?"

"You. I can't help it. I think you feel just as awful over the loss of the letters as over the death of your father."

Pia's eyes bored into mine. She said, her voice quivering with emotion, "Jette Wulff was a strong, independent, wonderful human being who had big problems to overcome—a lot bigger than most women today have. She was nicer than my father, and she means more to me than he ever did."

That was a eulogy of sorts, over two people.

She snatched up a Kleenex and blew loudly into it.

I asked her how Christian's mother was taking the theft. After all, finding Jette Wulff's stuff—as Mary Vedel had pointed out—must have been the coup of Denise Donnelly's life as a collector.

"I haven't seen her, but we talked on the phone," Pia said. "She called to tell me how sorry she was about my father. She sounded miserable, but sometimes you never know with her. She's very emotional—she reads a lot of romance novels, according to Christian. He says she's spent a lot of time in bed since Saturday."

I asked her if she had any thoughts about who might have hated her father enough to want to kill him.

"No!" Absently, she braided a thick strand of hair. "I didn't know him very well, actually," she went on, more quietly. "Now if it had happened in Denmark, it might have been some kind of personal thing—jealousy, or something—but here . . ." An idea struck her. "Unless somebody he knew in Denmark waited until he got here to kill him, just to confuse everybody? The police ought to be able to find out, if somebody who came here for the symposium had a feud going with Daddy in Denmark, right?"

I said Buck was looking into that possibility. I glanced at my watch. It was getting late. I told Pia I wanted to go down to the symposium and circulate among the participants for a while, see what I could pick up in the way of gossip.

"You've met some of them," I said. "And some of them know who you are, too. How about coming down and introducing me as a Scandinavian scholar or something."

Her tear-stained face lit up at the idea. "Sure, I can do that, although frankly, you don't look as scholarly as you might, though having been sick a couple of months helps a little. Try to move carefully, like you're afraid you might spill an idea."

Her face darkened and she chewed a strand of hair angrily. Then she dropped it disgustedly and got up. "I can't believe anybody in there could kill anybody, no matter for what!"

As we walked down the hall to the conference rooms, I asked her how her father had seemed when she'd seen him on Saturday.

"I only saw him for a couple of minutes," she answered. "I stopped in at the symposium for a while, but he was always surrounded by admiring scholars who knew him by his books and wanted to meet him, or people he'd known before but didn't see very often."

"He brushed you off," I said, flatly.

She turned and looked at me. "Not exactly, Peggy. He never actually did that, you know. He just treated me the same way he treated people he didn't have much interest in. He was very polite and introduced me to the people he was talking to, but then he talked only to them. So I didn't hang around very long."

"He didn't seem worried or anything?"

"Worried? No. If anything, he seemed kind of upbeat—kind of the way he was when we picked him up to take him to the banquet Friday, you know? Like he was happy to be the center of attention." She sighed. "I wish we'd been able to spend more time together. He never got to meet Christian. Isn't that terrible?"

I made noncommittal, sympathetic noises.

"I think it's too bad, Peggy. I think he would've liked Christian, if he'd gotten to know him—I really do. Not everybody's supposed to be a scholar like my father, who reads a hundred books just so he can write one more, you know."

"You don't have to tell me that!" I said with a laugh.

But I didn't think Jens Aage Lindemann would have liked Christian at all.

Eighteen

There were meeting rooms on both sides of the hall, where small groups of people sat on folding chairs and listened intently to panels or solo speakers talk about Hans Christian Andersen and children's literature, and seemed to be taking notes or doodling. In the main lounge, people were standing or milling around, or talking animatedly in little groups, holding paper cups of coffee and plates with horrid-looking doughnuts on them that were probably stale that late in the afternoon.

Almost as soon as we walked in, a man noticed Pia, said something to the people he was with, and came over and put a hand on her shoulder. The other people stared at her curiously.

"It is a terrible thing, your father's violent passing," he said. "But I am glad to see that you appear to be bearing up well. Not so, Miss Austin?"

"Thank you, Professor Meisling," Pia said in a mournful voice, and after a decent interval introduced us. "Miss O'Neill's come all the way from Berkeley for the symposium," she told him, lying with startling ease. "She's working on her Ph.D. in Danish literature there." She turned to me and, an evil glint in her eye, said, "Professor Meisling has written the book on Hans Christian Andersen's sex life, which apparently consisted entirely of masturbation. Not so, Professor Meisling?"

"I would like to think so," he said ambiguously. He offered me his hand, which I pretended not to see. Meisling was a middle-aged man with a perfectly round head, soft, pear-shaped body, a fringe of blondish hair, and granny glasses that kept sliding down his nose.

"Of course I know your work, Professor Meisling," I enthused, showing teeth and a little gum for good measure. "It's enriched my reading of Andersen's stories immensely."

He swelled up with pleasure.

"I have to get back to my own work," Pia said. "I'll leave you two to what I'll bet will be a really seminal discussion of the problem." She nodded to both of us, turned, and made her way hurriedly out of the room, glanced back one last time at me from the door and waved.

"She's very brave," I said, watching her go and wishing I could kick her. "Pushing on with her own work, in spite of her tragedy. Did you know her father well?"

"Not well, not well at all. He taught at the University of Copenhagen, you see, and I teach at Aarhus University—quite a ways away, really. But we saw one another often, of course, on scholarly occasions. He was not an easy man to get to know, unfortunately." He shook his head sadly. "The United States of America is a violent country, is it not, and life is cheap here. It could have been any one of us in that room when the thief broke in—I myself spent at least ten minutes in there, examining the various artifacts that that rather strange woman has collected or bought or made herself."

Then he chuckled, as another thought occurred to him. "It is ironic, not so, that Jens Aage, who hated this country and who resisted coming here for most of his life, should be murdered on his very first visit." He smacked his lips, tasting the irony and appearing to find it good.

"But surely you don't think some thug came in off the street to steal Andersen's letters, do you?"

"Why not?" He shrugged. "Your papers are full of even less rational crimes than this one! Some such person might have read about the letters in the paper—they were written up, I understand, when they were found—and thought he could get some money for them, for narcotics. Isn't that why you murder people here?"

A short, stubby man with a fringe of oily dark hair who'd been eavesdropping on us broke in. "In my opinion, Meisling, Jens Aage was not killed on account of the letters," he said. "Their theft was what I believe they call a 'red herring' in detective stories." He raised bushy eyebrows meaningfully.

"Oh? Then why was he killed, Hostrup?" Meisling demanded, looking down his nose at his colleague.

"What are the usual reasons men are murdered, Meisling?" Hostrup asked pedagogically. "Jealousy, professional or sexual; greed, for power or for money; and revenge." He ticked them off on plump fingers. "What else is there?"

"That's interesting," I said, contriving to appear to look up at a man several inches shorter than I, a knack I learned as a teenager and still keep for occasions like this. "Who would want Lindemann dead?"

"That I cannot tell you," Hostrup said. He gave Meisling a meaningful look.

"Me?"

Hostrup smiled grimly. "I have not forgotten what Jens Aage wrote about your book, Meisling, in his devastating review of it: 'Will the Meislings never cease tormenting poor Andersen?' Those were his exact words, were they not? It was quite an amusing review, as I recall."

Meisling tried to stammer something but couldn't get it through his indignation.

"Who are the Meislings?" I asked, sensing a clue.

Meisling sniffed and pretended not to hear my question.

"Simon Meisling was the headmaster of a school Hans Christian Andersen attended as a youth," Hostrup explained. "He made Andersen's life hell for several years— did everything he could to stamp out his creativity." Turning to Meisling, he said, a malicious glint in his eye, "Whether you would respond to such a devastating critique of your book with murder or not, Meisling, I don't know, but the fact remains that only a fool would want Andersen's letters to Henriette Wulff badly enough to steal them, especially at a time like this."

"There are such fools here," Meisling reminded him. "That crazy old fellow, what's his name? Vedel . . ."

Hostrup snorted. "Vedel, yes. Crazy, but much too old to break into that room through the window, or to kill Jens Aage."

"You think, then, that Lindemann was the real target?" I asked.

"I do, yes."

"If you're right," Meisling bleated, "I'm certainly not the only Andersen scholar here who has been unjustly attacked by Jens Aage!"

"Of course not—" Hostrup broke off, nudged Meisling, nodded at something behind me, and said something in Danish. I caught the word "Claussen."

I turned and looked. Eric Claussen, the Scandinavian professor Pia and I had sat with at the banquet, had just come into the room and was looking around uncertainly. Even from where I was standing, he looked pale and drawn.

I started to turn back to Meisling and Hostrup when I spotted somebody I knew all too well standing at the table: Floyd Hazard, in his retro forties trenchcoat, loading a paper plate with doughnuts.

Hostrup was asking me if I knew Claussen.

"Only by reputation," I replied absently. What the hell was Hazard doing here?

"Eric Claussen has been writing a book on Hans Christian Andersen for as long as I've known him—twelve, fifteen years."

"Longer than that," Meisling put in. "Whenever I speak to him—at literary conferences here and abroad—he tells me his book is due out next year." He made a noise that may have been a Danish snicker. "It's become a little joke in our field: Whenever something is promised for a long time—a book, an article, a review—and it keeps somehow not materializing, we say that 'He's writing a Claussen.' "

The two men were suddenly good friends again, chuckling over a colleague's misery.

When he'd recovered sufficiently, Hostrup went on to me, "Of course, we have not seen Claussen at conferences in the past several years. It must not be so easy to get travel money, when you are writing a Claussen." The two men chuckled together again.

I remembered that, at lunch the previous Wednesday, Lindemann had treated Claussen's forever forthcoming book as a joke. I asked Meisling and Hostrup if they'd known about the book Lindemann was supposed to write for our University Press.

Meisling's eyes behind the little round glasses twinkled. "Certainly! Jens Aage was not at all reticent about discussing it. He said he would probably not have come here, had he not wanted to go over the book contract in person with the editor of your press. Nobody believed that, of course. He came here because he was invited to give the keynote speech."

"However," Hostrup added slyly, "Professor Claussen did not leap onto a table and start dancing when he heard the news of Jens Aage's book."

I asked him why Claussen would care.

"Just how many 'definitive' studies of Andersen's life and work does the American reading public need?" he replied.

"Of course," Meisling said, "to be fair to Claussen, we don't know the publishing situation in your country. But I agree with Hostrup that he did not look terribly cheerful at Lindemann's good fortune."

In a loud, hearty voice, Meisling said, "Hello, Eric!"

Eric Claussen was suddenly standing next to me.

"Good to see you in such fine spirits so early in the morning," Hostrup said without a trace of shame. "Last night went on a bit long, did it not?"

Claussen gave an exaggerated groan. "Why do we do it?" he asked. "We're too old for nights like those!"

"Oh, well," Meisling said, patting him on the shoulder. "We deserve to cut loose now and again, Eric. Especially after the tragic event of Saturday night."

Claussen was staring at me. "You're a friend of Pia Austin's, aren't you? My wife and I sat with you at the banquet the other night. I think you said you're a campus policewoman?"

"A policewoman!" Meisling exclaimed, horrified. "I thought Lindemann's daughter said you were studying Danish literature at Berkeley, Miss O'Neill."

"That was just Pia's idea of a little joke," I said, throwing her to the wolves without hesitation. The truth is the best way to go on occasions like those, which, fortunately, have been rare in my life. "Excuse me, I see somebody I have to talk to." I smiled all around and faded into the crowd.

Hazard was standing alone over against a wall, glowering at the people milling around, many of whom seemed to be giving him a wide berth. I went over to him.

"What are you doing here, Hazard?"

"We ain't supposed to know each other," he said, talking out of the corner of his mouth and staring up at the ceiling. Apparently he thought that made him invisible.

"If only that were so. What's going on?"

"I'm supposed to play 'bad cop' to draw attention away from you. Where ya been?"

I ignored the question. "This was Bixler's idea, right?"

"Right."

I sighed. I had to admit it wasn't a completely loony idea, although Eric Claussen's having blown my cover to Meisling and Hostrup had seriously weakened the plan. Well, how long could I have gotten away with pretending to be an Andersen scholar, or a student of children's literature, anyway? Far better to use my winning personality, the way I'd always done in the past. It had sometimes worked, at least on the unwary.

I asked Hazard if he'd picked up anything useful.

His eyes narrowed in what a lifetime of television viewing had informed him meant intelligence. "Maybe yes; maybe no," he replied shrewdly. "How 'bout you?"

"I think they all ganged up on Lindemann," I told him conspiratorially. "I think they're all in it together."

"Oh, yeah—like in that Agatha Christie movie that takes place on a train." He gave it some thought, then rejected the idea, probably because Lindemann hadn't been murdered on a train. "Get serious, O'Neill." He chuckled moistly. "You know what this bunch of bozos do for a living, most of 'em? Read fairy tales!" He lowered his voice. "Speaking of fairies, guess who I met this morning?"

I just looked at him blankly.

"Christian Donnelly. You know, the quarterback. You're a friend of his girlfriend's, aren't ya? The daughter of the guy who was iced?"

"He's a fairy?"

"No—Jeez, Peggy, that's disgusting, even for you! But this morning I was in the murder room, you know? And there's the daughter, sitting at a desk over by the window— the window the guy who killed her father came through. Can you imagine, bein' in the room where your dad got killed so soon after? You think it's natural for a guy's daughter to do that?"

He shook his heavy head in amazement. "Anyway, there's Christian Donnelly standing there talking to her— large as life. And there was another guy with 'em—a fairy with a tennis racket, 'cept he didn't look like he came outta no kid's book!"

"Ooh!" I exclaimed. "I hope you arrested him."

"Nah—they're allowed in libraries." Hazard chuckled. "I told 'em who I was and wanted to know who they were and why they were there. I pretended I didn't know the room had been released by the homicide cops."

"Good thinking! And you met Christian Donnelly and Sam Allen," I said, to hurry him along.

"Yeah? You know this Allen character?"

"Yep."

"He's a friend of theirs—of Donnelly's and Donnelly's girlfriend! Hard to believe, ain't it?'

"He's a friend of mine, too," I said.

Hazard shrugged. "That don't surprise me. But why's he a friend of Donnelly's?"

"Why don't you ask Donnelly?"

Hazard chuckled, his eyes widening. "I don't guess I will. But I still think it's weird."

I watched him lumber off, then got myself a cup of old coffee and worked the room a little more. Apparently the word hadn't got around yet that I was a cop. I picked up a great deal of dubious theory about children's literature and Hans Christian Andersen, but it went in one ear and out the other, and I learned that nobody in the room was greatly mourning the death of Jens Aage Lindemann.

I also got the impression that, if we took a vote, most of the people in the room would have voted for the theory that Lindemann got between a thief and the letters, and paid for it with his life.

I wasn't enjoying my first day as a real detective. I wondered if I could apply for combat pay.

Nineteen

It had been a long day and I was glad to get home. Gary had got there before me. I let myself in, and sniffed the air: ramen noodles again.

"We have ramen every time you cook, damn it!" I hollered.

"Not every time," he hollered back, his voice coming from his room. "Last week I did macaroni and cheese. You said you loved it."

"Oh, right—sorry! But every other time you cook, you fix ramen. That's too often."

He came out, stood in the doorway. "But it's different tonight," he said. "It's got real shrimp in it—"

"Yeah, from one of those bags of tiny salad shrimp! Yuk!"

"And I added hot pepper paste."

"In a pathetic effort to overcome the sameness, he adds hot pepper paste," I told the wall. "How much?"

"More than a soupçon, less than a ladle. Sorry, Peggy, but I'm really bushed tonight—I spent the whole day interviewing Hmong farmers. I promise I'll do better on Friday. I found my old recipe box, I'll fix a great pumpkin soup—served right in the pumpkin. We'll eat it by the fireplace."

Gary was writing a series on the changing culture of Southeast Asians in the state—which didn't seem more urgent than dinner to me, especially since all I'd eaten since breakfast was a hamburger and fries.

"Besides," he said, "those pasta salads you make get kind of boring too, even if you do—"

"Let's don't quarrel, Gary, okay?" I said. Anyway, the pumpkin soup sounded promising.

I stumped into my bedroom and changed into more comfortable clothes. When I came out, he'd laid the table with a white linen tablecloth and candles. Two bowls of steaming ramen were at our places, little shrimp glistening on the surface among the vegetables and noodles.

"Oh, Gary!" I kissed him, sat down to eat, and smiled at him, seated across the table, through the candle flames. Oscar Levant was playing Gershwin on my CD player, softly. One of the things that had attracted me to Gary in the first place was that he'd read both of Levant's memoirs. I don't know very many people—our age, at least—who have.

The noodles were actually quite good—a balance of chewy and crunchy things, sweet and spicy tastes. Lots of practice had made Gary a master ramen cook, I had to give him that.

I remembered what Nancy Austin had told me that afternoon, of how Lindemann and she had dinner at a good restaurant every Sunday night. The idea was that they would each recount their sexual adventures with other people.

"Sex is as natural as drinking a glass of water," I said, in a fairly good parody of the late Lindemann's Danish accent.

Gary looked up, a noodle hanging from the corner of his mouth, his deep-set brown eyes startled. "I think of it more as dessert," he replied after he'd swallowed.

"It is the commingling of the spiritual and the physical," I persisted, in the same voice. "Or something."

"It's been a long day for you, hasn't it?"

"You just don't understand, Gary. You're so Victorian."

He leaned back in his chair, regarded me coolly. "I'll bet, if I beg you, you'll tell me what this is all about. Somehow, I don't think you're trying to lure me into bed with this line of patter."

I repeated what Nancy Austin had told me about

Lindemann having wanted an open marriage, in which they would meet at week's end, Sunday night, to relive the lurid details of their sexual adventures over cognac and candlelight.

Gary brooded on it for a minute or two. "It's interesting," he said finally, "that it would be on a Sunday night. Probably without realizing it, the man needed something to replace God, and settled on sex."

I told him how Lindemann had wanted to get together with his ex-wife on Sunday while he was here, but she'd got so upset she slammed—

"Sunday night!" I shouted.

"What about it?"

"Lindemann asked Nancy Austin to meet him for dinner Sunday night!"

Gary shrugged. "Maybe he had a really juicy affair he wanted to share with her, and in his excitement, forgot they were divorced."

I jumped up from the table, ran to the kitchen, dug the phone book out of the cupboard under the kitchen counter, and looked up Nancy Austin's number. When she came on the line I asked her to tell me again when Lindemann said he wanted to get together with her for dinner.

"The next night—Sunday night. He said he couldn't do it that night because he was going to the play."

I thanked her and broke the connection before she could ask me why I'd asked, and dialed Buck's number, which I know by heart. Even though it was after seven, he was still in his office.

"Lindemann asked Nancy Austin to have dinner with him Sunday night," I said.

It only took him a moment to get it. He swore—that may have been the first time I ever heard him do that—and wondered aloud why he hadn't thought to ask Nancy Austin when Lindemann had wanted to get together with her.

Because Lindemann's plane ticket, in the Property

Room at police headquarters downtown, had said he was returning to Denmark Sunday morning.

"I'll call you back when I've checked with the airline," Buck said, and hung up.

When he called back about five minutes later, he said, "Lindemann extended his stay a week. He had to pay a big penalty to do it."

"Not as big as the penalty he paid later," replied. "When did he call the airport?"

"Saturday morning."

"That was a busy day for him, wasn't it? He extended his stay, called his ex-wife to invite her out to dinner, and got murdered. I wonder what else he did."

"No need to jump to conclusions, Peggy. Those things don't have to be connected. He may have found the symposium more enjoyable than he thought it would be and decided to stay on."

"You'd suppose he would have mentioned it to somebody."

"Maybe he did," Buck replied. "We'll ask around, see if he mentioned it to any of his colleagues."

When I returned to the table, Gary said, "Finding a clue—especially one the police have overlooked—unites the spiritual and the physical in you a lot better than sex ever has! You should see your face. My God, you're beautiful!"

The soup was cold but still tasted pretty good, and dessert was wonderful.

Twenty

I spent the next morning circulating among the scholars, learning very little that I thought Buck's interviews probably hadn't caught—but I dutifully jotted down bits and pieces of gossip about people Lindemann had hurt, or who sounded as though they had a grudge against him. I also got the names of a few Danes who'd been especially angry that Denise Donnelly hadn't donated or sold the Andersen letters to some worthy Danish institution. Some people viewed me suspiciously, whispered behind my back, and shut up when I approached; others seemed not to know that I was a spy in their midst.

I was a little hampered by the number of people speaking foreign languages—I took two years of Required German, but still haven't met anybody who speaks it—but fortunately not a lot of people speak or understand Danish either, so unless it was Danes speaking among themselves, the language of the symposium was English.

I avoided Floyd ("Miss Marple") Hazard, bullying scholars with his stubby pencil, his notebook, and his trenchcoat. I'd just disengaged myself from a group of scholars in the lounge who were heatedly discussing Freud's theory that "The Emperor's New Clothes" was Hans Christian Andersen's sublimated dream of exhibiting himself, when suddenly Professor Claussen was standing in front of me, looking outraged.

He was a couple of inches taller than I, about five-eleven, bony and loose-limbed and wearing another version of the Ivy League professor's outfit he'd been wearing at the banquet on Friday: Oxford shirt, wool plaid tie, sweater vest, and a tweed jacket with leather elbow patches.

"I assume you are a part of the official investigation of Lindemann's murder, like that lout over there," he said, gesturing with a long, trembling finger in the general direction of where Hazard was tormenting another scholar. "I think his behavior is outrageous, and constitutes harrassment. I'm going to call your superiors and lodge a complaint. This is a gathering of *scholars*—doesn't he realize that?"

"He's investigating a murder," I reminded Claussen sternly. Is this what being a real detective means, I asked myself, defending Floyd Hazard?

"I'm aware of that!" Claussen snapped. "But the police must tread softly, softly—as they would in any holy place! That man has no idea of the prestige of some of the men—and women, too—he has bullied and insulted. Do you realize that he ordered me to account for everything I did Saturday night? I protested in vain that I had already done that. All he need do was consult the man who took my statement. But no! And because I could not account for every moment of my time—could he account for every moment of his? Could you?—he had the effrontery to hint that I was among what he called, with heavy emphasis, his 'prime suspects.' "

"Did he suggest a motive?" I asked, when he'd paused for breath.

"Of course! He claimed that I coveted those letters from Hans Christian Andersen. I demanded to know if he had any idea of the trivial nature of the correspondence between Andersen and that silly woman. I'm not sure he even knows who Hans Christian Andersen is!"

"Well, the sooner we catch the murderer, the sooner the police'll be out of your hair," I said, like the good cop I was. I spent a few minutes soothing Claussen's ruffled feathers. I'm pretty good at it, when I want to be.

When he'd calmed down, he said, "Have you turned up any suspects—besides me, I mean? I understand that Jens Aage's murder is a scandal in Denmark—the Danish newspapers are having a field day with it—even though, personally, I think the culprit is some local Danish-American anxious to add to his collection. Several scholars have left the symposium and returned home—cancelling their lectures!"

What a loss. "I'm sorry to hear that," I told him. "All I've really learned so far is that, if you'd wanted to kill Lindemann, you might have had to stand in line. He didn't seem to have many friends here."

Claussen shrugged. "It was nothing personal, with perhaps a few exceptions. It's just that Danish literary scholarship is so competitive, you see. So few Danish authors are known outside of Denmark. So any literary scholar who wants to make a name for himself beyond the 'duck pond,' as Denmark is called, finds himself fighting over very few names—Andersen being, by far, the best known."

"Crows fighting over the same roadkill," I said.

Claussen nodded and smiled, revealing a mouthful of teeth as small, even, and numerous as corn kernels. "A not entirely inappropriate metaphor, I think. Not all of us are willing to stoop to such undignified squabbling," he added.

No, I thought, some scholars preferred to "do a Claussen" instead.

"You were a close friend of Lindemann's, I suppose," I said.

He darted me a worried look, then pursed his lips and stroked his goatee thoughtfully, working it into a sharp point. "I can't really say I was, although I admired him very much—very much indeed. Jens Aage was the most prominent Andersen scholar in the world. Of course, he made his name twenty years ago, with his seminal study of Andersen's later tales. In my opinion, nothing he has done since has quite measured up to that remarkable work, but he continues—continued, I should say—to churn out books and articles of sufficient quality to keep his name as our greatest Andersen scholar."

Claussen lowered his voice: "However, Jens Aage's was an influential voice in Danish academic circles, and he sometimes used that voice ruthlessly. There are people, some of whom are in this building even as we speak, whose careers will not be hurt—to say the least—by his death."

I asked him if he could give me some names.

"I don't indulge in gossip." He took a closer look at me. "Do your questions mean that the police don't think Jens Aage's death was incidental to the commission of a theft?"

"That's still the most likely theory, of course. But we have to keep our minds open, don't we?" It felt almost natural, speaking of "we." I might even get used to it, I thought.

I told him that we'd just learned that Lindemann had extended his stay a week, and wondered if he knew anything about it.

" A week! Well, well, that's interesting. I got the impression that he only came here to give the keynote speech and then return home. A little arrogant and insulting, to my way of thinking."

"You have no idea why he changed his mind?"

"None at all, I'm afraid," Claussen said. "I understand he was to meet some colleagues for dinner the night he died, to discuss an Andersen conference in Europe or Asia or wherever. Perhaps other business came up that made him decide to extend his stay—or perhaps he wanted to see more of his daughter."

"You must have had a lot to do with the Danish-American community here," I said. "Can you think of anybody who might have wanted those Andersen letters badly enough to break into the library and steal them?"

He snorted. "I don't know anybody personally who would do anything of the sort! I've spent my entire academic career avoiding the Danish-Americans. They're mostly sentimental old fools who aren't serious about Danish culture, they only want to sit around drinking good Danish beer, dance the folk dances, and sing the native songs their parents and grandparents brought over with them in heavily accented Danish. To them, Denmark is a village with stork nests on thatched roofs surrounded by gently rolling fields and the occasional cow."

He shuddered. "The Danish-Americans don't like me, either. They think I've betrayed my heritage, because I'm interested in the serious study of Danish literature—I'm American-born, of course, third generation—I don't even speak Danish very well, I have to admit, although of course I read it fluently. I'm sure there are quite a few members of the older generation who would love to own something by Hans Christian Anderson, and would be willing to go to great lengths to get it. I'm not sure many of them still have the strength to climb through library windows, however."

"What about one of the people here for the symposium?"

"You mean Danish patriots who think those letters ought to be in Denmark? Not unlikely, not at all unlikely. I've overheard more than one Dane speak of that 'Andersen Room' of Gustav Lund's daughter with the greatest contempt. And it is sad that those letters, assumed lost for nearly a hundred and fifty years, should have to spend the rest of eternity in that horrid room, isn't it? Almost a fate worse than death." He chuckled again, showed his little teeth.

I suddenly decided I liked the Hans Christian Andersen Room. After all, Pia liked it enough to want to work in there—and for Denise Donnelly it had been a work of love. I even decided that Henriette Wulff, whom I didn't know at all, would have liked it too.

"I've heard that Lindemann signed a contract with the University Press to write a book on Hans Christian Andersen," I said, and watched to see how he reacted.

He turned a little pink and his little eyes darted to mine, as if to see if there were more to what I'd said than just the words.

"Yes," he said, "so he told me. He would have been a good man for the job—a very good man. As he explained it to me, it was to be the sort of general introduction to Andersen that Jens Aage was singularly equipped to write."

"But wouldn't it make more sense for an American to write a book like that?"

He pursed his lips thoughtfully. "No doubt, no doubt. An American scholar would certainly be better able to draw the relevant parallels between Andersen and his Anglo-American contemporaries. But I'm convinced that Jens Aage could write a very respectable book, very respectable indeed."

"Aren't you writing a book on Andersen?" I asked him, as innocently as I could.

His eyes flashed angrily for a moment and he tugged on his goatee with bony fingers. "Oh, we're all writing books on Andersen," he replied, flapping a hand in the general direction of his colleagues, some of whom were watching us. "If you're thinking that I might have suffered from professional jealousy, Officer O'Neill, I can assure you that nothing could be farther from the truth. My own research is much more specialized than Jens Aage's—much more theoretical, if you will. I hardly think my work would appeal to the same audience as his at all. In fact, the popularity of his book would almost certainly draw readers to my more difficult study—not that I'm out to attract the general reader, of course."

"It's too bad then," I said, "that Lindemann didn't live to write his book."

He replied that he thought so too.

I asked him if Lindemann had said anything at dinner on Thursday night that sounded as though he expected trouble.

"Jens Aage seemed quite pleased with himself. Not that there was anything very unusual about that—he always behaved like the cat that had just swallowed the canary. We talked about Denmark and the marvelous sabbatical year Julie and I spent there twenty-two years ago. And, of course, we talked about Hans Christian Andersen and the various scholarly irons we have in the fire. He gave no indication that he expected trouble of any sort whatsoever."

Claussen chuckled stuffily. "We talked about American football too—because of that athlete his daughter is involved with, you know—what's his name. My wife knew enough about the game to satisfy his curiosity."

"How'd he feel about Pia's involvement with Christian?"

"He thought it was absurd—as, indeed, I do, myself—that a daughter of his should be living with such a person, may even intend to marry him! But he also found it amusing. 'The ugly duckling,' he said, 'manages somehow to win the prince and, eventually, half the kingdom. Only in America!' I assume he was referring to the Lund family money."

I remembered that Pia had called herself the ugly duckling to Christian the first time I saw them together. Christian had told her she was a swan.

Claussen looked at his watch. "And now, Officer, I hope I've answered all your questions satisfactorily, for I must leave you. I have a panel to moderate, on Andersen and Postmodernism. The sparks are truly going to fly!" He nodded gravely, turned and marched purposefully off, as to war.

"Thanks for your time," I called after him.

I've always assumed that fatuity is catching—how else do you explain its epidemic proportions at institutions of higher learning? I just prayed I wouldn't catch it from that carrier.

Twenty-one

I spent ten minutes extricating myself from the clutches of a French feminist scholar who was going to give a paper on "Hans Christian Andersen's Colonization of Woman's Body."

"It is impossible for a man to look at a woman without leering," she told me, "just as it is impossible for a male author to create a female character that is not an act of sexual violence against women. Both are acts of colonization of woman's body."

"Andersen created lots of female characters, didn't he?" I said. "You've got a lot of grist for your mill."

"Precisely." Her thin black mustache quivered, her eyebrows rose and fell, pregnant with meaning.

"I suppose Andersen could be called a kind of verbal serial killer," I mused.

"That would not be putting it too strongly," she agreed. "And—to make it even more terrible—many of his fictional females were *children.*" She licked her lips and gave me a hard, knowing leer.

I found it a little creepy to realize that, working together, the two of us were creating a monster. I managed to steer the conversation around to Lindemann. "A tragic loss," I said.

"Oh? Do you really think so?" She looked disappointed in me, then launched a massive Gallic shrug. "Jens Aage Lindemann wrote savage reviews of feminist interrogations of Andersen's patriarchal attitudes."

"You think that's why he was killed?"

Her laughter was shrill and contemptuous and caused an elderly man standing nearby to slop coffee down his front. "Of course not!" she replied. "We had nothing any longer to fear from him. But that is certainly why he won't be mourned within the feminist community."

I asked her who she thought might have killed him.

"I haven't wasted any time thinking about it. I suppose it was someone who wanted the Andersen letters for his private collection—or hers, sad to say, for there are still women capable of such sentimental crimes. It would be the height of irony, would it not, if such a woman—one of patriarchy's victims—killed a male Andersen scholar in order to acquire letters written by a sexist male author to one of his victims."

"Henriette Wulff was Hans Christian Andersen's victim?"

"Of course she was, poor thing! She was his friend only because she told him what he wanted to hear, she flattered him shamelessly, and she lived her life through him. What more does a man want in a woman, eh? She never questioned the unequal status in their relationship—indeed, like Andersen, she accepted it." She leaned into me, blowing the reek of European tobacco and poor digestion into my face. "Henriette Wulff believed that childbearing made women superior to men! How is *that* for turning reality on its head?"

I said I'd have to think about it. I excused myself and moved away—retreated in disarray, actually. I wrote down in my notebook: "Lindemann the victim of one of patriarchy's victims, or something."

Later, out of a kind of morbid curiosity, I decided to sit in on one of the sessions. I checked my program and chose a panel discussion of *The Little Mermaid,* perhaps because Lindemann had been murdered with a bronze statuette of her.

I found myself sitting next to Carl Vedel, who turned and stared at me suspiciously. He still looked like a failing shoe store clerk and was wearing the same dark, shiny suit he'd had on at the banquet, or one just like it.

The first panelist, a gaunt, haunted-looking young woman, argued with great earnestness that Andersen's story "problematizes the place of women in a phallocentric world." The second panelist, a young man who twitched a humorless smile whenever he wanted us to believe he'd made a point, argued with equal passion that the little mermaid was a slut who tried to seduce the prince in order to gain immortality, the way other women seduce men for diamonds and furs. The first panelist looked as though she'd kill the second if she had a weapon—say, a heavy statue of the sweet, if scaly, creature under discussion. The third panelist, a psychoanalytic critic who looked like one of the Smith Bros., argued that Andersen had projected his own fear of castration onto the poor mermaid.

I was becoming increasingly concerned about the sex lives of the panelists when Carl Vedel, who had been muttering to himself for some time, stood up noisily and stomped out of the room. A few minutes later, I slid quietly out after him.

I found him in the main lounge, his back to a wall, glaring at the scholars milling around, who were giving him a wide berth. I told him who I was and reminded him that we'd met at the banquet.

He nodded, said he remembered me. "After listenin' to that crap," he added, gesturing with a gnarled thumb in the direction of the room from which we'd just escaped, "I'm gonna take a bath soon's I get home. How 'bout you?"

I laughed, agreed that was a good idea. "What brings you here today?"

"Thought I'd try to catch up on what's goin' on in Denmark these days. Shoulda known better. Now I'm killin' time 'til my daughter can come and take me home."

"You were born in Denmark?"

"Yah, I was fifteen when I come here."

"And you've never been back?"

"Once, a couple years ago, me 'n Mary—she's my daughter—went over there. She teaches Danish, said she needed to hear real Danes speak it, to keep up her accent.

But my family's gone now—the ones I knew, so I didn't get much out of it."

He shoved his hands in his pants pockets and looked around the room. "It don't bother me none that old man Lund sank a lot of *his* money into this place. What gets my goat is that it's the taxpayers—you 'n me—who's gonna be stuck with the bill for heating it and cooling it and keeping it up." He shot me a glance. "You come to many of these kinds of things?"

"This is my first," I told him. "I think it's also going to be my last."

"Me, too." He chuckled. "You think old Gus'll ask for his money back, since the University did such a piss-poor job of guarding those letters his daughter stole from me? If it weren't for Denise, he wouldn'a given the U a penny. I wonder how Denise is holdin' up." Although Carl Vedel didn't resemble his daughter Mary in many ways, they did share the same malicious smirk.

I said I hadn't heard, and asked him who he thought might have stolen the letters.

A look of indignation appeared on his undistinguished face. "The idiotic police think I did—or Mary! They think one of us climbed through that window, cracked Lindemann over the head with the mermaid, and made off with 'em!" He chuckled angrily. "They even asked us if we'd let 'em have samples of our blood—can you believe it? Oh, they asked politely enough, all right. But I told 'em I'd fight 'em all the way to the Supreme Court before I'd let 'em stick a needle in me or my daughter! And Mary said the same thing."

"I suppose it would help them eliminate suspects," I said.

He glared at me. "That's what they said! But I told 'em they'd have to get blood from all the distinguished perfessers here first."

I had to agree he had a good point.

He shook his head in disgust. "Not more'n an hour ago, some damn fool claiming he's a detective cornered me and tried to make me tell him where I was Saturday night. I made him show me identification and then told him to arrest me or go away. He went away."

"What makes the police think you stole the letters?" I asked him.

"On account of them letters is mine, that's why—partly mine, anyway—and I haven't bothered to hide what I think about it from nobody! Gus Lund and Denise as good as stole 'em from me." He looked at me narrowly. "You must know that, Sis, you was there Friday night when Gus and I were arguing about it. I don't forget hair the color of yours."

People don't. "I was just curious to hear your side of the story," I said.

"Old Gus and I go back a long ways. He collects Danish furniture—the stuff the immigrants brought over with 'em. Me, I've got an antique shop, and I've kinda specialized in Danish antiques. It's getting almost impossible to find any now, that's not in a museum or owned by somebody who knows the worth of what he's got, but if you know where to look—and I do—you can sometimes pick up some good pieces still.

"Anyways, about a year ago, I come across some stuff at a farm outstate—the owners'd died. Junk mostly, but I was able to restore a few pieces of furniture. I'm pretty damn good at restoring old furniture, I do say so myself, and I've taught Mary the tricks of the trade too—she's a quick learner. She's not gonna be teaching Danish much longer, so she'll need something to fall back on. Anyway, one of the pieces I restored looked like the kind of thing old Gus Lund is always on the lookout for—a cupboard, just about the ugliest thing you'd ever wanna see. So when he calls me one morning, askin' if I have anything he'd be interested in, I describe it to him, and he says he'll take a look at it, next time him and Denise is out our way. So a week or so later, out they come. Soon's he sees the cupboard, he wants it."

Vedel's eyes narrowed shrewdly. "I pretended I was

havin' second thoughts about selling it, naturally," he went on, "to jack the price up a little, you know—and we haggled about it. While we was doin' that, Denise is wandering around the garage, poking into this and that.

" 'What's this, Carl?' she asks me. She's down on her knees, goin' through a pile of crap in a corner. 'Old Bibles and prayer books, Denise,' I says. 'Can I have 'em?' she asks, and I laugh and say okay, and give 'em to her just for the taking. Old Bibles and prayer books aren't worth the paper they're printed on anymore. 'Can I have 'em?' she says," he repeated, as if the words were significant.

I raised my eyebrows knowingly, not understanding a thing, but eyebrow-raising is important when you're discussing conspiracies.

"There was something odd in her voice when she says that," he continued, "but I didn't smell a rat at the time, of course. Later, though, after I read in the paper what she'd 'found,' I realized she must've spotted them Andersen letters right away. Her hands were filthy, as though she'd been thumbing through those books—and who thumbs through old Bibles? Everybody knows what's in 'em already, don't they?

"Sombitch," Vedel went on after a pause for emotion. "A man of honor and decency—the kind of man I always thought Gus Lund was—would've sold that stuff for a lot of money in Denmark and offered to split the money with me. But no, instead of money, Denise wants those letters in that room of hers down the hall, with 'Donated by Denise Lund Donnelly' on it."

Carl Vedel chuckled suddenly and stared in the direction of the Andersen Room, a pleased expression on his face.

"And you'd gone through those books—those Bibles and things—yourself, and didn't see the letters?"

"Sure I did," he said, his eyes moving away from mine. "And I didn't see 'em. It looked to me like just the usual religious stuff the immigrants brought with 'em. I'm not an expert, the way Denise is, or thinks she is, but don't you think I'd a known a packet of old letters and a picture if I seen one?" He shook his head. "It's just a mystery to me, that's all."

"You might have just thought it was letters from some immigrant," I suggested.

He glared at me, started to say something, then glanced up. "Oh, there you are, Mary—about time. I'm hungry, let's go home. And I won't be comin' back to this place again neither!"

Mary gazed down at me with her little eyes, like raisins in a pudding. "You're a policewoman, aren't you? Professor Claussen told me that. Yesterday you tried to get me to incriminate myself, and now it's my father's turn."

"You're a cop, too?" Vedel said. "Goddamn, they're all over the place, like rats. You can't use anything I said against me, you know—you didn't warn me! I know my rights."

"You didn't say anything incriminating," I pointed out as soothingly as possible. "I only wanted to get your opinion, as president of Sons of Denmark, on who might want those letters badly enough to break into the Andersen room and steal them."

"Well, I can't think of anybody," he replied, as his daughter started to pull him away from me.

"That's hard to believe," I said, following them. "Those letters were the real thing. They completed a long correspondence between Andersen and his best friend. Surely it must have been a temptation to somebody, especially since the Hans Christian Andersen Room was so poorly guarded."

He listened to me, his eyes never leaving my face.

"Come on, Father," Mary said, still pulling on him. "You don't have to talk to her."

He shook her off. "Wait a second, Mary." To me he said, "I know that. I been in the antique game long enough to know how crazy people can get over crap that nobody else would look at twice. But the people I know who might want those letters badly enough to steal 'em, they wouldn't kill anybody. Hell, if Lindemann'd caught 'em, they'd just push him aside and walk out. Or surrender and wait for the police. I've already told you who done it—one a these idiots." He waved at the people in the room. "Somebody here for the conference, or somebody who's pretending to be here for the conference, but who really came to steal them letters and sell 'em to a rich collector in Denmark."

He stuck a finger up under my nose and shook it. "You check the luggage of the people who went back to Denmark right after that fella was murdered. One of them's the one who done it, you'll see."

He let his daughter lead him off. They looked like a battleship and a tugboat, their roles reversed.

Twenty-two

After a few more hours I'd finally had all I could take of
the conference and drifted down to the Andersen Room to
see Pia. She was at her desk by the boarded-up window,
bent over her books and papers. One of the thick faded
blue volumes of the correspondence between Hans Christian Andersen and Jette Wulff was propped open against
the windowsill, a multi-volume Danish-English dictionary
on a nearby shelf, and her fingers were dancing on the
keyboard of her word processor. I knocked softly on
the doorframe.

"Hi, Peggy," she said, waving me over.

"Sorry to bring you out of the 1850s," I said. I peered
over her shoulder and read a few sentences of her translation on the computer screen.

"These two people are *so* sweet!" she exclaimed with a
sigh, flopping back in her chair. "You wouldn't believe it.
Andersen was smart and clever, but I don't think he had an
intellectual bone in his body. He was just curious about
everything and he had one of the richest imaginations of
anybody who ever lived. He even imagined that someday
people would fly between Europe and America, did you
know that?"

"No!" I said, throwing my hands up.

"He wasn't interested in *analyzing* everything to death,
Peggy," she said, giving me her stern look. "He could live
himself into the life of almost anything—darning needles,
dung beetles, tin soldiers, trees, ducks, you name it."

"*Dung* beetles?"

"That's why he wasn't cynical and skeptical, unlike *certain* people I could name," Pia pressed on, ignoring the interruption. "Since he could imagine how it must feel to be just about anything, he could accept and forgive almost anything too. And that's why children love him so much, too—or they would, if their parents would just turn off their TVs and start reading the stories to them."

"Civilization as we know it would collapse, if everybody was like that," I said.

" 'As we know it,' " Pia flared. "Exactly!"

"I'll bet he couldn't empathize with those creatures out there," I said, waving in the general direction of the Andersen conference.

"Actually, you're right," Pia admitted. "Scholars don't come off very well in Andersen's stories."

I was glad to hear he had a bottom line, even if it was well below mine. I told Pia some of the things I'd heard at the panel on "The Little Mermaid" and from circulating among the scholars.

"They're *so* disgusting!" she said. "You know, Peggy, Andersen was lucky. He never felt at home with his own class, the lowest class in Danish society. He was too creative for that. And the upper classes wouldn't let him feel at home among them, no matter how famous he became. So he lived his entire life as something in between."

"Maybe that's what we should all do," I said.

She gave me a hard look, to see if I was laughing at her. I wasn't. "That's what Sam says too," she went on, chewing hair. "Being gay, and out, he's in between. He's not locked into or trying to hide behind a gender role that most people are just handed at birth. 'Here, take this, this is what you are, this is how you're supposed to act, rehearse until you get it right for life.' He thinks that's what makes him a very good observer, and that's why he's such a good writer and director too."

"It's probably why he's a good actor, too," I said. "He knows he's always on stage and being talked about, just as we're talking about him now. I suppose your friend Jette

Wulff was in between too. Being crippled, nobody would marry her, so she had no gender role—she had to invent a role for herself, and she must have been tough and creative enough to do it."

Pia's face brightened, probably at the progress I was making as her student. "That's right," she said. "That's why she and Andersen got along so well. She didn't get along very well with most people, you know. If she hadn't been crippled, she would have married and had children and died and been forgotten like all ordinary people do who just go along with the crowd. I mean, with a mother like hers . . ."

She waited for me to ask her what kind of mother Jette Wulff had. When I did, suppressing a grin, she plunged on, "Her mother wrote to Andersen once, 'You imagine, dear Andersen, that you were born to be a great writer. Well, you weren't, and you mustn't think you were.' "

"That's awful!" I said, horrified in spite of myself.

"So you can imagine what Jette would probably have been, if she could've been like her mother."

"I wonder, though," I said, "if she'd had the choice . . ."

"Like most people, she would've probably taken the easy way. But she didn't have a choice. Andersen once told her that, because she was his friend, she was going to be immortal along with him. That sounds terribly egotistical, doesn't it—but why shouldn't he have said that? He was only telling the truth."

I told her what the bemustached French feminist had breathed hideously into my face, that Jette had thought women were superior to men because they could have babies.

"A lot of women thought like that back then!" Pia hollered, flying into a rage. "Contraception was still very primitive, Peggy—and it was condemned by both the church and the state. And abortions were dangerous and illegal too. And not very many women could support themselves without being married, you know. So they had to glorify what they couldn't get out of. It's perfectly understandable—except to people who don't consider how hard it was to be a woman a hundred years ago—or a man, for that matter. Men and women create the myths they live by together, you know."

"If Jette believed childbearing made women superior to men," I said, "she must have felt inferior herself, since she wasn't able to marry and have kids."

Pia looked sad. "I'm sure she did, subconsciously. Women who couldn't get married for whatever reason were made to feel that they'd betrayed their true destiny— with a capital T and D. That's why so many unmarried women in the nineteenth century were happy to be gover- nesses and nursemaids. By helping another woman take care of her children, they were somehow atoning for their own failure. Luckily, Jette didn't have to support herself. Her family was well off."

I peered over Pia's shoulder at her computer screen. "Where are you now—you and Hans Christian and Jette?"

"He's in Copenhagen," she said, falling back into the nineteenth century and the idyllic world of a man of ge- nius and a woman of means. "It's raining, and cold and windy. Jette's in Naples, where it's springtime. Isn't it lucky they travelled so much? Otherwise, there wouldn't be all these letters." She looked at her watch, then closed down her word processor. "Your partner was here about an hour ago. If he was supposed to soften me up for you, it didn't work."

"My—? You mean Floyd Hazard?"

"Is that his name? He smells like a dirty ashtray and acts like Fearless Fosdick. I told him he had to stand across the room if he wanted to talk to me."

"Good. What did he want?"

"I'm not sure. He asked me some questions about my father, but he also wanted to know all about how Christian and I got together, and if we were engaged—stuff like that. He's a football fan, naturally. I finally hinted strongly that I had to get some work done and he finally went away.

Are all the campus cops—except you, of course—so hideous?"

I assured her that most of us were decent and fairly hygienic.

"So what do you want, Peggy?"

"The morning of the day he died," I said, "your dad called the airline and extended his stay a week."

Pia's eyes grew huge. Apparently Buck hadn't got around to asking her about it yet. "He did?"

"You didn't know?"

"Huh-unh. I would've told you, if I had."

"Think, Pia. Didn't he give you any indication that something unusual had come up?"

She wound a strand of hair around a finger and stared at it cross-eyed. "No, honest. I didn't see all that much of him when he was here. You've got eyes, you saw how he didn't feel comfortable around me. On account of my diabetes, probably, or it could've been 'cause he never got a chance to really know me—on account of the divorce and Mom moving us back here and all. I don't know!" she added loudly, as though speaking to somebody inside her who'd been interrogating her about it. Her eyes were glittering with tears.

I suddenly wondered what I was doing trying to find out who killed her father. Some days, even obstetricians must wonder why they bother going to work, given what most babies grow up to be, but they have to make mortgage payments too, and pay for their kids' orthodontia and private schools. Maybe only undertakers never question what they do, maybe they're the happiest toilers.

Shaking off such thoughts, I pressed on: "Professor Claussen's been writing a book on Andersen for years. I've heard the book your dad was supposed to write might've come as an unpleasant surprise to him. It might've made his unpublishable. You know anything about that?"

She shook her head. "Huh-unh."

"But you were Claussen's assistant for a couple of

years. You must have some idea about what he thought of your dad."

"Well," she replied doubtfully, "Claussen's always spoken highly of him—and it was Claussen who suggested inviting my father to be the keynote speaker at the symposium. When I was working for him, he would sometimes ask me what Daddy was working on and told me to be sure to give him his regards when I wrote to him.

"I don't know, Peggy," she went on, "I always felt kind of squirmy whenever Claussen brought up my father. I don't think he really liked him, I think he was just trying to suck up to him through me. Of course, it must have been awkward for him too, having Jens Aage Lindemann's daughter as his flunky. It's odd, you know: Claussen's wife mentioned at the banquet that they'd seen me in Denmark when I was just a baby. Claussen never told me that, even though I worked for him for two years."

"He probably didn't remember," I said. "Men don't usually pay much attention to other people's babies."

I asked her if her father and Claussen saw each other very often.

"They must've met at conferences and things like that in Europe, I suppose. When I told my mom I was going to be Claussen's assistant for the Andersen course, she said she remembered meeting him and his wife when she was still married to Dad—my father. And you heard my father at lunch the other day, talking about Claussen. He didn't think very highly of him."

She absently dipped a finger into her hair again and twirled a strand around it. "Anyway, I seriously doubt Professor Claussen could kill anybody, if that's what you're thinking," she went on. "I've read some of his reviews of other people's work. They're nasty, in a sneaky kind of way. I mean, he uses double negatives like "a not unimpressive study" and "not without merit," to try to put other scholars down. I think that's the only way he would kill somebody—with words."

"Except that Claussen's words wouldn't have any effect

on a man like your father," I reminded her. "He might have to use a stronger weapon."

She frowned. "I remember reading a review he wrote of one of my father's books. It was quite respectful—for Claussen."

I asked her why she was doing her honors thesis with Edith Silberman, instead of with Claussen.

"Because I'm a humanities, not a Scandinavian major," she said. "But Claussen's on the committee that's going to evaluate my work, since Professor Silberman doesn't read Danish and can't really evaluate my translation. She's working with me on the introduction."

"Has Claussen seen what you've done on your thesis so far?"

She shook her head. "He didn't want to see it, said he was too busy. I didn't press the issue. He's got a nasty temper—flies off the handle at the drop of a hat. Never with me—probably because of my father—but I wouldn't want to test that."

I called Buck and told him I thought I'd figured out who'd done it.

"Who?"

"The Little Mermaid. She came to life and struck down one of her tormenters as a kind of protest."

" 'The Mermaid's Revenge,' " he said. "It doesn't sound like Andersen somehow."

"Do you realize, Buck, that if I hadn't bruised my spleen, I'd be home now, sleeping the sleep of the innocent after a hard night patrolling the campus in a fine, icy mist? There's something clean and honest about that. There's nothing redeeming in what I'm doing here, in daytime, among these pompous asses."

"You ought to try a stakeout, Peggy, if you think a gathering of scholars is boring." He was laughing at me.

"A stakeout would probably be more intellectually stimulating," I retorted.

"Besides," he said, "you wouldn't be the star of a play,

if you hadn't gotten beaten up. You got a nice review in the *Daily.*"

"That's true," I admitted, wondering why my mother was right and you have to take the bad with the good in life. "Okay, Buck, if you don't buy the Little Mermaid as the perp, how about Mogens Madsen?"

"Who or what is Mogens Madsen?"

"Who, not what." I told him a piece of gossip I'd picked up that morning. "Mogens Madsen's a Dane. He teaches Danish language and culture in Sydney, Australia. I gather it's not a plum of an assignment. Apparently, he'd applied for a job teaching at a university someplace in Denmark and Lindemann blocked the appointment—Madsen had dared to question Lindemann's interpretation of an Andersen story. The best Madsen could do was get one of the jobs the Danish Foreign Office arranges for Danish scholars, spreading Danish language and culture in obscure places—probably to keep them off the Danish streets."

"And so, surrounded by kangaroos, this Madsen character snapped, came here, and did in Lindemann, did he?"

"According to the gossip, Madsen did threaten to kill Lindemann about a year ago. He was drunk at the time. Now, with Lindemann out of the way, Madsen's chances of getting a university position in Denmark will increase tremendously."

I heard paper rustling on Buck's end of the line. "He's not on the list of participants in the symposium," he said.

"No. But you might want to get Interpol to try to locate him and check his passport to see if he was here Saturday."

Buck sighed. "How do you spell 'Mogens Madsen'?"

When I'd spelled it for him, I asked him what he'd done with the fact that Lindemann had postponed his return to Denmark. He said he had detectives talking to the people Lindemann had been closest to here, to see if they knew anything about it. So far, nothing. They'd also talked to

Nancy Austin, but she continued to deny that she knew anything about Lindemann's plans.

"Pia doesn't know anything about it either," I said. "You'd think he'd have told somebody, if he was planning to stay on."

"Pia *says* she doesn't know anything about it," Buck corrected me.

"She doesn't know anything about her father's death, Buck," I told him firmly. Before he could say anything to that, I asked him if Eric Claussen had an alibi for the time Lindemann was killed.

"No, he doesn't—nothing he can prove, anyway. According to him, he left the symposium a little early—around four. He walked across campus to his office in Frye Hall, to do some work."

"On Saturday?"

"Uh-huh. He said that the symposium had caused him to neglect his duties as chairman of the Scandinavian department, so he went in Saturday evening to catch up."

"How late did he stay? Did he go to the play?"

"He says he worked until nine or so, got home around nine-thirty. Apparently he shares with the late Professor Lindemann an aversion to dramatic adaptations of Hans Christian Andersen's stories."

I pointed out that if Lindemann had attended the play, he wouldn't have been murdered. A kind of poetic justice.

"At least, he might not have been murdered in the Andersen Room," Buck replied.

I asked him if anybody had seen Claussen in his office the night of the murder.

"Nobody," he said. "Not too many people work in Frye Hall on Saturday nights."

"You've done a pretty thorough job of checking his alibi, Buck. How come?"

"Claussen was at the symposium. That would be reason enough. But he's known Lindemann for over twenty years, and had him over for dinner a few nights before he was murdered—another very good reason."

"I may have another one for you," I said, and told him about Lindemann's book and the gossip I'd picked up, that Claussen had become a joke in his field because of how slow his own book on Andersen was to appear.

"It's a pretty good motive," I said, "at least for an academic—to kill Lindemann to keep him from publishing a book that might make Claussen's superfluous. Pia Austin also thinks Claussen was jealous of her father—and she told me it was Claussen who proposed Lindemann as the keynote speaker."

"Interesting—I hadn't heard that, either. That's good work, Peggy. If that's the case, I guess we can say that Claussen's responsible for Lindemann's death. I wonder if that was his intention. Maybe it's time we had another talk with Professor Claussen."

"Of course, that doesn't explain why Lindemann extended his stay here a week."

"He may only have wanted to spend more time with his colleagues or his daughter. It might have been a surprise for Pia."

"No," I told him, flatly. "Jens Aage Lindemann wasn't into happy surprises."

Buck laughed. "You just can't stand the thought of innocent bystanders getting murdered."

"Lindemann wasn't an innocent bystander. He wasn't a very nice man and he'd earned a lot of bad karma over the years."

" 'Bad karma,' Peggy?"

"You know what I mean. People like Lindemann don't get murdered just because they happen to be in the wrong place at the wrong time. That's how good people die, not bad people."

"You'd like to think so, Peggy, because, in spite of knowing better, you want the world to be just and rational. But it's not."

"I see!"

"According to the *Daily* review," Buck said, laughing, "that's one of the play's funniest scenes. Making that line sound convincing must have taken some real acting on your part." He turned serious. "Peggy, we live in a society where the Supreme Court—the last court of appeal, composed of human beings who presumably love their children and bounce their grandchildren on their knees— recently decided that it's okay to execute an innocent man just so long as you dot all the i's and cross all the t's. How's that for being in the wrong place at the wrong time!"

"Why?" I asked, appalled.

"Because nothing in the US Constitution says you can't kill an innocent person as long as you've followed due process. The legal system isn't about justice, Peggy. It's about law. Human beings aren't big enough to dispense justice. That's for God, if there is one."

"That's bullshit," I said.

"The system works," he replied, a little lamely, I thought, "most of the time."

"I see!" When he didn't reply to that, I said, "Buck?"

"What?"

"I'm on this case officially, right?"

"Right."

"I'm not going to catch a killer by talking to those people at the symposium. If one of them did it, the only chance you have of solving the case is through Interpol turning up something from the past, or inconsistencies in their statements that I'm sure your computers are working on even as we speak."

"You're not quitting, are you?"

"No—not yet. One thing I'm going to do is try to find out more about Eric Claussen's long-awaited Hans Christian Andersen book—see if he had any reason for wanting Lindemann dead."

"How are you going to do that?"

"I'm going to talk to Edith Silberman first, find out if she knows anything about Claussen. Then I'll play it by ear."

"Okay, Peggy," he said, after he'd thought about that for

a minute. "Give Professor Silberman my best," he added, a touch of irony in his voice.

Buck once arrested Edith on a murder charge. I got her off. Their relationship isn't a warm one.

Twenty-three

Edith was teaching until three, so I walked around the Old Campus, getting some fresh air and exercise. It was a windy November afternoon, cold, but the sun poking through the clouds made the ivy licking up the sides of the old buildings glow like fire.

At three I walked into the Humanities Building, where Edith has her office. Inside, the dark halls are lined with heavily veined Italian marble, which always gives me the sense that I'm entering a shaft that goes deep underground.

Edith Silberman was my favorite teacher when I was a student. A love of literature and the ability to read critically and write clearly are Edith's only absolute criteria for a human being. She's lived to see the University taken over by a new breed of teachers who have no love of literature at all, but use it only as a way to gain power over each other and to turn their students off reading.

She hollered "Come in!" and I opened her door and entered her cluttered office with its wall-to-wall books. She had her back to me, stirring powdered coffee into the hot water in her cracked mug. She glanced over her shoulder, saw the large container of coffee in my hand, and laughed. "Planning on being here awhile, are you?" she asked. I'd stopped at the little sandwich truck outside the building before coming in and bought a cup of coffee, because all Edith serves is instant coffee in hot tap water.

She beckoned me to the old couch in the back of her long, narrow room and she took the matching overstuffed chair that faced it. Between us was a scarred coffee table piled high with student papers that were decorated with Edith's red marginal comments, many punctuated with exclamation marks.

"Pia's father's murder," she said. "You've decided to catch his killer." Edith's a short woman, although she doesn't seem aware of it, with threads of gray beginning to take over her dark hair and a burst of white like a carnation at her temple.

"Did Pia tell you that?" I asked.

"I haven't talked to Pia since the murder, but I knew you were friends, of course. Superficially an unlikely duo, I might add, but underneath you have a great deal in common: You don't think you have a sentimental bone in your body and Pia doesn't know how tough she is. As soon as I heard about her father's murder, I wondered where you were."

I told her I'd been with Pia when she found his body.

"Not much fun, I imagine—for either of you." Edith knows the story of my father's death too. "So what's your problem? Find who's got the stolen Hans Christian Andersen goods, you've found the killer."

"Maybe so. But it's also possible the real crime was the murder of Jens Aage Lindemann," I said.

"Is that what you think?"

"I don't know what to think yet." I told her about how unpopular Lindemann was among his colleagues.

She shrugged. "It's the same everywhere, isn't it? But academics rarely pay with their lives, or anything else, for being unpopular. Why are you involved, Peggy? I thought you were on sick leave."

"Lindemann's murder's given the University a black eye abroad, I guess," I said, "so the administration wants it cleared up fast. Captain DiPrima, the campus police chief, asked me to help out, since I'd met Lindemann and have a kind of in at the Andersen symposium." I grinned. "I agreed—on condition they make me a detective when I go back on duty. I'm even being paid for snooping this time."

"Huh!" Edith has mixed feelings about my career as a cop. "So if you get killed, it won't be as a meddling fool, but as an officially meddling fool. What do you want with me? Until I met Pia Austin, I didn't know anything about Hans Christian Andersen except what I saw in that movie they made about him—Danny Kaye, wasn't it? Pia has disabused me of the notion that Andersen wore wooden shoes, danced and sang on cobbled streets with little cottages with thatched roofs and storks on them and thought he was a swan hatched from a duck egg. She thinks I should read him seriously."

"She's tried to work her spell on me, too," I said. "Tell me what you know about the Scandinavian Department."

She raised her eyes. "The Scandinavian Department? I don't think there's much to say about it." She got up, went over to her desk, and brought back the University staff directory. "It was one of those departments they set up in the sixties, when the University was rolling in the green stuff and thought it could appeal to every interest and ethnic group. It thrived for a while, but I've heard it probably won't survive the next budget cut. Ah, here it is."

Her eyes scanned the page, then she looked up and said, "I thought so. The department's down to only three professors—a native Norwegian, a native Swede, and Claussen, who's the chairman. I think he's American-born. The other two are untenured assistant professors who probably weren't able to get jobs in Scandinavia for one or another reason."

"If the department folds, what'll happen to them?"

Edith shrugged. "They'll shoo the Scandinavians back where they came from and dump Claussen into the German Department, or—God help us!—force the Humanities

Department to take him in. That's all the University thinks we're good for nowadays—as a dumpster for the detritus left behind by departments that go under. What's your interest in Claussen, Peggy? Did the murder victim—Lindemann, is it?—try to snatch a piece of meat away from him at feeding time, or something? He must have been small and weak for Eric Claussen to risk attacking him."

"I've heard a rumor that Claussen's been working on a book on Andersen that never gets published," I said.

"Still? Eight or nine years ago, I served on the college's promotion committee when Claussen came up for promotion to full professor. I didn't think he had enough publications to justify it, but he claimed he was working on the definitive English-language study of Hans Christian Andersen and it had taken up all his energy for years, which was why he hadn't published much else. He probably called it 'seminal'—male professors really like that word." Edith stuck a finger in her mouth and made a gagging noise before going on.

"I voted against him, of course, but the wimps on the committee saw to it that he got his promotion in spite of me."

She laughed scornfully. "So I was right—he never did finish the thing. Well, he's not the only one. We've got quite a few aging prodigies going around claiming they're working on the seminal study of this or that—maybe it fools their wives."

I told her that a Danish professor had told me they called a project that never seemed to get completed "writing a Claussen."

"Poor man!" Edith said with a groan. "I'll bet you anything they've let him know it, too."

"You think it might be a motive for murder," I asked, "if he'd just about finished his book, and then learned that the University Press had offered a rival a contract to write a similar book?"

"And this Lindemann was the rival?" When I nodded, she said, "That would be a motive for some people—I think I even know some of them." She was silent for a few moments, thinking. "I know Claussen well enough to say hello to when I pass him on the Mall—his office is in Frye Hall, and I don't get over there much. He sometimes nods back, sometimes doesn't, depending on how deep in thought he's pretending to be at the moment. A self-important little man with a mustache and goatee who wears out-of-date tweed jackets with leather patches. Students have told me he has a quick temper."

I told her Pia had mentioned that too.

"Pia! Now there's a remarkable woman," Edith said. "I suppose you've met her boyfriend, the jock."

"Sure. I like him—at least, I think I do. I don't see much of him on account of the football season."

She nodded. "He doesn't read," she said flatly. That's just about the worst thing Edith can say about a person. "I wonder what they talk about, when they're alone?"

I laughed because she looked as if she'd really like to know. "They care about each other a lot," I said.

"That's not enough, Peggy," Edith retorted. "Brothers and sisters do that, but you don't want to live with them, do you, after you've grown up?"

I asked her if she'd ever met Christian. Her answer surprised me. She'd never met him, but she enjoyed watching him play football sometimes. "He's a remarkable athlete," she added, sipping her miserable instant coffee.

"You go to football games, Edith?" I asked skeptically.

"No—you can't see anything that way! But I watch the team when they're on television now and then. Christian Donnelly's the best football player I've ever seen at this stage of his career. Someday he's going to be a great quarterback."

This was a side of Edith I hadn't encountered before. "You sound like you know what you're talking about," I said.

"I do. When I came to the University, I was the first woman professor hired by the Humanities Department. During the football season, all the male faculty members talked about on Monday mornings in the faculty lounge was the football games they'd watched on television over the weekend. I decided I'd better start watching football too, so I'd have something to talk to them about. I sat in front of the television every Sunday afternoon for a month, watching the games. Paul fled to his study, and didn't come out until the last game was over." Paul was her husband. He'd died a couple of years ago.

"And you became one of the boys?" I asked, laughing.

"Guess again! I'd totally misjudged the meaning of football. Men don't talk football because they're interested in the game itself, Peggy. Football exists almost solely to exclude women from the lives of men, just as the necessary brutality of the game itself excludes women from participation. When I started to talk knowingly about games I'd watched, the guys in the faculty lounge stared at me as though I was trying to use a urinal!"

She shook her head in resignation. "It took me a while to catch on. Before I did, though, I learned a lot about the game, enough to know how good Christian Donnelly is. But no matter how good he is, I can't believe an intelligent and sensitive woman like Pia would have anything to talk to him about after a couple of years of marriage."

"Oh," I said, "there's probably more to Christian than what you can see from watching him perform on the football field."

As I said that, I remembered that Pia's father had said something similar as we were driving him to the banquet the night before he was killed. "Do you think I'd be with him if there wasn't?" Pia had demanded scornfully.

There was a knock on Edith's door. Edith looked at her watch. "That's probably Tessa—she always comes early. C'mon in!" she hollered.

A student opened the door and stepped into the room,

holding a paper in her hand, looking earnest and ready to do battle. It could've been me a few years earlier. I thanked Edith for her time, we agreed it was her turn to have me over for dinner, and I left.

Twenty-four

I wanted to talk to Julie Land, Eric Claussen's wife, but it was late afternoon and I didn't want Claussen coming home while I was there, so I went home and read until it was time to fix dinner. It was my turn. From the freezer I took a container of pea soup that I'd made a large batch of last week and thawed it in the microwave.

Gary and I ate it with cheese sandwiches, but without candles, and talked about how our day had gone just like a married couple that's still on speaking terms. Scary, but nice too, as long as I have my own room and people have to knock first before coming in—assuming, that is, I say it's okay to come in.

That night was supposed to have been a cocktail reception for the participants at the symposium. However, it had been reconstituted as a memorial service for Jens Aage Lindemann. Gary agreed to go with me. As I waited my turn to use the bathroom before we left, I wondered how much it would cost to add a new bathroom—assuming Mrs. Hammer, my landlady, would let me. Maybe I should consider buying a house. The look I gave Gary as I took my turn in the bathroom probably puzzled him, but he didn't say anything.

The memorial service was held in one of the University's smaller auditoriums. We found Mrs. Donnelly and her father, Gus Lund, standing in a corner of the room with Pia. I was surprised to see Christian and Sam there too, probably as moral support for Pia, who I didn't think needed it, but it was a nice gesture anyway. Gus Lund was wearing a black band on one sleeve—either for Pia's father or Jette Wulff's letters from Andersen—and divided his time between Pia and Denise Donnelly.

I hadn't seen Mrs. Donnelly since the night of the banquet. To judge by her face and behavior, she didn't look as though she was taking the theft of the Andersen letters well. She was pale, so it looked as though she'd applied rouge and lipstick too heavily. There were dark bruises under her eyes that indicated she hadn't been getting enough sleep and she also looked as though she'd lost weight. Sam was as solicitous to her as her father was. Her husband, Clay Donnelly, seemed to be in some world of his own, probably watching replays of great sports moments.

The University president and his entourage stood in a cluster on the raised platform at the front of the room, looking grim, determined, and a little nervous. A thin gray man in an expensively tailored suit and with a mane of perfectly groomed white hair too large for his head came up to Pia, bowed, and introduced himself. I recognized him as the Danish consul general, who'd spoken at the banquet Friday night. He asked Pia if she wanted to say a few words about her father to the assembled people.

"Yes," she told him, and he nodded and went back and joined President Hightower and the other University officials.

Professor Claussen and his wife came up to Pia and expressed their condolences. Claussen nodded curtly to me. Mary Vedel loomed behind them like a load of guilt, the mean glitter in her eyes contradicting the sorrowful curve on her little mouth.

"You must be devastated," she said to Denise Donnelly, clutching her hand. "Those letters must have meant the world to you. My father sends his condolences, too."

Mrs. Donnelly pulled her hand out of Mary Vedel's grip. "Thank you, Mary," she said weakly.

"But you have a new interest now, don't you? Hans Christian Andersen's mother. I can't imagine why you'd be interested in a woman like that, Denise, as I told your son's lover yesterday"—she shot Pia a wary glance—"since you have so little in common. She was little more than a whore, wasn't she?"

There was a shocked silence. Denise Donnelly turned pale and then drew her hand back, obviously intending to slap or hit Mary Vedel, but Sam stepped quickly between them.

"That's a very nice cross you have there on your bosom, Miss Vedel," he said to Mary. "It looks old; has it been in your family long?"

Ignoring him, Mary spoke over his shoulder to Mrs. Donnelly, her eyes glittering slivers of malice. "But Andersen's poor, dear mother couldn't write, so you're unlikely to 'stumble across' letters from her to her son in an antique shop, aren't you, Denise?"

She turned and looked Christian up and down. "So you are the product of the marriage between Denise Lund and Clay Donnelly. It's very nice to meet you finally. I was once a friend of your mother's, and of your father's too."

Her gaze swept slowly across all of us, as if to see if she'd missed anybody with her seething rage, and then she turned and disappeared into the crowd of scholars.

Mrs. Donnelly was trembling with suppressed anger and, at the same time, struggling not to cry. Christian put his arm around her and pulled her to him.

At the front of the room President Hightower cleared his throat into the microphone to get our attention.

Hightower expressed his regret to the symposium participants for the terrible incident that had disturbed but not deterred their "celebration of the child in literature," extended his deepest sympathies to Pia, and asked the consul general to convey his apologies to the Danish people for the distressing way in which Jens Aage Lindemann—a cultural giant among cultural giants in his own country and the world—had met his end. He vowed that he, personally, would not rest easily in his bed until the guilty party or parties had been brought to justice.

The consul general replaced Hightower at the microphone. He reminded us grimly of what an irreparable loss Jens Aage Lindemann was to Danish—indeed, world—scholarship on children's literature, made pointed allusions to the violence now endemic in a country that had once been the model for all freedom-loving peoples, and then looked over at us, one eyebrow raised questioningly.

Pia made her way to the front of the room, climbed onto the platform, and turned and looked out at the crowd. She was wearing a black wool dress, its long sleeves covering her pale arms, and black high-top shoes that made her legs look skinnier than they actually were. I'd never seen her wear makeup or jewelry and she wasn't wearing any that night either.

"I'm Pia Austin, Professor Lindemann's daughter," she began, "and I didn't know my father very well." She stared down at the floor, as if trying to decide where to go from there. Then she looked up and, in a steady voice, continued, "That's because, whenever I visited him, he was away at a conference like this one, giving papers on Hans Christian Andersen. Or, if he was home, he was in his study with the door closed, writing one of the books or articles that made him the leading Hans Christian Andersen scholar of his time. I learned not to disturb him." She paused again while she poured water into a glass and drank some of it. Her hand was trembling slightly.

"Well," she continued brusquely, "a lot of ambitious men—and women too, now that they finally have the opportunity—are like that. It just seems funny to me that what my father neglected me for was to write about a man who wrote stories for children—and for adults who keep the wonder of childhood alive in themselves. He had no time to read to me, or do the other things that,

I later discovered, lots of fathers do with their children.

"For a long time, I hated Hans Christian Andersen because I thought he'd stolen my father away from me. So I didn't read his stories. Then one day, the last time I visited him in Copenhagen, I got so bored hanging around my father's apartment that I picked up a book about Andersen that had just come in the mail. I glanced through it and read a passage that described how Andersen liked to sit with kids and entertain them, in the upper-class homes where he visited. He thought that was a worthy thing for a man to do. Imagine that!

"The author described how Andersen had a long pair of scissors—it gives me goosepimples when I think what some of you have probably made of that long pair of scissors!—and he would make intricate papercuts for the children, and make up stories about them as he went along. He even cut out figures, and blew on them to make them dance." Pia laughed, as though seeing it, instead of us, before her.

"In my imagination," she went on, "I saw him sitting there—that gawky, comic figure of a man—bringing characters and scenes to life with words and scissors, and always leaving the children richer than they'd been before, full of memories they'd never forget. I thought of that as I sat there in my father's living room, hearing the brittle clack of his typewriter behind his closed study door."

She lowered her voice, almost to a growl. "And as Andersen was entertaining the children, the other men were sitting in their studies with their port and sherry and long cigars, discussing the important issues of the day."

She paused and stared out at the people standing there, her large eyes glowing. "What did *they* have to discuss that was so important? I'll bet no one, except maybe a few dried-up Danish historians—can think of one single thing those patrons of Hans Christian Andersen could have discussed, or one single thing they accomplished in their whole lives!

"What did my father have to do that was so much more important than spending time with me? In ten years, his books and articles will be forgotten—replaced by the books and articles of some of you in this room tonight—whose books and articles and papers will be forgotten ten years after that! Why don't you go to the University library sometime and see what *your* books on Andersen'll look like in twenty years!"

Steady, Pia! I thought, not knowing whether to applaud or cry.

The room was deathly still for a few moments, and then she went on, more calmly. "The best of Andersen's tales were written for children and adults alike, and for men as well as for women. I think Andersen united the adult and the child, male and female, in one person—himself—without conflict, without tension. No wonder you can't understand him. My father couldn't, either."

She looked over our way. "When Mrs. Donnelly—Denise Donnelly—found the letters from Andersen to Henriette Wulff, she told me about Jette and her relationship to Andersen. Mrs. Donnelly had no 'scholarly' interest in their relationship at all, which means, she didn't want to analyze it to death, use their perfectly human need for one another to diminish them, turn them into patients in an asylum."

Mrs. Donnelly, standing next to me, sniffed loudly.

"She got me interested in reading about their relationship through their letters," Pia went on, "which is the only place it exists, because no 'scholar' thinks it's worth writing about. And that's probably a good thing, considering the nature of the crap people write about Andersen these days! And what I learned of Hans Christian Andersen from their correspondence made me love him even more—for being such a friend to her, and for bringing out the best in her, just as she brought out the best in him, something he freely admitted.

"The letters are gone now, stolen as a part of the violence that destroyed my father too. Their theft reminds me of a story that most of the Danish scholars in this room have heard before, but I'm going to tell it anyway."

Pia paused to take another sip of water. "In the late eighteenth century," she continued, "a Danish farmer was plowing a field. He turned up a large drinking horn made of gold. It was from the Viking Age—a thousand years old—with intricate designs on it, and Runic writing. A few years later, in nearly the same place, a simple farm girl found another golden horn just like it, just as beautiful and in just as perfect condition.

"It was a miracle that those horns turned up like that after all that time—and they were found by uneducated people, too, not by scholars! They were put in a museum and, a few years later—they disappeared without a trace. Some people thought the old gods had come and taken them back because the Danes weren't worthy of them, they couldn't understand them as they were meant to be understood."

Pia smiled across the room at Mrs. Donnelly, who was sniffling into a handkerchief. "I think that's what happened here," she said. "Nobody in this room but you and I, Mrs. Donnelly, could really appreciate those letters. And just like Andersen entertaining the children, here we are, surrounded by our intellectual 'betters,' who are laughing up their sleeves at us. In the end, though, it's going to be people like us who have the last laugh."

She stood at the microphone a minute longer without saying anything, then she jumped off the platform and returned to where we were standing. People got out of her way.

Somebody laughed nervously somewhere, a shrill, high-pitched noise that broke the silence, and then the room was full of the jabber of outraged academics.

Sam wrapped Pia in a bear hug and exclaimed, "What a performance!"

"Hey, let me in too," Christian said, and inserted himself into the hug.

"Let's get out of here before they lynch Pia," Gus Lund said, and shooed us towards the door.

Twenty-five

Outside, in the cold, clean night air, Gus announced that he wanted dessert and asked if anybody knew a place not too far away.

"Oh, Dad," Mrs. Donnelly protested. "Not tonight. Let's just go home."

"Nonsense, Denise! A piece of chocolate cake'll do you a world of good. You can't mourn for those letters forever, y'know!"

"Gus is right, Mom," Christian said. "Besides, you've been off your feed lately. You need dessert to keep up your strength. Starving to death won't bring the letters back."

"I know a place whose pastry chef does cakes and pies the way Miller and Williams did plays," Sam said. "It's not far and it's open late to catch the theater crowd—which won't be out yet." He pointed to Mrs. Donnelly. "You will be driving with me, Denise, the rest can trail along behind." He gave the rest of us directions, took Mrs. Donnelly's arm, and marched her down the sidewalk.

I said Gary and I didn't want to horn in on a family affair. That wasn't quite true, since Gary was sticking to Christian like a leech, talking post-season football prospects with him and his father. The three of them seemed to be getting along well, so when Pia insisted we join them, I said okay.

Gary, Sam, and I sat across the table from the Donnellys, Gus Lund, and Pia, where I could watch the interplay among them. I've always been interested in seeing how families get along among themselves.

Christian obviously loved his mother a great deal, and was concerned about her. And Gus Lund clearly loved both Christian and Pia, and tried to provide the male warmth that Clay Donnelly couldn't or wouldn't give. If it wasn't about sports, Donnelly didn't seem to have much to say on the subject.

Christian patted his mother's hand and murmured, "It's not the end of the world, Mom."

She turned and gazed at him sorrowfully. "Oh, I know, Christian," she replied. She looked at Pia and her eyes filled with tears. "It's so selfish of me, thinking of the loss of Henriette Wulff's things, when your loss is so much greater."

Gus Lund said, gruffly, "That was a beautiful story you told up there, Pia, about how those Viking horns appeared mysteriously and then disappeared just as mysteriously. Whatever the facts, those miserable scholars didn't deserve Andersen's letters."

I'd heard Carl Vedel's story of how Mrs. Donnelly had found the Andersen letters, and I was curious to know what her version was. Since the subject had come up anyway, I asked her how she'd found them.

Her father answered. "It was a miracle, all right," he said, "no matter how you cut it. About a year ago, old Carl Vedel calls me and tells me he's just finished restoring a cupboard I might be interested in, a beautiful piece he'd picked up at a farm somewhere. I told him I'd drive out and see it on Saturday—me and Denise were planning to spend the day antiquing. Well, Carl was right for once, the cupboard was a beaut, so I made him an offer. You tell Peggy what happened next, Denise."

"While Dad and Mr. Vedel were haggling over the price," she said, "I browsed through a pile of old books on the floor over in a corner of the basement. You never know what you're going to find among things like that, so I got down on my hands and knees and started going through them."

"Mom likes cast-off things," Christian interrupted. "Thank God," he added, giving her a smile and a wink.

"Oh, Christian!" she exclaimed. She was looking better, either on account of the cake or the story she was telling. "Anyway, Mr. Vedel saw what I was doing and asked me if I was interested in buying the books. He said they'd come with the other things he'd picked up at the farm where he'd got the cupboard Dad was interested in. I could see they were old religious books—Danish Bibles, hymnals, and books of sermons, mostly—but they can sometimes be interesting. I like to read the names and dates of the people who owned them through the years, and the births and confirmations and deaths so faithfully recorded in the Bibles. Sometimes you can guess the kinds of lives they had, you know—their joys and sorrows."

She smiled at me, almost apologetically. "I think it's a shame that things that were once so precious to people are ending up in dumps—which was what Mr. Vedel had in mind for those books too. They were already damp and moldy from being down in that basement for so long. So I said I'd take the whole pile." Denise smiled at her father. "You didn't like the idea much, did you, Dad?"

"I admit it," he said, grinning back at her. "You're too damned sentimental, Denise. Anyway, Carl named a price and I just laughed, said we'd take 'em off his hands for nothing, or else he'd have to haul 'em to the dump himself. In the end, he gave 'em to us for nothing, but I paid more for the cupboard than I needed to. The next day, I sent one of my men over to Carl's place with a company truck, and he brought the cupboard and the books out to my place. A couple of weeks later, when Denise was out to the house, she went through 'em. You should've seen the look on her face when she came in with those letters!"

"I couldn't believe what I'd found," Mrs. Donnelly said.

I smiled to myself. Their version of the story differed in a couple of significant ways from Vedel's. For one thing, Carl Vedel claimed he'd called Gus Lund, not the other way around, and that Mrs. Donnelly had brought up the subject of buying the old books first, not him—but I suspected it would take more than a grilling under hot lights to get the truth out of any of them. I wondered if it mattered.

"They came so close to being lost forever," Mrs. Donnelly went on. Her face crumpled. "And now, they are lost forever!" she wailed. "Maybe it's a judgment—maybe I should have shared the credit for finding them with Mr. Vedel, or paid him something for them."

"That's crap, Denise," Gus Lund growled. "The fool was just gonna haul 'em off to a landfill if you hadn't of taken them off his hands! Besides, those letters'll show up again someday. Maybe Peggy'll find who stole 'em and bring 'em back. Right, Peggy?"

I said I hoped somebody would.

"Then again, maybe Pia's right," Sam said, taking her hand. "Maybe the gods came and took them away."

"Or one of Hans Christian Andersen's *fairies,*" Clay Donnelly muttered, and shoved a piece of apple pie into his mouth.

"Save that for the Sports Boosters, Dad," Christian snapped.

Donnelly looked up at him, surprised, then returned to his pie.

"Actually, Mr. Donnelly," Sam said, switching into his gay voice, "there aren't that many fairies in Hans Christian Andersen's stories. Just ask Pia, if you don't believe me."

"Sam," Christian said warningly.

Gus Lund looked up at Sam, his eyes twinkling under the bushy brows, and winked.

I asked Mrs. Donnelly where she'd found the letters.

"In an old book of Bible stories for children," she replied. "Assuming Mr. Vedel even bothered to go through all those books, they would have been easy to overlook. The book's binding was loose and pages were falling out. I almost missed seeing the letters myself."

"Did you try to find out anything about the farmer who'd had those books?"

Mrs. Donnelly smiled sadly. "Of course I did. That's the only reason I told Mr. Vedel I'd found the letters among the things he'd given me. I wanted to know as much as I could about the background. But the trail ended at the farm. The farmer and his wife were dead and the present owners didn't know anything about the books. They weren't even Danes."

"You have any reason for being so curious?" Clay Donnelly asked me suddenly.

"Do I need a reason?" I asked him. Two can play the game of brusque questions.

"I just wondered if maybe you were here on business."

"Peggy's here because we invited her, Clay," Gus Lund said to his son-in-law.

"Besides, a good cop's always on business," Sam said.

On the way home that night, Gary said, "What're you thinking, Peggy?"

"That I'd like to know a little more about those letters."

"You don't believe the Little Match Girl came down from heaven and took 'em away because the scholars of today are clowns?"

I pointed out that the Little Match Girl probably wouldn't have bashed Jens Aage Lindemann over the head first; it wouldn't have been in character.

"But I'll bet she would've given him a hotfoot," Gary said. He changed the subject. "The relationship between Christian and his father's interesting, don't you think?"

"How so?"

"Donnelly's so surly. He can rattle off statistics and opinions about everything relating to football, in a voice that sounds like an assault rifle, but he doesn't show any warmth towards Christian at all. Sometimes he looks at him as though he can't figure out where he came from."

"Sam once told me that he failed to make the football team when he was a student," I said, "so maybe he's jealous of Christian. Or maybe he just doesn't know how to express his feelings."

"If I had a son like Christian," Gary said, "I'd be so proud, I'd glow in the dark."

Twenty-six

The next morning, as I was sitting at the breakfast table, spooning microwaved shredded wheat into my mouth and chasing it with coffee, hands fell onto my shoulders and something cold and wet landed on my neck. I almost jumped out of my skin.

"Damn it, Gary!" He came around and pulled up the chair opposite me.

"Sorry," he said, pouring himself a cup of coffee and re-filling mine, and not looking as sorry as he might. "A penny for your thoughts."

"I can't believe you said that," I snarled, resisting the urge to rub the kiss off my neck, which seemed to linger there. I've never responded well to physical shows of affection, although I expect others to respond to mine—which are rare enough. Besides, I'd only had one cup of coffee, never enough to brace me for banter in the morning.

"It's what my mother always said," he said.

"Mine, too."

We glared at each other across the table and then both started laughing.

"You think it's time for me to find a place of my own?" he asked, suddenly serious.

"No!" I said, too quickly, then added, "We'll talk about it again when the season's over."

"Huh?"

Gary's question had reminded me of the first words I'd heard Pia speak to Christian. She'd asked him if he wanted her to move out. He didn't, he said, and then she'd ended the conversation by saying they'd talk about it again when the season ended.

When I told Gary about it, he said, "Strange conversation. Is that what you were brooding on when I came into the room a moment ago?"

"No. I was thinking about the stolen letters. Mrs. Donnelly's and her father's version of how she found them differs from Carl Vedel's."

"You think it's important to find out who's telling the truth?"

I shrugged. "How'll I know until I've checked it out?"

There was also something mysterious about the sudden appearance of the letters, just as there was about their disappearance. I doubted that divine intervention would explain either mystery. Call me cynical and skeptical. Pia had.

"You also don't want to go back to the Hans Christian Andersen symposium," Gary said, sighting at me down the length of a spoon.

"You're right. Let Floyd Hazard waste his time stomping around among those dreary people."

I got up and took my breakfast things to the sink. On the way back, I planted a kiss on his neck, a warm, wet one, but I think he was expecting it, since he didn't jump. Of course, Gary'd lived in tropical jungles, where you have to expect warm, wet things to fall out of trees onto your neck periodically, so maybe he didn't even notice.

Gary went off to the newspaper and I sat at the kitchen table and considered what to do next. I wanted to talk to Julie Land, Eric Claussen's wife, about the evening they'd spent with Lindemann a few nights before he was murdered, but I didn't want Claussen to know about it, since I was hoping to pump her for her husband's reaction to the news of Lindemann's book on Hans Christian Andersen, the book that might make Claussen's superfluous. It was still too early to call her and be sure of getting her instead of her husband.

I drove to the University and parked in the staff lot behind the library, hoping that if a campus cop came by she or he would recognize my old Rabbit and leave it alone. When I became a real detective, I thought, maybe I'd be issued a sticker that would let me park anywhere.

I took the elevator to the Rare Books Room and asked the receptionist if I could see the director. Thick, dark carpeting absorbed the sounds of our passage as she led me across an oak-panelled room furnished with rows of tables that were occupied by men and women bent reverently over old books and manuscripts. She knocked at a door and opened it without waiting for a response, and introduced me to the director, Gordon Brill, an appropriately elderly, fragile-looking man.

I identified myself and told him I was working on the murder of Jens Aage Lindemann and the theft of the Hans Christian Andersen letters.

"A tragedy," he said, shaking his head, "a terrible loss. What can I do to help?"

I told him I'd like to get some idea of the value of the letters.

He rubbed his hands together, making dry, autumnal sounds that were loud in the room, and said, "I'm sorry, I really can't tell you. I understand that Mrs. Donnelly was offered a great deal of money for them by a collector in Denmark, but—" He broke off, shrugged.

"But the University must have insured them. For how much?"

"How do you insure something irreplaceable?" Brill asked. "The glass in the case was insured, and the window—but not the letters."

I asked him if Mrs. Donnelly had given the letters to the library or just loaned them. He said they were a gift.

"But she took a tax write-off for them, didn't she?"

"I'm sure I couldn't tell you that," he replied.

"You don't know?"

"That's correct. It was no concern of ours."

"But she could have taken a write-off if she'd wanted to?"

"Of course, but she would have had to get the letters appraised first."

"Didn't she?"

He spread his hands, shrugged again.

"You don't know that, either? If she'd had them appraised, somebody here would've done it, wouldn't they?"

Brill coughed discreetly, or perhaps it was a discreet laugh. "The Internal Revenue Service, Miss O'Neill, would view with suspicion a price assigned to a gift by either the donor or the recipient. I'm sure that, with your knowledge of the darker sides of human nature, you can understand why. A gift has to be appraised by a bona-fide appraiser with ties to neither party to the transaction. I don't know if Mrs. Donnelly had the Andersen letters appraised or not."

As Gordon Brill sat and waited patiently, I, with my knowledge of the darker sides of human nature, thought about the implications of that for a moment. "How would an appraiser go about putting a monetary value on the letters?" I asked finally.

"He would base his appraisal on how much similar letters had sold for in the recent past."

"And there's a record of that?"

"Of course," he replied, suddenly full of competence and useful information. "I could show it to you, if you'd like."

I told him I would.

He excused himself and left the room, returning a few minutes later with a fat book: *American Book Prices Current*. He thumbed through it until he found what he wanted, studied it for a minute, and then turned it so I could read it. It was a list of books, manuscripts, and letters by Hans Christian Andersen that had recently been sold at auction, in British pounds, German marks, Danish *kroner*.

"Translated into dollars," he said after a minute, "Hans Christian Andersen's letters typically bring anywhere from eight hundred to five thousand dollars, depending on the number of pages, the subject matter, and—a fairly subjective category—their importance. Also, don't forget that these are wholesale prices. The buyers may have bought these things with the expectation of selling them to private collectors or museums at much higher prices."

"Just as a guess," I said, "what price do you think an appraiser would have put on the seven stolen letters?"

"As I already told you, somebody in Denmark offered Mrs. Donnelly a great deal of money for them—I believe I heard the sum of forty-five thousand dollars mentioned. Unofficially, I think that would be a fair evaluation for tax purposes. But, of course, Mrs. Donnelly preferred to make the letters the centerpiece of her Andersen Room. And she certainly didn't need the money."

But Carl and Mary Vedel might have, I thought, and Carl Vedel, at least, thought the letters were his.

I gave Gordon Brill my nicest smile. "You didn't really care—you or anybody else at the University—about the letters, did you? You accepted them from Mrs. Donnelly, and built the Hans Christian Andersen Room to house them and the other Danish things she'd collected, only because you had to, to get her father's money. She could have filled that room with Hummel figurines or 'Precious Moments,' for all you cared, as long as you got Gustav Lund's dough. That's why the University hadn't got around to installing burglar alarms in the Anderson Room yet."

Brill had the grace to blush, bringing needed color to his parchmentlike skin, and his pale eyes searched the room, perhaps in search of a circumlocution. Then he pursed his lips, to indicate that discretion was the order of the day, and said, "The Hans Christian Andersen Room was Mrs. Donnelly's pet project, Miss O'Neill. If it made her happy to have it, and if it got the University the money it needed to build the children's library, a valuable addition to its research and teaching mission, what harm was there in it? It's really quite a nice room, isn't it?"

"Yes, indeed," I said. "And it made quite an atmospheric murder room, too." I enjoyed seeing him wince. I dragged my chair closer to him and, staring into his face, asked, "Mr. Brill, how difficult would it have been to forge the Andersen letters?"

"Forge!" he exclaimed, horrified at my use of the "F word."

"Forge," I repeated.

"Surely a professional forger wouldn't bother forging letters like those, would he?" he stammered. "So much work for such a little reward, relatively speaking."

Not everybody wants to be rewarded with money, I thought. Some people just want a room of their own, as it were.

"But since you didn't care enough about the letters to have them authenticated yourself," I said, "we'll never know if they're real or not—unless Mrs. Donnelly had them appraised. And you didn't answer my question."

"How difficult—?" He tapped his long, thin nose. "Getting hold of paper from Andersen's time would not be hard. The ink would be a greater problem, of course, but the chemistry is known and could be duplicated—if you had the money to spend on it. And there are many ways to age things artificially, I'm sorry to have to say."

"What about Andersen's handwriting?"

He shrugged. "If you had the necessary skill, possible—with practice. Because the letters were relatively unimportant, they would probably not be subjected to the severest tests, even by a professional appraiser."

Mrs. Donnelly had a lot of time and money, and she'd dug through a lot of old junk from Andersen's time over the years. She'd even taught herself to copy Andersen's own elaborate paper cuts.

Of course, Carl Vedel and his daughter Mary had similar interests, and access to old Danish things too, and time.

I thanked Gordon Brill for his help and he followed me

out of his office and across the still room, perhaps to make sure I didn't take anything. For some reason, he seemed happy to see me go.

I went back down to the first floor and walked over to the children's library. As I approached the Andersen Room, Floyd Hazard swung out the door and strode down the hall toward me, his face blotchy with anger. When he saw me, he tried to go around.

"Hey, what's your hurry?" I stepped in front of him. "About to make an arrest?"

His attempt at a casual laugh hit the floor like a hairball. "Huh-unh. How about you?" His eyes wouldn't meet mine, and he looked eager to get away, normally something I'd encourage.

"The secret's buried in the distant past," I said, my voice hushed.

"What'd'ya mean by that?"

"Nothing," I said. "Anybody in the Andersen Room?"

"The what?"

"The room you just barrelled out of."

"Oh. Yeah, those friends of yours—and Christian Donnelly."

"You get his autograph this time?"

"I gotta go, O'Neill. I don't have time for chitchat."

"Sorry!" I stood aside and, puzzled, watched him disappear around a corner, trenchcoat flapping in his wake.

As I stepped into the Andersen Room, Christian said, with mock disgust in his voice, "Another cop!" He was standing behind Pia, reading something on the desk over her shoulder. He was wearing a matching sweatshirt and pants and carrying a tennis racket.

"Tennis anybody?" That was Sam, sprawled in the chair under the Hans Christian Andersen portrait, a tennis racket across his bare knees. He was dressed in ragged cutoffs and an old t-shirt with a beer advertisement just barely legible on the front, under a windbreaker with the University football team's logo on it.

"What did he want?" I asked, gesturing over my shoulder with a thumb.

"Do you realize," Sam said, his eyes wide with shock, "that that man's name is Floyd Hazard? Someday, when I get a moment, I'm going to write an article on the determining factor of names not only on the formation of character, but also on physical characteristics. Had his name been Chandler St. Claire, do you think for a moment his brow would have been so low, so sloped and so ridged?"

"He started out talking to Christian about the football season," Pia said, "and what Christian thought the team's chances were of getting into a bowl game. Christian didn't encourage the friendship, exactly, so he turned to Sam and asked him if he was a big football fan. Sam's response was a shocked '*Moi?*' "

"You'd suppose he'd have more urgent things to worry about than whether or not I support the team, wouldn't you?" Sam said. "But perhaps he was thrown off by this windbreaker, which—if you must know—I won in a poker game. Your man Hazard also asked me if I was related to either Pia or Christian," he added, darkly.

"So Sam had to go into his queer act, of course," Christian said, laughing. "He fondled Hazard's jacket and told him he envies men who look good in polyester."

Sam shook his head sadly. "After a while, he stomped out in a huff, I can't imagine why. I suppose you're his replacement, Peggy—the good cop on the heels of the bad, or some such devious and complex strategy. Pia says you're an official part of the case now and absolutely ruthless. I hope that's not going to interfere with your acting career. I couldn't find anybody capable of doing a self-deluded cop as well as you on short notice—unless, perhaps, I could convince Floyd Hazard to try his hand at the histrionic art—he seems to have time to kill."

I assured Sam that my sleuthing wouldn't interfere with my acting career.

Pia asked me if I was making any progress. I didn't want to tell her what I'd heard from Gordon Brill, so I shrugged and said I wasn't sure. "I haven't met an Andersen scholar out there yet who doesn't hate Andersen, or patronize him, or want to cure him," I added. "One obnoxious little gnome told me it was too bad Andersen didn't live long enough to be psychoanalyzed. 'How much a trained therapist could have told him about himself!' he said ruefully."

"It's because of shrinks that so few people know themselves anymore," Sam said.

"Aren't you putting the cart before the horse?" Christian asked him.

"What do you know?" Sam retorted. "You're just a football player."

"Andersen was among the half dozen most creative people in the world of his time," Pia stuck in. "He was successful beyond most creative people's wildest dreams, he never hurt anybody, he was happy and he knew how to deal with his problems, so is it any wonder that literary scholars treat him like a mental case or a child?"

"There is nobody more hated by ordinary people than a person who's successful and happy," Sam pronounced. "I don't fear stupidity as such, I fear the righteously mediocre."

"As opposed to the righteously superior," Christian said.

"You got it, man," Sam said, doing a scary imitation of one of Christian's offensive linesmen, either Howitzer or Danielli, take your pick.

"When Andersen was made an honorary professor," Pia said, "Jette Wulff wrote to congratulate him. She added that she really ought to be congratulating the professors on Andersen now being one."

"Pia has assured us that it sounds hilarious in Danish," Sam said.

She glared at him.

"Let's not get Pia started on Jette and Andersen," Christian said. "She's bad enough at home."

Andy Blake—the emperor—came in then. "Hey, guys,"

he said in his deep voice, giving us all his big smile. "What's goin' on?"

"Andy and I are going out for lunch," Pia told me, "since Sam and Christian have a tennis match. You want to come along, Peggy?"

"Or watch me make a monkey out of Christian," Sam said.

"Is he that good, Christian?" I asked.

"No, he plays dirty. You ought to come and watch. You'd lose all respect for the man."

"Not Peggy," Sam said. "She respects the devious."

"I can't," I said. "I've got things to do. I want to talk to Pia about the Andersen letters. Are you going to be here later?"

"Sure." She took a second look at me. "What about them?"

"I'd like to know a little bit about their history."

"Boy, have you come to the right place!" Andy exclaimed.

I asked her if I could come back that afternoon around two and she said okay.

I walked out of the building with the four of them, watched them cross the Mall together, then split up and each pair go its own way. Andy had his cap on backwards, as usual, and his jeans had holes in the knees and seat— his underwear showed.

I remembered the smear of greasepaint on Pia's cheek the night her father was killed, but the thought that strayed through my mind was unworthy even of me.

Twenty-seven

I called Buck and asked him for the Donnellys' address. As he looked it up, he asked me why I wanted it.

"I've acquired an avid interest in Henriette Wulff."

"Why?" He sounded a little skeptical.

"I'm not sure the stolen letters are genuine."

"Doesn't the University know?"

"The University doesn't care. It just wanted Gustav Lund's money. Mrs. Donnelly could probably have put her son's athletic trophies in that room, as long as her father coughed up the dough for the children's library."

"You think Mrs. Donnelly faked them? Why?"

"If they're fakes, she's the likeliest culprit. Finding them was the triumph of her life."

"So you think Lindemann found out they were phony and Mrs. Donnelly killed him to keep him from exposing them and making her look foolish. Then she decided she'd better get rid of the letters too, so nobody else would be able to discover her deception."

"It's possible, isn't it?" I remembered what Sam Allen had once told me: Denise Donnelly was tougher than she looked. I wondered if she could be cleverer than she looked, too.

"She's too short to climb through that window," Buck pointed out.

"But her husband isn't. Do you know where he was the night of the murder?"

"No. We never considered him a suspect—or her, either, for that matter. I'll find out."

It was hard to imagine Clay Donnelly climbing into the Andersen room through a window and stealing the letters just to keep his wife from being seriously embarrassed, but you never knew. The family fortune was hers, not his, and he might jump through flaming hoops if she told him to.

I told Buck of my conversations with Carl and Mary Vedel. "I got the feeling that both Vedel and his daughter are resentful of Gustav Lund and his daughter's money and position. And on top of that, they think the letters are rightfully theirs. Also, Mary Vedel may think Clay Donnelly dumped her for Denise."

"Not all the weird stuff you turn up in a murder investigation is relevant," Buck reminded me. "It'll be hard to prove the letters are fakes, now that they're gone."

"I know that. And Mrs. Donnelly claims she didn't make photocopies of them, just typescripts. That supports my suspicions about them."

"I agree. But even if they are forgeries, Peggy, it doesn't mean Mrs. Donnelly was involved in stealing them. A thief would have assumed they were genuine."

"Let's just say I'll do anything to avoid going back to that symposium and talking to any more scholars," I told him, and hung up before he could raise any more objections. I didn't know what I was going to find out by talking to Denise Donnelly, but if I did know, I wouldn't need to talk to her, would I?

I went around the library to my car. A note on the windshield said "Next time get a permit, Crimebuster!" It was signed "Lawrence." Lawrence Fitzpatrick, who'd saved my life two months earlier, carrying me out of a burning building as guns were going off and Paula Hendersen was kicking shit out of bad guys.

Now he'd passed up the chance to give me a ticket.

I owed him a lot.

Although it wasn't done in polite circles, I showed up at the Donnellys' without calling first, exploiting to the full my new freedom as a real detective. They lived in one of the older suburbs, in a beautifully preserved Victorian mansion with gingerbread, turrets, and leaded windows, set way back on a large and beautifully landscaped lawn. The Scandinavian furniture business had been good to them—just as marrying "the rich man's daughter," as Mary Vedel had put it, had been good to Clay Donnelly.

I was surprised when Mrs. Donnelly opened the door herself. I'd expected a servant. "This is a surprise, Peggy," she said, smiling up at me politely. "What brings you here?" She still looked like she wasn't eating enough, or getting enough sleep.

"I'd like to ask you some questions about the Henriette Wulff letters," I said.

"Henriette's—? Why?"

"Just routine," I said, because that's what detectives say on television and in books. "May I come in? I won't keep you long."

She sighed. "All right." She stepped back to let me in. As I followed her down the hall, she asked me if I wanted coffee or tea.

She didn't sound enthusiastic about getting either, so I said no.

A grandfather clock guarded the entryway to the living room, turning time into a dirge. Why do people own such tedious things? The living room was large and high-ceilinged, with a beautifully finished hardwood floor, a fireplace that looked as though it was never used, area rugs and furniture that looked old and uncomfortable. It was a cold room and looked unlived in.

A china cabinet in a corner was full of figurines sitting on little lace doilies, and paintings on the walls depicted aspects of rural life, probably Danish, but how would you know? Cows are cows.

"What's this?" I asked, standing by something that looked like a chaise lounge in the center of the room.

"A Danish fainting couch from the middle of the nine-teenth century," she replied. "Women fainted a lot back then, you see, and it was useful to be close to one of these when you did."

"A little calculating, though, wasn't it?"

She laughed, some color coming into her face. "Of course! But haven't we women always been calculating, Peggy? Haven't we had to be?" She sat down on the edge of the couch, gestured me to an ethnic-looking chair across the coffee table from it, and gave me an expectant smile.

I started off by asking her how she'd got interested in Henriette Wulff.

"I've always been interested in Danish culture," she said. "It's my heritage, just as Hans Christian Andersen is. When I learned to read Danish, I read everything I could get my hands on about him that's not available in English translation. Then one day, ten or twelve years ago, I came across the published correspondence between Andersen and Henriette in a used bookstore in Copenhagen, and I became fascinated with her."

"Why?" I asked. "According to Pia, she wasn't happy in Denmark and didn't get along very well with her Danish acquaintances—except Andersen. That's why she was emigrating to this country when she died. You seem to really love Denmark."

Color suddenly appeared in her cheeks and her eyes darted nervously around the room. "It is odd, isn't it?" She gave a little laugh. "I can't explain it. I love Denmark— but I love Henriette Wulff too."

"Because she loved Hans Christian Andersen," I said.

"I suppose so," she replied uncertainly, looking down at her hands, clasped in her lap.

"There was a lot of pressure on you to return the letters to Denmark, wasn't there?"

She smiled, nodded. "Yes, there was."

"I suppose you thought that would be a betrayal of Jette—since, after all, she was turning her back on Denmark?"

She gave that a moment's thought, watching me as if it

might be a trick question. "I didn't think of that," she said finally.

"Quite a remarkable coincidence," I said, "that those letters should appear to just you, who loved Jette Wulff so much."

She stared hard at me for a moment and there was an edge to her voice when she said, "They might have appeared to many people over the years, Peggy, but nobody recognized them for what they were until I saw them. There are lots of old letters rotting in old books, you know."

It sounded lonely. I asked her if she'd had the letters appraised.

She shook her head and fiddled with her wedding and engagement rings, sliding them on and off her finger. "They're—they were priceless. It somehow seemed disrespectful to even consider it."

"For such things as tax write-offs," I said, "people often try to put a price on the priceless."

"Oh, I see what you mean." I wondered if she could really be that disingenuous. She shook her head. "But I didn't use them as a tax write-off."

"Why not?"

She looked around her living room, as if the answer were obvious. "Clay and I are quite well off, as you must know. We don't need to deduct every little donation we make."

"I didn't think people got rich, thinking that way, Mrs. Donnelly."

"I didn't get rich, Peggy. My father did."

"So the letters have never been authenticated."

"No, they—" Her already large eyes widened as what I was getting at dawned on her. "You think I forged those letters, don't you? That's what you're here to try to find out!"

"I just think it's odd you didn't show them to an expert, or make photostatic copies—"

"I didn't show them to an expert because it never occurred to me they might be forged," she interrupted me, her voice rising. "Who would forge such letters? They aren't—weren't—valuable enough to make it worth a forger's time. We're not talking about copies of the Magna Carta or the Gettysburg Address, after all! And as far as making photostatic copies go, if any Dane cared enough about Henriette to want to see the letters, I wanted them to have to come here to do it—to *my* Hans Christian Andersen Room," she added fiercely, her eyes glowing.

"Was Jette Wulff as angry at Denmark as you are?" I asked.

She gave me an astonished look. "Angry at Denmark—me? You don't know what you're saying. I love Denmark and I always have!" She put a concerned look on her face. "What's the point of all this, Peggy? Even if the letters were forgeries—which they aren't—it doesn't change the fact that a thief killed Professor Lindemann and stole them. Does it?" she added in a small voice.

Instead of answering that one, I said, "Lindemann had originally planned to return to Denmark on Sunday. But on Saturday morning of the day he was killed, he extended his stay another week."

"Really? Why?"

"I don't know. We're asking everybody connected with Lindemann or the letters if they know anything that could help us."

Mrs. Donnelly leaned forward on the fainting couch, her eyes angry and her voice no longer weak and tired. "Professor Lindemann didn't give a damn about those letters! He didn't give a damn about anything real—you heard what Pia, his own daughter, said about him last night! Do you think he suspected the letters were forgeries, and he needed to stay here another week to prove it?" She laughed scornfully. "The police must be desperate, to come up with a theory as silly as that. Or is this just a bee you've got in your bonnet, Peggy?"

"It's my bee," I said with an apologetic smile. "And

yes, the police are feeling a lot of pressure to solve Lindemann's murder."

"Lindemann was killed by a thief who thought the letters were genuine," she said flatly. "And they were."

"Carl Vedel thinks you and your dad stole the letters from him," I said, "and Mary Vedel thinks you stole Clay from her. It's possible the two of them decided to get something of their own back."

"No! Mary wouldn't do any such thing on her own, and her father would never permit it, even if she wanted to! *He's* not crazy, just eccentric. They had nothing to do with the theft of the letters." Her vehemence surprised me, considering how close to hitting Mary Vedel she'd come the night before.

"One of them could have forged the letters, for some purpose of their own," I said, "and you ended up with them by mistake. They wanted them back."

"Impossible!" she said, shaking her head, making her hair fly. "There was no reason for anybody to forge the letters."

"Was Mary Vedel right? Did you steal Clay from her?"

In spite of herself, Denise Donnelly smiled. "No. Mary had a crush on him in Denmark, but he never encouraged her. She's always been a little odd, even when we were children. She didn't make any friends in Denmark and didn't even get along with her host family. And she always acted as though the rest of us were doing things we shouldn't—because she was left out so much." She made a face. "I suppose we were cruel to her, but she asked for it. She didn't even stay the entire year in Denmark, she came home before the winter ended." Mrs. Donnelly shook her head, as though she couldn't understand behavior that strange. "I understand she's a terrible Danish teacher too. I'm not surprised. How could somebody like that make anybody want to learn Danish?"

"I remember you said at the banquet that Lindemann came into your class and spoke about Andersen when you were an exchange student."

"It was Mary who remembered that," she corrected me. "I'd forgotten all about it. Mary said we found him boring, but I don't remember that, either, although the speech he gave at the banquet Friday night was certainly boring enough. So she was probably right."

"Speaking of boring Andersen scholars, how well do you know Eric Claussen?"

"I don't know him at all. Pia's told me some dreadful stories about him, though. Apparently he's just putting in his time until he can retire, and he doesn't change his lectures from year to year. If they paid me to teach a course on Hans Christian Andersen, I'd consider it a privilege, and do the very best I could."

She relaxed back onto the arm of the fainting couch and stared into the distance. "I wonder why his wife stays with him," she went on. "She's a very successful artist—although I've seen her work and I can't really say I care for that kind of art. Julie Land, her name is. She bears a striking resemblance to Greta Garbo—I don't suppose you'd notice something like that, would you? But I thought so the first time I met her, in Denmark years ago, and at the banquet Friday night she'd hardly changed at all. I suspect she cultivates the resemblance deliberately."

"You'd suppose Professor Claussen would have contacted me when I discovered the Andersen letters," she went on. "After all, it was a feather in our University's cap to have them. But not a word. Pia says he has no interest in that kind of 'sentimental trivia.' "

"And now," I said, "you're collecting things about Hans Christian Andersen's mother. Are you going to put a room in the children's library in her honor too?"

"Not a room, no," she answered, shaking her head. "She didn't leave enough behind for that—just a few letters to her son after he moved to Copenhagen, and she didn't even write those herself. You heard what Mary Vedel said about her—she called her a whore. That was mean."

Something seemed to occur to her and a wicked glint appeared in her eyes. "I think I'm going to have to do something about that," she said thoughtfully. "Perhaps, if the letters from Andersen to Henriette Wulff aren't recovered, I'll put a display about his mother and her family in that case. His mother, you know, was one of three illegitimate children herself. Her mother served time in prison for immorality. And, as Mary reminded me last night, Andersen had an illegitimate half-sister who was probably a prostitute, and one of his mother's sisters was a madam in a brothel in Copenhagen."

Denise Donnelly laughed out loud. Color had appeared in her cheeks and she was looking better than I'd seen her since before Lindemann's murder. "Maybe I'll call it 'The Duck Yard,' " she said. "You know—the yard Andersen grew up in, before he became a swan. And we'll see how Mary Vedel and all the other good people in the world like *that* display!"

This was a side of Denise Donnelly I hadn't seen before. I laughed with her and said I was looking forward to seeing it.

As she walked me to the door, I asked her how well she knew Pia's mother.

"Not very well. We don't have a lot in common. Because of her experience of being married to Professor Lindemann, which must have been terrible, she seems to hate everything Danish." She shook her head sadly and glanced up at me. "I think Denmark's a lovely country— beautiful, clean, the people so warm and friendly. The year I spent there as an exchange student was the happiest year of my life, and it seems—in memory, at least —that the sun was always shining."

She looked at me sternly, as though I were a cloud threatening to pass across that Danish sun. "You were quite wrong, Peggy, to imagine for a moment that I could hate Denmark."

I liked her better when she was planning her memorial

to the Andersen family women and wondered if she would be able to carry it off.

It was starting to rain when I got outside, a fine, cold mist. On the car radio, the weather report said it might turn to snow by tomorrow night.

Twenty-eight

I got back to the University at a little after two and found another illegal parking spot. This time the Andersen Room door was ajar and Pia was in there alone, staring at her computer monitor.

"Wait a second," she said. I pulled a chair up to her desk and watched as she typed something, studied it a moment on the monitor, then highlighted and erased it. She sighed and turned to me.

I asked her how much more work she had to do on her thesis. She said the translation was done, now she was polishing the preface before showing it to Edith Silberman. Edith was hell on sloppy writing. She thought she'd be finished in about a week, max. She'd have to be, if she wanted to graduate *summa* at the end of winter quarter.

I looked idly through one of the three volumes of letters Andersen and Jette had written to each other so long ago, the books that had gotten Denise Donnelly interested in Jette Wulff and led her to the discovery of the seven letters—or to their creation.

I asked Pia why Jette had only seven letters from Andersen with her when her ship sank.

" 'Cause she left most of her stuff in Copenhagen," she answered. "She took only what was absolutely necessary for the trip, and planned to send for everything else when she got settled here. It's a good thing, too! If she'd taken everything, all of Andersen's letters to her would've been lost—two hundred and sixteen of them."

"Or else Mrs. Donnelly would have found a much larger packet in Carl Vedel's basement," I said dryly.

Pia darted me a glance. "Yeah, right. The seven letters she had with her were ones Andersen wrote to her after she left Copenhagen for the last time, and she was travelling around Europe before her ship sailed, saying goodbye to friends."

"Where are the originals of all these?" I asked, nodding at the three volumes.

Pia frowned. "Somebody in her family eventually sold them and they ended up in libraries and private collections all over the place. There's even a few in the Library of Congress in Washington. A hundred and forty and a half are in the Andersen museum in Odense, Andersen's birthplace—"

"A hundred and forty and a *half?*"

"Yeah!" She laughed disgustedly. "Can you believe it? A money-hungry bookseller cut one long letter in half, then sold one piece to the Andersen Museum in Odense and the other to a collector—who eventually gave his collection, thirty-two and a half letters, to the Royal Library."

"So Jette wandered around Europe for a while before sailing to the United States."

"Right. And you know what, Peggy? Just before her ship sailed from England, she wrote to her sister, telling her that there wasn't anybody on the ship who looked interesting at all, so she was tempted not to go. But she added that she felt ashamed of being so weak, so she was going to go anyway."

"She should have listened to that inner voice," I said, shaking my head and tsk-ing. "As my mother would say, it just shows to go."

Pia gave me her much-practiced glare of disapproval.

I wondered if Jens Aage Lindemann would have died last week if Jette Wulff had decided to stay in Denmark in 1857.

"And while she was wandering around Europe," I said,

"she received seven letters from Andersen. And then the ship burned up and so did she. And everybody thought her belongings burned up too."

Pia nodded, watching me and chewing hair.

"I assume there were survivors."

"Sixty-nine—only six of them women, by the way—out of five hundred and forty-two people on board. So much for 'women and children first'! Here, let me show you something."

She picked up one of the thick volumes, opened it, and paged through it until she found what she was looking for, then turned it so I could see.

It was a full-page picture, an etching of the kind you see in very old books, of a ship in flames. A mob of people were pressed against the railing, driven there by the fire and smoke. Some of them were falling or jumping overboard, others were trying to escape the fire by climbing a mast. People clung to a broken spar that had fallen into the sea, while others were in the water, clinging to debris or trying to climb into already overloaded lifeboats. On the side of the burning ship was the name *Austria.*

"It's an illustration from a German newspaper at the time," Pia said, "an artist's rendering based on eyewitness accounts."

"That's the ship she was on, right?" When she nodded, I said, "It looks like a scene of complete panic and chaos."

"Yeah, it was. The fire started below deck and it was out of control in minutes. Here's what the book says."

She flipped quickly to the page she wanted. " 'Scenes of the most indescribable horror were played out. Many passengers jumped into the sea and drowned. Only one of the ship's eight lifeboats made it into the water—and then capsized. The crew was unable to stop the engines, so the blazing ship kept moving full steam ahead.' God—doesn't that sound spooky!" Pia whispered, looking up in horror from the book.

"Were there any survivors who saw what happened to Jette?"

She shook her head. "Huh-unh, but Andersen asked a mutual friend of his and Jette's to write to one of the survivors, a man named Alfred Vezin from Philadelphia. He was on the *Austria* with his mother and two sisters—they all died—but he was rescued after being in the water for four hours. He wrote back that Jette usually returned to her room after breakfast and took a nap. So Andersen hoped she'd been asleep when the fire broke out and was overcome by the smoke and didn't suffer very much. It horrified him to imagine her struggling to save herself all alone in that panic-stricken mob. She was so tiny."

I stared down at the illustration of the burning ship, tried to imagine how it must have been. "She had no friends on board," I said. "She was probably alone in her room when the ship burned up—and yet the letters and a photograph survived."

"Maybe she met somebody she liked," Pia said. "After all, they'd been at sea nine days. She must have made some friends—obviously this guy Alfred Vezin knew her. When the fire broke out, he was in the back end—aft end?—of the ship, smoking a cigar and reading."

"Reading Andersen's letters, which Jette just happened to loan him before she toddled off to her cabin to take her nap?" I said. "Or maybe she and Alfred were having a shipboard romance and they were in her cabin together and, when he smelled smoke, he— "

"Peggy!" said Pia, thinning her lips disapprovingly.

"Sorry."

"They could've been in a suitcase that floated away from the ship and was picked up later," she went on. "What're you after, Peggy? You can't solve my father's murder, so you're working on a mystery that happened a hundred and thirty-five years ago?"

"Maybe that's it," I agreed. "You and Mrs. Donnelly think it was a miracle that those letters turned up after all those years. I think the biggest miracle was that they survived that day in the Atlantic."

She didn't say anything, just continued to look at me.

"When I first met your father," I said, "he dismissed the letters as unimportant—said they didn't add anything to what we already know about Andersen. Is that true?"

She pulled a strand of hair across her face under her nose. "They add a little bit—for people who want to see it—but not a whole lot, really. You see, Peggy, for months before she left for America, Jette kept begging Andersen to visit her. They were both travelling around in Europe at the time, not too far apart. But he refused. Some Andersen scholars get pretty snotty about that. They think it shows how selfish he was, but I think he was right. I mean, he knew what was good for him and what wasn't and he wouldn't budge once he'd made up his mind that something wasn't good for him. Most people aren't like that, you know, and they don't like people who are.

"People are always saying Andersen was egotistical and self-centered—and he was! If he hadn't been, he never would've left the slum he grew up in. He would've taken the crummy jobs the other kids his age were taking—God knows, his mother wanted him to and they could've used the extra income!—instead of staying home and playing with his doll theater and sewing doll clothes. He—"

"Pia!" I said. I can thin my lips disapprovingly too.

"Sorry."

"I take it the seven letters Mrs. Donnelly found do put Andersen in a better light," I said dryly.

"Well, I think they do," Pia replied. "For example, at one time, just before she was about to sail to America, Jette and Andersen were only about a six-hour train ride apart, somewhere in Germany. She wanted him to come and see her really badly and told him so in a very emotional letter, but he refused. The Danish scholars—who don't give a damn about Jette, really—dump all over Andersen for that—they're always finding excuses to try to reduce him to their size.

"Besides," she rushed on before I could get a word in, "why couldn't Jette have visited *him?* I'll tell you why—because she hated trains! She was just as self-centered as Andersen—which is why they understood each other so well. Some scholars claim Jette was the model for the 'Princess on the Pea,' did you know that?"

She flipped through the pages of one of the books containing Andersen's correspondence with Jette. "Here's what somebody wrote about Andersen's refusal to visit Jette: 'It was a great disappointment to Henriette Wulff, a disappointment she should have been spared.' Really!"

Pia snorted, her eyes blazing. "Who's got any right to say that, I'd just like to know? In one of the letters Denise found, Andersen makes it clear he was ill at the time—he had boils under his arms, and he was travelling with a guy who was a real pain in the ass, one of his patron's sons. He told Jette it would be a nightmare if he had to travel those six hours by train, and he wouldn't have enjoyed himself anyway."

"Of course," Pia went on, apparently driven by the need for complete honesty, "all the time he was suffering so horribly from boils under the arms, he was attending theater performances—but that doesn't really change anything! It's one thing to attend a play when you're feeling horrible—especially since he got in free—and it's another to ride on the kind of trains they had in those days for six hours with a travelling companion who's a pain in the ass."

"But," I said, also feeling the need to be honest, "if it was to bring a little sunshine into the life of his dearest friend, a tiny, crippled woman about to depart for America?"

"You're just as horrible as the scholars, Peggy O'Neill," Pia bellowed. "He didn't know it was going to be forever! He promised Jette in one of those letters that they'd meet again someday, and he also tried to kid her out of her disappointment by telling her he was certain she wouldn't just bury herself in America and never go travelling again—and he told her that he would probably visit America someday soon himself.

"And you know, Peggy," she said, calming down, "he was right on both counts. Jette was a lifelong traveller— she never really felt at home anywhere, just like him. She wouldn't have holed up here in America for the rest of her life. She would've gone back to Denmark to visit, maybe even to stay, or else they would've met someplace else— in Spain or Portugal or Italy or somewhere.

"Another thing," she plowed on, "if Jette hadn't burned to death on that ship, Andersen would have come here, sooner or later. You wouldn't believe how popular he was here by then, and he wanted to come. But her death haunted him for the rest of his life and was the main reason he never did come here."

"And did Jette accept his excuses for not coming to visit her and let her place warm poultices or leeches on his boils?" I asked.

"Yes and no—and don't pretend you're not interested, Peggy. You just keep encouraging me. Her letters are full of reassurances that she's not mad at him—but you can read between the lines that she is, and quite disappointed too. But she signs her last letter to him 'As always, your sisterly Jette.'"

"Prim and proper, right to the end," I said. Denise Donnelly's smiling face, as she was telling me about Andersen's mother, grandmother, aunt, and sister, popped suddenly into my mind.

"What was the moral of 'The Ugly Duckling'?" I asked Pia.

"Why?"

"Just wondered."

" 'It doesn't matter if you were born in a duck yard, if you were hatched from a swan's egg.' "

"I wonder if Andersen ever longed for the duck yard," I said.

"You're weird, Peggy. You know that?"

"Yeah." We sat there for a while, thinking our own thoughts. "Well," I said finally, "I probably wouldn't want to sit on a train for six hours if I had boils under my arms, either. Before Mrs. Donnelly found those letters, was most of what's in them known? I mean, the stuff about the boils and the wretched travelling companion, for example?"

"Oh, sure. Andersen put everything he did in his diary, even including who he wrote letters to. Also, we have Jette's replies to the seven letters—they're in here," she added, patting one of the blue volumes. "The originals are in the Royal Library in Copenhagen."

Leaving a paper trail like that would make it easy for somebody to forge the letters, I thought—especially if you planned to donate the results to a library that didn't care one way or the other, and gave only typescripts to other libraries.

"Why are you interested in Jette Wulff all of a sudden?" Pia asked, giving me a suspicious glare.

"I guess she's catching," I said.

She smiled, shook her head. "You can't fool me, Peggy. I know what you're thinking."

"What?" I tried to look innocent.

"You're thinking that Mrs. Donnelly forged those letters."

I nodded. "I think she would've had them authenticated, if they were genuine. She told me she couldn't be bothered."

"But that would be just like her!" Pia said. "Denise has never had to worry about money, so it wouldn't even occur to her that she could take them off her income tax when she donated them to the University. And it wouldn't occur to her that the letters would be anything but real anyway—I mean, who'd forge them?"

"But you'd think her husband would want the tax deduction."

"Denise doesn't ask Clay's permission to do what she wants, and he doesn't care what she does with her money—or if he does, he keeps quiet about it. If anything, it's the other way around: She's got money, he's got a salary."

"You've thought of this, too, haven't you?"

"Of course I have, Peggy. I'm not quite as naive as you think I am, you know! I *want* those letters to be genuine. To have been genuine, I mean. But that doesn't make it true, what I want."

"You realize what that might mean, though."

She laughed. "That Da—my father somehow figured out the letters were forgeries and threatened to expose Denise, so she killed him and stole the letters back? Give me a break! There's nothing in the letters that would indicate to anybody they were forgeries, and my father didn't pay any attention to them—you were there, you saw how bored he was when I showed them to him. And unless he was the one who broke into the case himself, before getting killed, he never handled them."

"It's just a loose end," I said, "and loose ends bother me. A distinguished Hans Christian Andersen scholar is killed in a room that just happens to contain letters that might be forgeries. That's quite a coincidence."

"You've got it backwards, Peggy! The letters were stolen by somebody who thought they were real—which they probably are—and my father died because he surprised the thief."

"Yeah, I guess so." We were back to the original theory again. The only progress anybody seemed to have made since Lindemann's murder was Pia, who was no longer calling him "Daddy." I could only approve.

"That was a beautiful story you told last night at the

memorial service," I said, as I got up to leave, "about the golden drinking horns. Was it true?"

"Oh, sure, it's true all right."

"The horns just disappeared, without a trace? The gods took them back?"

She glanced up at me and smiled. "Not exactly, Peggy. They were stolen—by common, ordinary thieves, who melted them down for the gold."

Twenty-nine

"Everything in that room's phony," I said.

I was in my easy chair, staring morosely out the picture window in my living room. In the daytime, you can see a piece of Lake Eleanor from that window, but it was night and all I could see was Gary's and my reflection in the dark, rain-streaked glass.

"Everything?" Gary was horizontal on the couch, using his laptop to work on the last installment of his series on the problems southeast Asian immigrants were having adapting to American culture in the Midwest. I wondered if, in a hundred years, an organization of sentimental Asian-Americans would belong to "The Sons of Vietnam," replacing organizations like the Sons of Denmark. If so, I wondered what they'd make of the Andersen Room, or put in its place.

"Everything. The heavy-lidded portrait of Hans Christian Andersen pretending to be a Romantic poet," I said aloud, "the portrait of Henriette Wulff with her large luminous eyes, the papercuts, *The Little Mermaid,* who's now locked up in the crime lab—everything, and most especially, the letters to Jette Wulff—false, all of it! False!"

The word had a hollow ring to it that sounded good on such a cold, wet night, so I said it again: "False!"

"Stop being melodramatic," Gary said. "You're just being dreary and with winter coming on, we don't need that."

"We don't need that—!" I repeated in disbelief under my breath. *"We—"*

220

"You don't know for sure the letters are phony," Gary went on. "Besides, Pia spends a lot of time in that room, and she's not phony. And neither are Christian and Sam."

I didn't say anything for a minute or two, just sat and stared at my reflection in the window, found a kind of pleasure in the grimness of my rain-streaked features.

"Pia's not what she seems to be, either," I said finally, surprising myself as well as Gary.

"Pia? For Christ's sake, Peggy—nobody's more what she seems to be than Pia! You're really in a wretched mood tonight, aren't you? Would a back rub help?"

"She's cheating on Christian."

Gary's voice took on an edge. "Pia loves Christian— that's as clear as the nose on my face." Gary's got a prominent nose.

He was right, of course, Pia did love Christian. Which meant that what I suspected didn't make sense.

Gary couldn't resist asking who I thought the other man was. "Not Sam, surely."

"No, Andy Blake. You haven't met him. He plays the emperor in 'The Emperor's New Clothes.' The night of her father's murder, just after the play ended, he kissed her."

"What kind of kiss?"

"I didn't see it. I just saw his makeup smeared on her face."

"Oh, well. It was probably just a congratulatory kiss, the kind theater people are always smearing on one another."

"And I've seen the way they look at each other on other occasions too. And the way they walk side by side, the way their eyes meet. Lovers can't walk side by side without giving themselves away, even if they don't touch. I can spot them a mile off."

"You've just got a lurid imagination," Gary said. "But even if it's true, it doesn't make Pia a phony. Didn't a lover of yours once find his way into your unresisting arms before he'd notified the woman he was going with at the time that they were finished?"

"That was different—that was a spontaneous thing! And besides, Al and Dierdre were on the verge of breaking up."

"Oh yeah? Well, they're happily married now, I believe?"

"What's your point?" I snarled, vowing never again to blab about my past to a lover, assuming I'd ever have another one.

"That Al was unfaithful to Dierdre with you, which didn't make him a phony. So if Pia's being unfaithful to Christian, that doesn't make her a phony."

"Pia's not like people like Al and me."

"Sure she is. You just want her to be different— meaning 'not human.' But even though she looks like you could blow her over with a sneeze, she's just as much a creature of flesh and blood as you are. Is it Christian you're worried about? He's a nice guy, but if she dumps him he'll land on his feet. I just hope she waits until the season's over—not that I believe for a minute that you're right about her," he added quickly. "It might distract him—what's the matter?"

Wait until the season's over. The first words I'd heard from Pia to Christian, again.

"Nothing," I said, but I was lying. I jumped up, went over to the closet and threw on my raincoat, headed out the door.

"Where are you going?"

"Out."

"Where?"

"To pay a visit to Pia and Christian."

"Business or pleasure?"

"I don't know."

I parked in front of their place and ran to the entrance through the rain, punched the buzzer, and waited for somebody to ask who it was. Nobody did. After a few minutes, I went around behind the apartment building and looked up at their windows—only a hall light was on. Either Christian and Pia were in bed, or else they weren't home. The latter seemed more likely, since it was only eight-thirty.

I went back to my car and drove to a convenience store and looked up Sam's address in the phone book. I could talk to him as well as to Pia and Christian.

He lived a few blocks north of the Old Campus, in an area of large old apartment buildings with names like "Alameda," "The Seville," and "Catalina" carved above their entrances, suggesting exotic places that the neighborhood, city, and state belied. I'd found a corpse in one of those buildings once.

Something about Sam's address was pricking at the edges of my mind, trying to tell me something, and it had nothing to do with my previous experience with the neighborhood.

I looked for a parking space, slowed when I saw one that I thought I might be able to fit my Rabbit into. It was too small. As I started to accelerate, a match flared in a car parked across the street, the flame etching Floyd Hazard's face onto the darkness even through the rain-streaked windshield.

I averted my face as I drove past, hoping the darkness would conceal me. I parked around the corner and sat in my car for a few minutes to collect my thoughts. I didn't have to wonder why Hazard was there. He must have come to the same conclusion I had—and for reasons not much more deplorable than mine too, I supposed—and he was hoping to be able to prove it that night.

I got out of my car, pulled the hood of my raincoat up over my head, and walked back to Sam's apartment building, head down, shuffling a little like an old woman as I passed Hazard's car on the other side of the street. Once in the vestibule, I pressed the button next to Sam's name and waited until his voice asked who it was. I told him.

"Peggy!" his metallic voice exclaimed. "A surprise! Cover your ears!" A blast of sound told me to push the door open. I did, then climbed to the third floor and walked down the hall to where Sam was standing waiting for me.

"Come on in," he said. "What brings you over here on a night like this? You'll forgive me if I tell you that you're not looking in the party mode, won't you?"

I stepped into his apartment, wasn't surprised at what I saw, given Hazard's presence outside. On a sofa on one side of a small fireplace, Pia and Andy Blake were sitting together, holding plates with sandwiches on them, their knees touching. Christian Donnelly was sprawled barefoot on a matching sofa on the other side, watching me with his sleepy eyes.

Pia looked concerned, her face even paler than usual. Andy looked wary and uncomfortable. He was still wearing his cap—on backwards as always. Classical guitar music drizzled softly from little speakers mounted on the ceiling above the front windows and a little fire crackled in the fireplace. It was a cozy scene.

"You look like you're here on a mission," Christian said. He took a sip of beer and watched me over the top of the can. "Does anybody besides me think Peggy O'Neill has come up with an idea—and dread to think what it might be?"

"Why are you here, Peggy?" Pia demanded, her dark eyes boring coldly into mine.

"How long have you and Sam been lovers, Christian?" I asked him.

Pia's hand flew to her mouth. Christian didn't look particularly surprised. "A Kodak moment," he murmured dryly.

"You're out of your mind, Peggy," Andy said, his voice vibrant with the emperor's sincerity. It occurred to me the emperor might have said that to the child. Would the child have swallowed it?

Sam dragged a dining room chair over in front of the fireplace and said, "You sit here, Peggy. It's not very comfortable, but you can keep an eagle eye on all of us from it, and leap up faster than we can if you have to." He went over to Christian, lifted Christian's feet up off the couch, slid under them, and put them down in his lap and made himself comfortable.

"Start by telling us what gave us away," he said. "Don't be shy, Peggy, and speak up."

I decided not to tell them about my belief that I can spot lovers just by watching them as they walk side by side, as I'd watched Christian and Sam do that afternoon when they were on their way to their tennis match. "A smear of Andy's greasepaint on Pia's face, for one thing," I said, "the night her father was killed."

Pia glared accusingly at Andy. Andy blushed.

"I just don't happen to think Pia would cheat on you, Christian. She'd break it off with you before starting anything with anybody else."

"You could be wrong about that, you know, Peggy," Pia said.

"I'm not, though. You're too decent. That's why I denied the evidence of my eyes when I saw the greasepaint. But also, the way you sometimes look at Andy, Pia. You don't look at Christian that way. You look at him more like a younger brother."

Andy turned and stuck his tongue out at her.

"Is that all?" Christian asked.

"Your bedroom," I told him. "If Pia slept there, it wouldn't look like a junior high boy's room waiting for mom to come in and clean it up."

"I've warned you about your slovenliness, Christian," Sam said accusingly. "Anything else?"

"No."

He shook his head, smiling sadly. "No, Peggy, it was more than that, I'm afraid. You're too cynical to really believe that a common, garden-variety, heterosexual football player—especially one as handsome and successful as Christian Donnelly—could love a woman like Pia."

"Or vice versa," I said.

"But we *do* love each other!" Pia exclaimed. Her dark eyes darted to Christian.

He gave her his grin, the grin that I was sure would sell products on national television someday. "And you couldn't believe a guy like me could have a friend like Sam, either," he said to me.

"Or vice versa," I repeated.

"That's too bad."

"It's too bad the world's like that," I said, "not that I'm the way I am."

"Hey, you sound like one of us!" Christian said with a laugh.

"Someday that cynicism of yours is going to get you in a lot of trouble, Peggy!" Pia said.

I stared at her, not knowing whether to laugh or cry. Instead of doing either, I said, "How did your father find out about Christian? He was here less than a week."

"I knew that was coming," Christian said.

"My father never knew, Peggy!"

"Pia, give me a break! He had to have known. He found out somehow, and threatened to expose Christian—and got killed for his pains."

Christian sat up suddenly, planting his feet firmly on the rug. "Then one of us must have done it," he said. "Isn't that right, Peggy? And now you've walked into the lion's den. Do you think you're going to get out of here alive—or are the cops waiting outside the door for us to try to murder you?"

"Take it easy, Christian," Sam said. "You're wrong, Peggy. There's no way Pia's father could have known. Christian and I have always been careful. Sure, we're taking a risk just being seen together—but it's almost always with Pia, so it's a very slight risk, and mostly confined to Christian's teammates, who don't want to believe what they see any more than you did. It's in their best interest, in a lot of ways, not to."

"And the fact that Christian and I are living together keeps them from thinking about Sam too," Pia added.

"They're too dumb to imagine a man could live with a woman without fucking her." She tried to make the word sound ugly, but couldn't manage it. "Besides," she added, "my father never met Christian or Sam."

"I'm supposed to take your word for that?" I asked, struggling to keep a jeering tone out of my voice.

"Oh, Peggy, I'm sorry we tried to fool you," she said, looking miserable.

"Another thing," Sam said. "Suppose Pia's father had learned the truth somehow. What could he have done with it? Who would he have told? If he'd gone to the media with it they wouldn't have published it without proof. And where's the proof?"

"Just the rumor of Christian being gay could destroy his career."

"Sure, but who'd listen to an old Danish professor?" Christian put in.

"Besides," Sam said, "it gets whispered around that a lot of athletes are gay, but as long as they don't come out, and as long as they do well on the field, they're okay."

"Maybe Peggy thinks your father had pictures, Pia," Christian said, "and Sam and I had to kill him to get 'em back. Is that what you think, Peggy?"

"No, I don't think that," I replied. "I don't know what to think."

Not very long ago, Sam had spent hours coaching me in how to say "I see." I wondered if they were all doing that to me now.

"It was very shrewd of you," Sam said, "finding us out. But Pia's father never did—he wasn't here long enough, for one thing, and he never met me or Christian for another. But even if he had known about us, he couldn't have done anything to hurt Christian."

"And he wouldn't have wanted to anyway," Pia stuck in.

I turned to Christian. "Your father knows, doesn't he? That's why he treats you so standoffish."

He nodded, surprised that I'd guessed that too. "Is that

the word for it—standoffish? Oh, yeah, Dad knows. He's the weakest actor in the comedy. He can't hide how much he hates Sam, he can barely hide how much the thought of Sam and me sickens him. But he can't keep away from me, either. His Sports Booster buddies wouldn't understand if he up and disowned me."

"He wouldn't do that, Christian," Pia protested. "He loves you."

Christian made a face. "Right!"

"How'd he find out?"

"I don't mind telling you the story, Peggy," he replied, "it's just that these guys have heard it already and I don't want to bore them."

"Go on, Christian," Sam said, "tell her."

"Well." He scrunched the beer can in his hand into a small shape and stared at it a moment, his beautiful face suddenly old and bleak.

Pia asked him if he wanted another beer.

"Thanks, no." He moved his eyes to me. "It was after my last high school game. I set a record for total yardage—passing and running—and we beat the shit out of the other team. Big upset. My teammates carried me off the field on their shoulders—very corny, but nice too. I liked it.

"I'd never seen Dad so happy before in my life. When I got home from the team party afterwards, he was still up, waiting for me. He was still high on my victory and, for the first time in my life, he told me he loved me."

Christian stopped, tried to go on, couldn't for a moment. Pia was clutching Andy's hand so hard, her knuckles were white.

"So I reciprocated," Christian continued. "I told him I loved him too." His mouth twisted into an ugly smile. "And then I had to go and ruin it—I told him I was gay. Bad decision, Peggy, very bad. At first he wouldn't believe me, then he believed I'd had sex with men but he thought it was a phase—I just needed a woman. He'd get me one, he said, one who'd knock my socks off and show me what real sex is like. No thanks, Dad. Then he decided I was sick—he'd find me a therapist. No, Dad.

"Then he hauled off and slugged me." Christian rubbed the side of his face. "I can still feel it. All in all, an unforgettable night, I guess you'd say. I'd gone from the best game I've ever quarterbacked, and being carried around on my teammates' shoulders, to lying on the floor at my father's feet with a bloody mouth. I hadn't seen it coming or I'd have ducked, of course," he added, because he had to, and then twitched a smile, because he knew why he'd had to.

"Mom came into the room then, to see what the racket was. He screamed at her that it was her fault." His face softened. "It hit her pretty hard, but she got over it. She accepts me the way I am.

"My father warned me that my chances of making it in college football and the pros would be zero if anybody found out—as if I didn't know that! I told him I didn't give a shit, football had been his idea in the first place, not mine. I was ready to come out, tell the world what I was."

He laughed. "I thought he'd have a heart attack! I couldn't do that, he screamed. Think of the shame! Think of Grampa Gus—it'd kill him, if he found out. He was thinking of himself, of course," Christian added with a smile. "*His* shame, if his friends found out his son was gay."

Long pause. A log shifted in the fireplace. Sparks flew.

"I didn't come out. I decided I didn't want to cut myself off from playing football in college or professionally just because my dad had rejected me. I wasn't *sure* that's what I wanted to do with my life—go on being a football player, I mean—but I knew I wasn't ready to toss it all away just to hurt *him*. What good would that have done?

"I don't think it would've hurt Gus, either, if he found out. In fact, I think Gus knows—and he likes Sam a lot. But I haven't talked to him about it. Why should I? He'd probably be offended. Heteros don't go to their grandparents and sit them down and tell them about it, do they? I think that's how Gus would think.

"Dad lives in fear that I'll come out," he went on with a bitter laugh. "He dies a little every time I run out onto the field, because he thinks that if I get a career-ending injury, I'd come out. He's right, too: I'd move in with Sam the next day."

"It would depend a lot on the injury, of course," Sam said.

Christian turned and shoved him backwards off the couch. There was a loud thump as Sam hit the floor.

"My back's broken!"

"And Dad lives in fear I'll give up football and decide to do something else with my life," Christian went on.

"I wish you would," Sam said, emerging from behind the couch, "before you wind up in permanent traction."

"Christian's dad's life is the Sports Boosters," Pia said to me. "He's been a member from the day he could afford the initiation fee. Isn't that right, Christian?"

"Which means from the day after he and Mom got home from their honeymoon," Christian said. "I've gone to some of the Sports Boosters dinners—I've done it for Dad. It would look odd if I didn't let him show me off to his cronies. You can't imagine the homophobia among those people, Peggy. You wouldn't believe the level of the jokes they tell. It's as though they're drawn to each other—man-to-man, you know—but they have to tell fag jokes to reassure themselves that they aren't queer themselves.

"After one particularly dumb gay-bashing joke, I couldn't help it, I just blurted it out: 'I think you're all protesting too much.' Dad choked on his food, and the other men thought I was making a joke—or pretended to—and roared with laughter."

"They probably know the truth," Sam said, "but they've convinced themselves they don't."

"Like the people in 'The Emperor's New Clothes,' " Andy stuck in.

Pia patted him on his cap, said, "Good, Andy."

"And that was when I made up my mind what I'm going to do," Christian said.

"What's that?" I asked.

"I'm going to win the Super Bowl. I'm going to be carried off the field by my teammates and voted the Most Valuable Player. And when I stand up there in front of all the television cameras—flanked by the owner of the team, the coach, and the football commissioner, my teammates behind me spraying champagne—and some jerk sports announcer asks me what I think the key to the victory was, I'm going to say: 'The love and support of a good man—Sam Allen.' "

"Everyone must have a dream," Sam said. "Mine is to get the film rights."

Thirty

"What are you going to do now, Peggy?" That was Pia.

I didn't answer. I stared into the fire, thinking.

"You're not going to tell that homicide cop friend of yours, are you?"

"I have to," I said.

"No, you don't! Christian's and Sam's being gay doesn't have any connection with my father's murder. Don't you think I'd tell you if I thought it did?"

"No, I don't think you would, Pia. Damn it, you guys!" I exploded. "You've been deceiving me for over a month and a half! How can I trust any of you now?"

"I was going to tell you, Peggy," Pia said, "but I kept putting it off. You wanted so much to believe Christian and I were a couple, and I didn't want to destroy your dream world."

My dream world!

"We talked about it," Christian put in, "but Sam said no. You're living with a journalist, and you can't trust a secret like that to a journalist."

"And when my father got killed," Pia said, before I could say anything in defense of Gary, "I was afraid to tell you, because I knew you'd think it might be related."

"Anyway," Sam said, "what are lies, but truth in masquerade?"

"What's that supposed to mean?" Andy asked.

"You'll have to ask Lord Byron, I'm sure *I* don't know."

"Does your mom know about this, Pia?"

"Sure, and so does my stepdad."

I'd never felt like such an outsider before in my life.

As she'd done before, Pia read my mind. "Welcome to the family, Peggy," she said, and gave me a hopeful smile.

They sat there, watching me and waiting, and I sat there too, confused and weighed down by the truth.

If I told him, what would Buck do with the knowledge? I knew him well enough to know he wouldn't spread it around for its own sake. But Buck went by the book. In fact, in the past I'd sometimes suspected that one reason why he'd let me get involved in murder cases—while pretending even to himself, I think, he was trying to discourage me—was because I didn't go by the book, wasn't even sure what the book was.

If I told him about Christian, he might feel he had to report it to his superiors. And several of them—the chief of police, among others—were Sports Boosters, according to Gary. In any case, with so much pressure on them to solve Lindemann's murder, one of Buck's superiors might use the information in a ham-fisted manner and destroy Christian's football career.

Funny. There was only one team sport I found less appealing than football—professional hockey, mindlessly stupid and without any redeeming grace at all—but I was contemplating withholding a potentially big clue to save a football player's career.

But, after all, only that morning Buck had told me that not all the strange stuff you turn up in a murder investigation is relevant. If I was still going around investigating on my own, I could decide what was relevant and what wasn't, couldn't I? I wasn't officially a detective—Floyd Hazard, sitting outside in his car, tarring his lungs and freezing his butt, was the detective.

Now I was lying to myself, something I generally try not to do. Because although I didn't have the title of detective, I had been officially assigned to investigate Jens Aage Lindemann's murder, and put back on the payroll for that purpose.

I glanced up to see four sets of eyes watching me.

Of course, I hadn't been paid yet—and I didn't have to tell Buck right away, did I? These people weren't going anyplace—they had no place to go. Also, it wouldn't be fair to Buck either, to put him on the spot like that, when Christian's sexual preference might not be relevant at all.

With a heavy sigh, I got up and retrieved my raincoat. As I shrugged into it, I said, "That campus cop who's been hanging around, Floyd Hazard, is sitting in a car across the street."

"What!" That was all of them.

"Don't look," I said. "I guess he's a little like me. He can't get over the fact that Christian's living with a woman who couldn't make it as a *Playboy* bunny, and hangs out with a queer. As far as I know, that's the only reason he's out there. I don't know if he's running some homophobic errand of his own, or if he thinks he's on the trail of Lindemann's killer, but he must have followed Christian and Pia over here—probably not to get Christian's autograph. I don't know what your plans were for tonight, but I don't think it would be a good idea for Pia and Andy to leave here together, and Christian and Sam to stay."

"No," Sam said thoughtfully, "that would surely raise the fellow's eyebrows all the way up into his low-slung hairline. We'll just have to put on a show for him."

He put the director's look on his face that I knew so well. "After Peggy goes, Christian and Pia will leave, arm in arm." He turned to Andy. "You and I will stand in the front window and watch them go. When they get a few steps down the street, they will turn and wave up to us— just to make sure the dogsbody doesn't fail to notice us. We'll wave back, and then turn and, staring tenderly into one another's eyes—"

"No," Andy said.

"If it weren't for a Higher Purpose," Sam said, "I wouldn't do it myself, I can assure you of that! But we have the future of pro football to think about, so we can't afford to be squeamish. Besides, it was one of your kisses that started Peggy thinking nasty thoughts about us all."

"It's a good thing she did," Pia said, "so she could warn us of that clown down there."

Sam led me down the back stairs and out the back door into the alley. "Thanks, Peggy," he said, ignoring the cold drizzle and engulfing me in a huge hug. "Don't look so worried. It's going to be okay. Christian's being gay had nothing to do with Lindemann's death." He smiled and added, "I can promise you that."

"How, Sam?" I asked, pulling away from him. "How can you promise me that?"

His eyes tried to meet mine and then darted away suddenly. "You know what I mean," he said.

But I didn't, I only knew what he said.

I walked down the rain-slicked cobblestones of the alley and out onto the street. At the intersection, I saw that Hazard's car was still there and, inside, the intermittent glow of a cigarette told me Hazard was still in it, and awake. I glanced up at the brightly lit front window of Sam's apartment, then walked to my car and drove home.

What if, in spite of Christian's denials, Lindemann had somehow discovered he was gay? Would he have cared? No. More likely, he would only have laughed at the thought of his daughter fronting for a gay athlete. If he'd wanted to expose the absurdity of a campus sports hero being gay, he would have waited until he got back to Denmark, then written an article in a newspaper or magazine. He wouldn't have needed to stay here an extra week.

But he had shown an interest in Christian. He'd talked to the Claussens about American football, tuned into a sports program—the same program I'd watched with Gary—and come to the banquet Friday night full of knowledge about Christian. Well, you'd expect that kind of interest in your daughter's boyfriend from a conventional father.

It was just that Jens Aage Lindemann hadn't been a conventional father.

* * *

When I got back home, Gary asked me what I'd found out.

"Nothing important," I said, hoping that was true. Gary's journalistic integrity might be greater than mine as a cop, as Christian had suggested.

"You were checking out who Pia was sleeping with?"

"I guess so," I said, "in a way."

"And she's in the right bed and with the right partner?"

I had to laugh in spite of myself. "Not tonight," I answered, "but eventually I suppose she will be."

Gary pondered that answer for a minute, then shrugged. "Buck called, wants you to call him back. He's still at his office."

It was almost ten. I didn't want to talk to Buck, but if I didn't, he'd wonder why I hadn't returned his call, and I didn't want him doing too much wondering about me now.

"Gary said you rushed out of the house as though pursued by demons," he said. "What were you after?"

"It was a wild goose chase."

"What did the goose look like?"

"Your average, run-of-the-mill gray goose. Feathers, beak."

Like Gary before him, Buck was silent a minute as he weighed my answer. My heart felt like lead in my chest. This was the first time I'd ever lied to him.

But it wasn't really a lie, I told myself. As far as I knew, Christian's and Sam's relationship had nothing to do with Lindemann's murder. As far as I knew . . .

"This wild goose chase," he pressed on. "Did it have anything to do with the Andersen letters?"

"The—?" I didn't know what he was talking about for a second. "Oh, no," I replied, glad to get onto another, safer subject.

"That's why I called," he said. "To see what you learned about them."

"I'm pretty much convinced they're fake," I said, "and that Mrs. Donnelly faked them. But it's possible Carl

Vedel—or his daughter, Mary—faked them too and Mrs. Donnelly got them by mistake."

I told him about my talk with Mrs. Donnelly and also summarized Pia's description of the death of Henriette Wulff.

"It does sound pretty suspicious," Buck said. "Oh, by the way, Mrs. Donnelly's husband's got an alibi for Saturday night. He was at a sports bar with his Sports Booster colleagues, watching the game on one of those giant screens, and then stayed on to eat dinner and talk football and get bombed. It's airtight."

Buck said he would talk to some of the Andersen experts at the symposium about the Jette Wulff letters, but it sounded hopeless. Without them, he couldn't prove they were fakes. With them, he couldn't prove they had anything to do with Lindemann's murder.

Thirty-one

Until my curiosity about the missing letters distracted me, I'd planned to talk to Eric Claussen's wife, Julie Land. I assumed that, since her husband was a colleague of his, she must have seen Lindemann off and on over the years. Claussen hadn't been any help to me, but wives often observe more than their husbands, especially wives with artists' eyes. Also, Lindemann had talked to Claussen about the book on Andersen he was going to write for the University Press. Claussen assured me he hadn't felt threatened by it, but I wondered if his wife might have a different opinion—and if I could get it out of her if she did.

Before I left the house the next morning, I dialed the Claussens' phone number, hoping Claussen had already left for the University. When Julie Land answered the phone, I told her who I was and reminded her of when we'd met before. I asked her if I could come over and discuss Lindemann's murder with her.

"What's to discuss?" she asked. "The man got between a thief and his prize, and killed for his pains, didn't he?"

"That's the most likely explanation," I agreed. "But we're looking at other possibilities as well."

"Such as?"

"Could we discuss it in person?"

She said she had nothing to add to what she'd already told a very earnest and pleasant detective a few days after the murder. "I told him that, on Thursday night at our house, Lindemann didn't act as though he had a care in the world, much less some dark secret that would lead to his death."

I gave the standard reply, that the police like to go over the same territory more than once, hoping to pick up details that might have been missed the first time.

"Especially when you're stumped, right?"

"Right."

"Well, I'm going to be out until around three. If you want to come over then, I suppose I can give you some time."

Since I didn't have to be at the theater for the Friday night performance of "The Emperor's New Clothes" until about seven-thirty, I told her that would be fine.

Although it was the last day of the symposium, I was in no hurry to return to it, so I caught up on my share of the housework and did some errands, then drove to the University to check in with Pia in the Andersen Room to see how the charade with Floyd Hazard had gone the night before.

"Poor man!" she said, laughing. "Christian and I stayed at Sam's until around midnight and then left arm in arm, stopping to embrace passionately just as we came up to Hazard's car. When Sam and Andy saw us, they did the same thing, up in front of Sam's window. Sam told Andy to pretend they were Mafia dons greeting each other at a mob funeral. Before Christian and I even got my car started, Hazard roared by in a cloud of exhaust fumes— everything about that man pollutes the environment, doesn't it? You should've seen his face, Peggy! He looked like he'd eaten a piece of bad fish." She turned suddenly serious. "You're still not going to tell your homicide cop friend about Christian?"

"Not unless I think it has something to do with your father's death."

"It doesn't. Honest."

" 'Honest,' right. I suppose the story you told me of how you and Christian got together was all made up too."

"Not all of it. I really did wait until after he'd passed

the Andersen course before I moved in with him—and he really did earn the A I gave him."

" 'The truth in masquerade,' " I said. I felt like crying, couldn't help laughing.

"Ah, Peggy, I'm sorry. I wanted to tell you, but . . ."

"I know, I know. Sam. How long are you and Christian going to keep up the pretense of being lovers?"

"I don't know." She made a face, squinted hard at a strand of hair, and then let it drop. "Christian has another year until he graduates, but Andy is hassling me to get a place with him now. Once Christian gets a pro contract, he won't have to be always hanging around the other football players in his free time. And even if people do wonder about him—why he's not married or divorced or shacked up with a bimbo—they'll kid themselves that he's not what he appears to be. So he won't need a beard."

"A what?"

"A beard. That's what women like me are called. It's disgusting."

"Especially since you're more like a fuzz."

"Thanks a lot! I really do love living with Christian, though." She laughed, remembering something. "When we were furnishing our apartment, I wanted to get bunk beds so we could fight over who gets the top one, the way kids do when they're little, but that wouldn't have been a smart idea."

"Not for a beard, anyway. What's Sam going to do when Christian gets a pro contract and moves away?"

"Oh, you know Sam! He's sure he can get a job with a theater anywhere—or start his own, if Christian goes with some team that's in a town without theaters. Sam's starved for his art before, he says, but with Christian's big bucks, he'll probably be able to start his own theater."

"Right." I had to laugh at her confidence in Christian's bright future. "And you and Andy?"

"Andy's a nice guy," she said, crossing her eyes and gnawing on a nail, "and a wonderful actor. And he worships me, which is a plus. But I'm way too young to think of marriage. We'll see. I'm thinking of writing a novel, about me and Jette—you know, a kind of dialogue between two women of different times and places. Until I write it and it becomes a bestseller, though, I'll live in an unheated garret and be terribly cold in the winter and unbearably hot in the summer."

"But soon you'll have your father's money," I reminded her.

"Yeah, I guess so. That's a downer! Maybe he didn't have very much," she added hopefully.

"Well, Christian can always subsidize you too—once he's gone to his Copenhagen, suffered terribly, and then becomes famous like his namesake."

"Oh, you're so cynical, Peggy—sometimes I think you're just like my father!"

Ouch!

"Fairy tales do come true sometimes," she went on. "They did for Hans Christian Andersen, after all. I'm kind of looking forward to being able to be seen openly with Andy—holding hands and stuff, I mean. But I don't know what I'll use as an excuse not to move in with him, if Christian and I split up."

"Just say no," I said.

"Now look who's talking."

After leaving Pia I walked through the children's library for one last look at the Hans Christian Andersen symposium. The meeting rooms were empty, their blackboards still littered with obscure scholarly graffiti, and not many people were left in the conference lounge either, but I recognized a few of the scholars I'd talked to, chatting together listlessly. Nobody turned pale and started to tremble with fear and guilt as I passed.

In the middle of the room, the large, pear-shaped Meisling was staring down at the stubby, gray Hostrup through granny glasses perched on the end of his little red nose. Hostrup's head was tilted back and he was poking Meisling in the chest with a stubby finger to make a point. Both scholars looked hung over and seemed to be going through the motions of quarrelling more out of habit than conviction. Pia had shown me a picture of the original Meisling, the one who had made Hans Christian Andersen's youth such a hell, and I was struck by how closely his descendant resembled him. Maybe this was the original Meisling, back to work off bad karma at an eternity of Andersen conventions.

I nodded as I walked by, but they didn't seem to recognize me.

In another part of the room, Eric Claussen was surrounded by a group of young scholars who, from their rapt expressions as they listened to him expound on something, didn't seem to have heard the phrase "to write a Claussen."

Floyd Hazard was sitting at a table in a corner with a pile of greasy-looking doughnuts and a styrofoam cup of coffee. He looked dispirited and tired, as though he'd been up late. I asked him how his investigation was going.

"Waste of fuckin' time," he said, speaking with his mouth full. "Whoever offed that sucker's sittin' somewhere with those fuckin' letters, laughin' up his fuckin' sleeve at us. How're you makin' out?"

"I'm close to an arrest," I said.

Thirty-two

At a little after three, I parked in front of the Claussen's home, a two-storied, white stucco house in a middle-class neighborhood a few miles from campus. Dark, rain-soaked leaves blurred the distinction between sidewalk and lawn and made walking a slippery business.

I rang the bell and after a minute Julie Land opened the door. She was wearing a gray sweatshirt over old jeans and tennis shoes, all splattered with oil paint. Today you had to look for her resemblance to Greta Garbo under her tousled hair and face without makeup. I wondered if Mrs. Donnelly's guess was correct, that she emphasized her resemblance to Garbo in public only to please her husband.

She led me through the house and then through a breezeway to a large room in the middle of the backyard. It was a studio, with skylights and big windows, and paintings hanging on the walls and stacked against them. It smelled of turpentine and paint, two of my favorite smells. A couple of my friends are artists, and I like to hang out in their studios when they let me.

"Help yourself to a chair," she said. "Coffee?"

I said sure, and as she poured it into two cracked, paint-smeared cups from an electric pot, I wandered around and looked at the paintings. They were large and seemed purely abstract at first, with vibrant blacks and whites predominating in all of them.

I stopped in front of a painting on the easel next to a big work table. Julie Claussen sat in a canvas-backed chair and watched me over her coffee cup.

"Maybe I've been around Hans Christian Andersen too long," I said finally, "but this one looks like a stork to me." I said it, even though I know how huffy abstract artists get when you try to find something real in their work.

"That's pretty good," she said. "It is a stork."

"You too, huh? I thought once I got away from the children's library, I'd get away from Andersen."

"I'm not a great fan of Andersen's stories—they're a little too sweet for my taste—but Eric had a book of his art lying around, and one day I glanced through it. I was amazed at how good an artist he was, and how far ahead of his time. He was doing collages and other kinds of modern art a good seventy years before the Cubists. Just from reading some of Andersen's stories, Van Gogh claimed he had the mind of a visual artist."

"Chalk up another convert for Hans Christian Andersen!" I said, laughing.

She smiled, shrugged. "Anyway, I decided to do a series of paintings based on Andersen's art and I'm really enjoying myself. I think it's odd that a writer of fairy tales for children is leading me back to realism."

I started to tell her what Pia had once told me, that Andersen's tales weren't meant only for children, but caught myself in time.

Once I'd spotted the stork, it wasn't hard to find other characters from Andersen's art concealed in the paintings, such as swans and dancing girls, harlequins and devils. "This is the 'stealer of hearts,' " I said, standing in front of a painting leaning against a wall. I wouldn't have known what to call it if I hadn't seen Denise Donnelly's copy of Andersen's original and gotten a lecture on it from Pia. It showed a gallows growing out of a heart, and a man—the 'stealer of hearts'—hanging from it. Pia had told me it was one of Andersen's favorite themes.

"Let's get down to business, shall we?" Julie said, glancing at her watch. "I'd like to get some more work done before Eric gets home. What do I call you? 'Officer O'Neill' seems a little too formal, even for a murder investigation. Call me Julie, unless you intend to arrest me right away."

"Peggy's fine," I said. I sat down in a metal folding chair across a little square table from her, and asked her how well she'd known Lindemann.

"Me?" She looked surprised at the question. "I didn't know him at all. I suppose Eric's seen him often enough over the years, at conferences and such, but I only saw him a few times, the year Eric and I spent in Denmark." She gave a mock shudder.

"What's the shudder for?"

"Just remembering that year—it's not something I do with pleasure."

"Why? What happened?"

"Nothing—that's what was horrible about it! I'd only just started to get a toehold in the art community here, I'd made a few artist friends and shared a studio with one of them—and then one night, out of the blue, Eric came home all excited from the University, waving a letter informing him he'd been awarded a Fulbright fellowship to spend a year in Denmark studying Hans Christian Andersen!"

"And you didn't want to go."

"Of course I didn't! To him it meant freedom—freedom from teaching for a whole year, the chance to get to know the big names in his field in Denmark, and to do research in the Danish libraries. But to me it meant exile."

"Why didn't you tell him to go alone?"

"I suggested it, but he was horrified—you'd think I'd proposed divorce. Eric was a very conservative man in those days—he still is, for that matter—and he expected his wife to follow her husband. And, after all, wasn't his salary supporting my artistic career? Didn't I owe it to him? Wouldn't he do the same for me, if the shoe were on the other foot?"

She laughed. "That was easy for him to say, of course, since he probably couldn't imagine a situation where the shoe would be on the other foot. But he was right, of course—his salary did allow me to work full time as an artist—so I went with him, hoping I could find a place to paint and other artists to talk to in Copenhagen."

She shook her head. "Not possible. We spent the year in a one-room apartment—and Eric's allergic to turpentine, which is why my studio's out here. We couldn't afford to rent a studio for me, and the Danish art community had no interest in a visiting American. The Vietnam War was on, too, and the few artists I did manage to meet seemed to hold me personally responsible for it."

"But you could have done *something* while you were there!" I said.

"Of course, and I did. I did a lot of watercolors and sketching—studies for the paintings I planned to do when I got back home—I accomplished a lot. Except for that, it was a wasted year for me, although I managed to hide the fact from Eric, I think. But it wasn't really a good year for him, either. The Danes are very possessive about their few well-known cultural figures, and they were suspicious and a little contemptuous of Eric—what did he think he was doing, trying to write a book on Hans Christian Andersen? After all, he hadn't got Andersen's stories with his mother's milk, the way they had!"

It was getting dark. The wind was blowing rain and sleet against the studio windows, and sleet was gathering in the corners of the skylights above us. Julie got up, turned on a floodlight, and aimed it at the painting on the easel so she could see it better.

When she returned to her chair, she said, "It was probably an omen that the year started out with one of the dreariest holidays of my life. It was our introduction to Denmark—and to Jens Aage Lindemann too. Eric and I had just arrived in Denmark and discovered that our apartment wasn't available yet. So we accepted an invitation to spend the Midsummer Eve holiday at a tourist hotel on the coast, south of Copenhagen somewhere.

"A bunch of American exchange students were there too. It was their last few days in Denmark, and the Danes

wanted them to end it on a high note—give 'em something
to remember the rest of their lives, you know! Ha!"

She jumped up, went over to the painting on the easel,
took a palette knife, and scraped paint off until some of
the canvas showed under it. An eye seemed to glare bale-
fully out, like the one in the stork in the Andersen room
that had presided over the murder of Jens Aage
Lindemann.

"Lindemann and his wife were there as chaperones,"
she went on.

"At the tourist hotel?"

"Yes. He wasn't the powerhouse in Danish literature
he became later, and he had to do things like that
occasionally—for international understanding, or something. They had their baby with them—your friend Pia."

I remembered that Julie had told Pia at the banquet that
she'd seen her as a baby.

She asked me if I knew about Midsummer Eve. I told
her I knew it was the longest night of the year and that
Shakespeare had written a play about it.

"Well, it's a very big thing in the Scandinavian countries, I suppose because their winters are so long and
gloomy. The Danes build bonfires on the beach and sit
around them and sing songs and get drunk. And in their
novels and films—so Eric tells me—if not in reality, the
kids drift off into the woods in pairs and lose their virginity and return to the bonfire with knowing smirks on their
round blond faces, and it's supposed to stay light all night
long."

I said I could think of worse ways to lose your virginity.

"Well, I doubt anybody lost theirs that Midsummer
Eve!" she said with a snort. "It was cold, and it drizzled
the entire time—just like now, except no sleet. We all huddled in the main room of the hotel and tried to pretend we
were having a wonderful time. Eric did have a good time,
because he was looking forward to the rest of the year.
The foreign students were miserable though, since they

were leaving the country in a couple of days. God, how I wished I could go with them!

"At dinner last Thursday night, Eric reminded Lindemann of that Midsummer holiday, but he said he couldn't remember it. I suppose he must have endured plenty of miserable Midsummers like it over the years, poor man, whereas I only had to live through that one. It often rains on Midsummer in Denmark, I guess. Eric brought out his photo album and showed Lindemann the pictures he'd taken."

She laughed without humor. "Lindemann said he didn't remember it, but I'll never forget it—or him either. He ignored Eric, participated in the student activities as little as possible, made a pass at me, and spent most of the time in a cottage away from the hotel, leaving his wife to entertain us. I did my best to help her, and the exchange students took turns taking care of Pia. She was a cute little thing—and she's beautiful now. I'd like to paint her."

"Could we back up a little way," I said, "to where you were listing things Lindemann did and didn't do? I think one of them was that he made a pass at you. Would you mind expanding on that?"

"Oh, dear me!" she said in mock horror. "You think Eric killed Lindemann on account of that—or I did—over two decades later, Peggy? You disappoint me." She gave a disgusted laugh. "I never even told Eric about it."

"I'd like to hear what happened anyway," I said. "I collect Lindemann stories."

"Sure, why not? It's kind of funny, I guess, in a sick way. It was Midsummer Eve itself—late afternoon, actually. I was lying on a couch over by the fireplace. Eric was across the room somewhere, poring over old magazines, the kind you find scattered around in tourist hotels everywhere. Lindemann strolled over to me and sat down at the other end of the couch, started chatting in that mealy-mouthed accent Danes have when they speak English. As we were talking—he was telling me he knew a lot of Danish artists and would be glad to introduce me to some—he picked up one of my feet and put it in his lap and, oh, ever so casually, began stroking it, as though it were a cat. I tried to get my foot out of his hand without making a big deal out of it, but he was holding it too firmly. He knew what I was trying to do, and I could see he was enjoying my struggle. After a while, he slid the stocking off my foot and began playing with my toes."

"You could have kicked him in the face," I said.

She laughed. "Now, of course, sure, I would. But twenty-two years ago, I doubt most 'well-brought-up women' would even have thought of it. Besides, I had Eric to consider. He was counting on Lindemann to help further his career, and if I did anything violent, the year might well have ended for Eric before it even began. So I had to proceed with great delicacy." She smiled at her own words.

"I tried to pretend I didn't notice—relax and enjoy it, right?—and tried to keep up my end of the conversation. It was rather unpleasant."

Just hearing about it, about something that had happened to a woman I hardly knew over two decades ago, made me angry, as if it were happening to me now. I had to remind myself that the cause of my anger was dead. Violently dead.

"How did it end?"

She showed her teeth in a smile. "Your friend Pia saved me from the fate worse than death, Peggy."

"Pia!"

"Yes, baby Pia." She laughed. "Lindemann, you see, had the use of a cottage down by the shore—he knew the people who owned it, I think—where he could work on his book without being disturbed by the American students or by his wife and baby. He asked me if I'd like to go down there with him—to get away from all the fuss. He said he could tell I didn't enjoy the spectacle of girls cooing over babies any more than he did. He would build a fire in the fireplace, he said, and we could sit in front of it and sip a little Danish aquavit, and I could tell him all about my art.

"What a joke! I hadn't tasted aquavit yet, but when I did, a month or so later, I realized that if I'd been dumb enough to follow Lindemann down to that quaint little fisherman's cottage, I'd've been a goner. That stuff sneaks up on you."

"How did Pia come to your rescue?"

"She rolled off a table that one of the students had put her on to change her. It was a low table and she wasn't seriously hurt, but she cut her chin. It was bleeding badly and she was screaming at the top of her lungs. I caught my breath dramatically, twisted my foot out of Lindemann's grip, jumped up, and ran across the room and into the crowd of kids that was gathering around Pia. I was grateful for the accident, to tell you the truth—I'd like to thank Pia for it but somehow I don't think she'd appreciate it. When I glanced over at the fireplace a few minutes later, Lindemann was gone. I didn't see him again until the next morning."

"And when he was here last week, he didn't remember that holiday at all?"

She shrugged. "I don't know. I caught him looking at me strangely once or twice, as if trying to place me, but who knows if he ever did? It was a long, long time ago, and nothing happened. I met him on a couple of other social occasions that year and he never tried anything with me again, or indicated he held anything against me. He was formal and pleasant, just as he was the other night. But he never invited us over to his place—or introduced me to any of his artist friends, and Eric didn't get much help from him either."

She paused for a minute, thinking. "He was a striking-looking man back then—almost beautiful. I would have liked to draw him, except I wouldn't have cared to spend any time alone with him. Pia has his mouth, you know. On her it's expressive and sensitive. On him it suggested vulnerability—the kind that seems to bring out the motherly instincts in certain unfortunate women—but I wasn't one of them, thank God! When I saw him last week, at dinner here and then at the banquet, his mouth had just become weak. I was surprised at how much he'd aged since that year."

"You hadn't seen him since then?"

"That's right."

"Don't you go with your husband to conferences abroad?"

"I went with him to Paris once, and once to Barcelona—both times just for a week or so—but I've never been back to Denmark. If by some miracle Eric ever gets another sabbatical—which he won't—and he wants me to spend another year with him in Denmark, we'll have some serious talking to do, because I won't go."

I asked her what they'd talked about at dinner Thursday night.

"American football! Lindemann seemed both disgusted and amused that a daughter of his would be living with a football player, and he wanted to know what football was all about. Eric's much too cultured to know anything about the game, of course, but I keep up on what's happening in the real world, so I could answer most of his questions."

"Lindemann didn't want to talk about Hans Christian Andersen?"

"Good heavens, no! What would a distinguished, world-renowned Andersen scholar have to discuss with Eric?"

"I've heard that Lindemann told your husband that night that he'd just signed a contract with our University Press to write an Andersen book."

Her large gray eyes didn't blink. "Did you?" She laughed, sprawled back in her chair. "And did you also hear that Eric got exceedingly upset and threatened to kill him if he went ahead and tried to write it?"

"No, I didn't hear that."

"Good, because it wouldn't be true. Eric wished him well."

"That's hard to believe. What about his own book on Andersen?"

She shook her head, smiled sadly. "It was going to be

the definitive work on Andersen in English. It was listed for years in academic journals as 'forthcoming,' but every time Eric was on the point of submitting it, he had to rewrite it—just *had* to add something more, something new he'd thought of. Like Topsy, the book grew and grew, came together, and then fell apart again. Finally he just gave up. Now all he does is write dry review articles that survey the year's scholarly output on Andersen, judiciously pitting the books and articles of the younger scholars who have taken over the field against one another. Eric's made quite an art of it," she added bitterly.

"Why would he want to murder Lindemann," she went on, "a scholar whose best work was behind him? Eric's over the hill too—except he didn't go over, I'm afraid, he went around."

Julie got up. "I'm sorry, Peggy. This has been—'not unpleasant,' as Eric would put it—but I have to get back to work now. If you came here hoping I'd tell you my husband killed Lindemann, I'm sorry to disappoint you. As a scholar, Eric's become a bit of a fraud now—I know that, I'd be surprised if his colleagues didn't—but he's no murderer. And I can assure you that he had no interest at all in those letters that were stolen."

I looked around at her paintings on the walls—powerful and expressive. "You don't seem to have any problems with creativity," I said.

She looked around her studio. "No," she replied, "I don't."

I followed her out of the studio and back into the house.

"What does your husband think of your success?" I asked, as we moved into the living room.

"He's always been very supportive, but the kind of art I do isn't to his taste."

I couldn't help it, I asked her why she'd stayed with him.

She looked surprised. "Because we're married, of course! Besides, he supported my art for many years, without complaint, before I made any money at it." Her eyes met mine. "We're very comfortable together."

Comfortable! I shook my head in amazement.

She asked me if I'd ever been married.

"No."

"Are you living with anybody?"

"Somebody's living with me."

She smiled at that. "Either way, Peggy, you ought to know the meaning of the word 'compromise.' "

It's not a synonym for resignation, I thought, but I didn't say it.

She laughed at my silence, maybe misinterpreted it. "We don't live in Hans Christian Andersen's fairy tale world, you know."

Lindemann had said that at the banquet. For some reason, he'd been baiting Clay Donnelly.

I stopped to look at an oil portrait hanging over the fireplace. At first I thought it was of Greta Garbo, then realized it was Julie Land's face as I'd seen it the night of the banquet. She was wearing one of those hats that were popular in the twenties and thirties—cloche? I don't know how it's pronounced—and she looked strikingly like Garbo in *Anna Christie*, a movie Ginny Raines and I had watched on VCR once, as a break from musicals.

"A portrait painter friend of mine did that fifteen years ago," she said, following my gaze. "I gave it to Eric as a birthday present. He thinks I look like Garbo, so I had the painter put me in something she would have worn in her heyday."

"When you dress up, you still look like her."

Julie held the door open for me and I started out. And then something occurred to me. I stopped and turned, puzzled.

"What's the matter?"

"You've only been in Denmark once?"

"Yes."

"You're sure?"

"It's not something a person would be apt to forget, is it?"

Denise Donnelly told me she'd seen Julie Land in Denmark, said she'd looked the same then as she did at the banquet.

"Twenty-two years ago?"

She nodded, watching me curiously.

"Right after you arrived in Denmark, you went to a tourist hotel for the Midsummer Eve holiday?" Part of me didn't like where this was heading. Another part—the cop part—did.

"That's right. I told you, Peggy, our apartment in Copenhagen wasn't ready when we arrived, so we accepted the invitation to spend Midsummer at that hotel—to experience the 'real' Denmark."

"You said your husband took pictures and showed them to Lindemann the other night. Could I see them?"

She looked at her watch. "I suppose so," she said reluctantly. "Eric hasn't even put the album away yet."

She went over to a table, picked up a large photo album, opened it, and handed it to me. "Eric only took a few pictures, because the weather was so abominable and he wasn't interested in keeping a photographic record of American students abroad."

I took the album over to a floor lamp, turned it on, and studied the pictures.

They were all five-by-seven color snapshots. One was of the hotel in the rain, a Danish flag hanging limply above the front door. There were also a few pictures of a gray shore, indistinct figures walking disconsolately along it.

"I think that's the cottage where Lindemann wanted to have his way with me," Julie said, pointing to a blurred little stone structure standing alone in the distance in one dreary snapshot. " 'My name is Might-have-been,' " she quoted, " 'I am also called No-more, Too-late, Farewell.' " She gave a mock sigh and laughed.

"Who wrote that?" I asked, glancing up.

"Rossetti—a poet who was also a painter."

"It could have been Jens Aage Lindemann's epitaph," I said.

The last of the photographs had been taken indoors, of about twenty people gathered in front of a large stone fireplace.

"That's Lindemann and his wife, and Pia," Julie said, "and Eric and me."

Once she'd pointed them out, I recognized Lindemann and Nancy Austin as they'd looked twenty-two years ago. Nancy was holding Pia on her lap, and didn't look much older than the students behind her. I also recognized Julie and her husband. She looked like the young Garbo with a headache, he looked young and eager to set about setting the world on fire.

The students were standing behind them in two rows—mostly young women, a few guys. They were all so blond, fair, and young—and so alike. I didn't recognize anybody. I would have been surprised if I had.

What had Lindemann seen when Eric Claussen had shown him this picture, I wondered.

"They look a little subdued, don't they?" Julie said quietly. "The last few days of their stay abroad, and it was cold and rainy the entire time. I wonder what was waiting for them when they got back home, and where they are now, and what they're doing."

None of the people in the photograph, certainly not Jens Aage Lindemann and his killer, could have imagined that the seeds of murder were with them that Midsummer holiday.

Thirty-three

As I sat behind the wheel of my car in front of the Claussens', the engine running, the wipers sweeping away the sleet-streaked rain, I pieced the whole puzzle together in my mind. The rubber edge of one of the blades was loose and flapped monotonously. I'd meant to get new blades before the onset of winter.

Feeling worse than I'd felt since I thought I was going to die two months before, I drove away from the curb and headed for the University, to see if I could find the only proof I would need to solve Lindemann's murder. I hoped it wouldn't be there.

I parked in the lot next to campus police headquarters and went in, gave Ron, the dispatcher that night, a wave, ignored his invitation to stop and talk, and hurried down the hall to Ginny Raines's office where the file cabinet containing the parking ticket carbons are kept—Ginny had already gone home for the night. I got out the carbons for the previous week and thumbed through them, looking for the tickets written the night of Lindemann's murder. One of the third-watch cops had written two tickets for cars parked illegally in the faculty parking lot behind the library during the first performance of "The Emperor's New Clothes."

I used Ginny's computer to call up Sam Allen's auto license from the Department of Motor Vehicles. It didn't match the license numbers on any of the tickets, yet when I'd met Sam coming from behind the library as I was walking to the theater, he told me he'd parked illegally in that lot and hoped his car wouldn't be ticketed or towed. It would have been, if he'd been parked there that night. . Last night, when I'd discovered that Sam lived just a short walk from the University, I should have wondered why he would have driven to campus the night of the opening of the play, risking an expensive ticket and getting his car towed too. Something had nagged at my consciousness, but the sight of Floyd Hazard parked outside Sam's apartment took my mind off trying to figure out what it was.

Bonnie Winkler had put the time of Lindemann's death at no later than six-thirty: What had Sam been doing behind the library an hour later?

I'd guessed the answer while sitting in front of the Claussens' home, and now I had the proof. I should have called Buck from Ginny's office, told him what I'd figured out, and let him take it from there. But I didn't want to read about the end of the story in the newspaper, or see it on television.

The porch light went on and Denise Donnelly opened the door herself as far as the chain would let her and peered out.

"Peggy! What're you doing here in this weather?"

I asked her if I could come in. She stared at me a moment, then closed the door, opened it again and stood aside to let me pass.

"Where's your husband?"

"Why? What's wrong?"

"Is he home?"

"No. Clay won't get home for another half hour or so. Why?"

"I have to talk to you." Without waiting for her answer, I walked down the hall and into the living room, the grandfather clock still marking time mindlessly at the entrance. A small fire burned in the center of the big fireplace, doing nothing about the chill in the room.

"Can I get you—?"

"No." I kept my coat on, and sat down in the uncomfortable chair I'd sat in before. Tentatively, Mrs. Donnelly sat down on the edge of the fainting couch, her eyes searching my face for the reason I was there.

"I just came from talking to Julie Land," I told her. "You remember her, Eric Claussen's wife."

"Yes, of course." She looked puzzled. "We talked about her yesterday."

"Yes, and you told me you'd seen her in Denmark years ago, and she hasn't changed at all."

"I know that, Peggy." She tried a smile. "My memory is quite good, thank you!"

"But you don't remember when you saw her in Denmark."

She shrugged. "No—nor where, for that matter. I've probably encountered her more than once." Her voice sharpened with sudden interest. "Why? Why are you looking so—so solemn?"

"Julie Land told me about a Midsummer Eve holiday she spent in a tourist hotel twenty-two years ago. It rained the whole time."

"So?"

"You must have been in Denmark for Midsummer Eve, Mrs. Donnelly, when you were an exchange student."

She sighed and looked sad. "No, regretfully. I wish I had, but I arrived in Denmark too late the one year, and left too early the next. Of course, I've experienced several lovely Midsummer Eves in Denmark since—but I missed it when I was a student, I'm sorry to say."

"You didn't miss it," I said. "You were there when Julie Land and her husband were."

She shook her head. "If she told you that, she's mistaken."

"Julie Land's only been in Denmark once, Mrs. Donnelly—twenty-two years ago."

It took her a moment to figure out what that meant—about as long as it had taken me. Then her eyes opened wide. "How could that be? Surely the wife of a Danish professor must have been in Denmark more than once!"

"Mrs. Donnelly, if Julie Land's telling the truth—and I can't imagine why she'd lie, can you?—the only time you could have seen her in Denmark was that Midsummer Eve holiday twenty-two years ago. She and her husband arrived in Denmark and almost immediately drove down to a tourist hotel on the coast south of Copenhagen. It rained and they were stuck indoors with a group of American students in the last days of their stay in Denmark."

Her eyes darted around the room, came to me, darted away again, and finally returned to me. "Well, what of it?" she said, almost whispering.

"The Lindemanns were there too."

She shook her head, her lips fixed in a thin, stubborn line. "I don't remember that."

"It would be strange if you'd forgotten—especially since Pia was also there and the American students took turns taking care of her. Where were you, Mrs. Donnelly?"

She didn't answer, just tried to look puzzled, but her acting was lousy. After playing one role for so long, she probably couldn't learn a new one.

"Pia and Christian have been friends practically since Nancy Austin moved back here," I continued, "and yet you never mentioned to Christian that you met Pia and her mother in Denmark. You probably even bounced Pia on your knee and played patty-cake with her. You may even have snapshots of that Midsummer Eve, as Professor Claussen does."

Her eyes widened. "You've seen them?"

"Yes, although I didn't recognize you in any of them—you've changed too much. But it doesn't matter, because once I'd figured out that you and the Lindemanns, and Pia, must have been there together that Midsummer Eve holiday, and you've never mentioned it to anybody, I knew why Lindemann was murdered."

"Why?" she asked, breathlessly, like a child who already knows the answer.

I took a deep breath and expelled it noisily. "Julie Land told me she thinks Pia takes after her father, especially around the mouth. But I think it's Christian who's got his eyes."

Thirty-four

She took it well, there on the fainting couch, her hands in her lap. "You'll never be able to prove it," she said. "But even if you could, it wouldn't necessarily mean I killed him. Anyway, I'm too short to climb through the Andersen Room window—or do you think I used a ladder, Peggy?" She smiled as though a funny idea had struck her. "Or did Clay lift me up?"

I shook my head. "You used Sam Allen. And I will be able to prove that."

"How?"

"He cut himself climbing through the broken window."

Her hand went to her mouth. "That wasn't mentioned in the newspaper!"

"That's right, it wasn't."

"You're bluffing!"

"No."

"Then Sam must have killed Professor Lindemann!"

"Is that how you want to play it? Okay. And Sam'll make a great fall guy too, if he's willing to play that role. It was probably some kind of queer thing: He made a pass at Lindemann, Lindemann rebuffed him, Sam reached for the statuette of the Little Mermaid. Or the other way around, of course. Sam could claim he was trying to protect his virtue. Sam's a nice guy, but I don't think he's nice enough to put himself through that for you and Christian. I sure hope he's not, at least."

She decided to give denial one last shot: "This is pure

speculation, Peggy. Even if what you think about Christian is true, I had no motive for killing Professor Lindemann."

"Oh yes, you did! To keep the knowledge of Christian's paternity from your husband."

"From Clay?" She laughed harshly. "I do love Clay, Peggy—but not enough to murder somebody to keep him from learning that Christian's not his son!"

"That's probably true. But if it became public knowledge that Clay Donnelly's wife had suckered him into raising another man's son as his own, he'd be the laughingstock of all right-thinking men—meaning the Sports Boosters. You killed Lindemann because you were afraid your husband would throw Christian to the wolves. You did it to protect your son, Mrs. Donnelly, not your husband."

"A mother has a right to protect her son!"

"We're talking about murdering somebody to protect a career in football!"

"No, we're not! You know better than that, Peggy—you must! We're talking about Christian's right to try to be whatever he wants! You know Christian, and you know how much he wants to be a professional quarterback—and you know how good he is at it too. Doesn't he have a right to do that? And do you think the Sports Boosters would let him, if they knew he was homosexual? If he tried to play after that, they'd see to it he got crippled or killed on the field, or hounded out of football!"

"I'm sorry, Mrs. Donnelly," I said, unable to meet her eyes.

Neither of us said anything for a minute, its seconds notched by the monotonous tick-tock of the grandfather clock.

I wanted to get up and get out of there. I cursed myself for getting involved in the first place. Pia's mother had told me to drop it. I wondered if she had any idea of Christian's paternity, and had guessed what I knew now.

I said, "I want you to tell me everything, Mrs. Donnelly."

"Everything?" she repeated, surprised. "You know everything."

"No I don't. I don't know what happened that Midsummer's Eve holiday in Denmark twenty-two years ago. And I don't know what happened between you and Lindemann in the Andersen Room last Saturday."

She stared at me for a long time, then began speaking. I listened carefully, trying to find the truth in her words.

She'd had such a happy year in Denmark, and she was looking forward to the Midsummer Eve holiday—she'd heard so many stories about how wonderful it could be. But it rained the whole time, and it was cold. The exchange students stayed mostly in the hotel, moaning about their bad luck, listlessly playing board games, helping Mrs. Lindemann with Pia.

"Then, on Midsummer Eve itself, Pia fell off a table or something and cut her chin. She was bleeding and crying and everybody was making a fuss over her. That wasn't how I wanted to remember my last days in Denmark, Peggy!"

Without telling anyone, she put on her raincoat and slipped out of the hotel and walked along the seashore in the rain and the mist.

"That can be so beautiful in Denmark too," she said with a little smile. "I could hear a foghorn far out in the bay, and the sand was so clean and so soft. I'll never forget how it was—never."

A man joined her then, coming up to her out of the mist. When he saw her, he asked her if she was one of the students staying at the hotel—he didn't recognize her. She said she was.

He told her he was escaping from the noise too. He didn't think a screaming baby was an appropriate Midsummer Eve song, he added with a chuckle.

He held up a bottle. Danish aquavit—she'd never tried it. He told her he'd got the use of a little cottage nearby to work in. He was writing his big book—the one on Hans Christian Andersen's influence on children's literature that made him so famous later. The cottage was cozy and had a fireplace—she could dry off and warm up in front of it, he said, and a little aquavit tasted good on a night like that too. She could stay as long as she wanted. He'd be writing, but she wouldn't disturb him.

She agreed.

"He built a fire in the fireplace, and then . . ."

She stopped to think about something that happened twenty-two years ago. And so did I.

"It was my first time," she went on, speaking so softly I had to strain to hear.

After a while, her voice clear and hard, she said, "I knew what I was doing, Peggy! I even gave a moment's thought to his wife and baby—to Pia. But I didn't try to stop him. I mean, I said no, and struggled a little, but only because a girl's supposed to—was supposed to, then."

"And you'd been drinking aquavit," I said.

"But I wasn't drunk—and it wasn't rape, if that's what you're thinking."

She'd been twenty. It was her last few days in Denmark and she'd been drinking. No, it wasn't rape. Men of culture and learning don't commit rape. They don't have to.

But I wondered why she didn't think it was rape now. This would be a good time to think of it that way.

"Afterwards," she continued, "he went back to working on his book. He told me I could stay there as long as I wanted, by the fire. He didn't seem to think we'd done anything out of the ordinary." She gave a little embarrassed laugh. "Then I did something dumb, Peggy, I asked him what it had meant to him, if anything. He turned and smiled down at me—he had a lovely smile. I was still on the floor in front of the fireplace, naked. He said it had been a wonderful moment, one he would remember for a long time, and he hoped I would remember it too as something good that two people had shared one cold and wet Danish Midsummer Eve. And then he returned to his work."

She shuddered, pulled her sweater tightly around her. "I

got up and dressed quickly, walked back to the hotel, and went straight to my room and I didn't go back downstairs until the next morning, when it was almost time to leave. Professor Lindemann wasn't there. Until the banquet last Friday night, I never saw him again."

"You could have got an abortion," I said.

She smiled and shook her head. "Abortions were illegal here then and I didn't know anybody who could help me find an abortionist either. Besides, I didn't want one."

And it wasn't rape and she wasn't drunk, either.

"So you married Clay," I said. "Didn't he wonder about the suddenness of it all? According to Mary Vedel, you two didn't even know each other until you got to Denmark."

She smiled. "Mary thinks I stole him away from her, so naturally she's bitter. But really, he fell in love with me and lost interest in her. I liked Clay very much, and we were close all that year in Denmark. I got him a summer job with Dad's firm while we were there. That's why he wasn't with us at Midsummer.

"Once I suspected I was pregnant, I—I put myself in his way. He invited me out, I let him get me a little drunk, and we ended up in his room." Mrs. Donnelly looked me straight in the eye. "We had to get married, Peggy. Luckily for me, Christian was a couple of weeks late. Clay thought he was a couple of weeks early."

"And you lived happily ever after—until the banquet."

"It was stupid of me to want to go. Twenty-two years ago, I wore glasses—big, clunky glasses. I wear contacts now. And I thought I'd changed enough in other ways so he wouldn't recognize me. Still, it was stupid.

"But I wanted to go!" she said, her voice rising. "I deserved it! *I* found those letters, *I* designed and furnished the Hans Christian Andersen Room, and Dad wouldn't have given the University the money to build the children's library if it hadn't been for *me!* Who deserved to sit at the head table more than I did, Peggy? Professor Jens Aage Lindemann?"

She wasn't certain until he ended his speech with the story about paternity that he knew he was Christian's father. He'd caught her alone afterwards, and told her he knew, but they didn't have time to talk about it that night.

"He said he'd seen Christian on television and his picture in the *Daily*. He said Christian looked like his mother—pictures of his mother, whom he'd never seen. She'd died at his birth."

And before watching Christian on television, he'd spent the evening with the Claussens, reliving Eric Claussen's wonderful sabbatical year in Denmark, looking at the photographs of that Midsummer Eve.

Mrs. Donnelly hadn't stood a chance.

He told her he didn't know what he wanted to do about it—it had come as such a surprise to him. But he promised to tell her before telling anybody else. He said he owed her that—courtesy.

She couldn't sleep that night, wondering what he'd decide to do. She stayed home all the next day, Saturday, too, waiting for him to call, but he never did. She even called him once, but his line was busy and she couldn't work up the courage to try again.

Saturday afternoon she went to the symposium, hung around on the fringes—nobody paid any attention to her. At four-thirty she watched Lindemann go into the Andersen Room. She went back outside and waited in the shadows of the oak tree next to the Andersen Room window, to see if he would come out alone. Pia came out alone instead, and soon the scholars started leaving the library too. She noticed that Pia had left the light on in the Andersen Room.

When Lindemann didn't appear, she went back into the library, knocked on the Andersen Room door. Nothing. Knocked again, louder. Then Lindemann asked who was there and when she told him, he opened the door and let her in.

"He didn't want to discuss with me whether to tell Christian," she said. "He only wanted to discuss when and how. He thought he was showing me consideration!"

"Did he tell you why?"

"Why?"

"Why he wanted to be acknowledged as Christian's father?"

"He said he couldn't explain it—not even to himself! He said he was surprised, even a little disappointed in himself, to suddenly discover how much he wanted a son, once he'd learned he had one. And he added that he wouldn't be able to live with himself if he knew he hadn't given Christian a *choice*—a choice Christian had never had, growing up thinking Clay was his father—of wasting his life on something as stupid and primitive as football or doing something worthwhile with his life."

"Like what?" I flared, suddenly feeling a little defensive about football. "Scholarship?"

"He didn't say." She paused for a moment. "He had another reason, Peggy," she went on. "He was furious with me for allowing Pia and Christian to live together as lovers."

"Well, that's what he thought they were," I said. "Incest is still pretty shocking to most people."

She laughed bitterly, shook her head. "You overestimate him, Peggy. He didn't care about incest—he said he didn't want Christian's children to inherit Pia's diabetes. She got diabetes through her mother's family."

"Go on," I said. "Finish the story."

"He'd been sitting in that chair under the portrait of Andersen. He got up and came across the room—my room!—and looked down at me and smiled and said I'd shown remarkable strength when I'd fooled Clay into thinking he was Christian's father, and kept up the fiction all these years. 'Show that same strength now, Denise, now that the truth is going to come out.'

" 'Denise!' he called me, as if I was still an exchange student in Denmark, twenty years old—I don't think he even knew my name in Denmark! I felt as naked as I'd felt—"

She stopped, swallowed. "I begged him to change his

mind but he cut me off with a wave of his hand. He looked at his watch and said he had to go to dinner and afterwards he was going to attend the play, 'The Emperor's New Clothes.' Then he tried to put his arm around me and as he did, he said, 'Be strong, Denise.' Those were his last words, Peggy: 'Be strong, Denise.' "

She got up suddenly and glared down at me, but I didn't think she saw me. "I jerked away from him, and stumbled and banged the little table with the mermaid on it with my hip. It hurt and I grabbed the table to keep from falling and the little mermaid toppled over. I caught it before it fell off the table and without thinking swung it with all my might and hit him with it!

"I just wanted to hurt him the way he'd hurt me and was going to hurt Christian! I didn't want to kill him—I mean, I did, of course I wanted to kill him, but I didn't *mean* to. But as he fell to his knees, I hit him again—and I think I hit him once more too, I don't remember for sure, but I think I did. The next thing I knew, he was sprawled on his face at my feet. It was horrible, the blood soaking the carpet and spreading around his battered head like a—like an *aura* growing larger and larger!"

She sat back down, and clasped her hands in her lap. The grandfather clock measured the silence with practiced indifference.

"I dropped the statuette and ran out of the room, out of the library. I didn't try to avoid people, Peggy, I just didn't see anybody and I guess nobody saw me either. But as I was driving home, I realized I must have left my fingerprints on the statuette and the table. I couldn't go back, and even if I did, I couldn't get back into the room—I didn't have a key. So I called Sam and told him everything. He was the only person I could think of to ask for help.

"He told me not to worry, that he'd take care of it. He broke in through the window and wiped away my fingerprints. He took Jette's letters and the photograph to make it look like that was the real reason for the crime. I wish he hadn't felt he had to do that," she added. "For one thing, it made poor Carl and Mary suspects. Sam didn't realize that might happen."

I was glad to learn that Sam didn't know everything.

I couldn't help asking her where the letters were.

"They will turn up again someday," she answered. "A long, long time from now."

Thirty-five

That was her story. Of course, by the time the case goes to trial, I thought, she'll have it polished, revised: She was nineteen, and drunk, and he raped her. And she'll cry in all the right places. Telling it to me, she didn't cry at all. I considered that a point in her favor, but, in my experience, juries prefer tears.

Then I realized she wouldn't change her story just to soften the heart of a jury and a judge. She would never let Christian's conception become the result of a rape or a drunken fling on the floor of a fisherman's hut, not even to shorten a prison term.

"Would you like me to call the police?"

I glanced up, startled.

"Or maybe you'd like to take me in yourself," she went on calmly. "I suppose that would be some kind of feather in your cap, Peggy, bringing in a murderess yourself, your first time out as a detective?"

"Do Christian and Pia know about this?"

She shook her head.

"Pia ought to know how her father died. And she and Christian should know they're half-brother and sister too."

"Sam and I discussed all that," she said. "I wanted to tell Pia everything right away, and let her decide if I should go to the police and confess, but Sam said I should wait until things quiet down. He pointed out that it was a decision that would affect the whole family, since Christian's life would be affected too, and Professor Lindemann was also his father."

270

"And when does Sam think would be a good time to spring it on them?" I asked dryly.

"On their birthday, in March—Christian and Pia have the same birthday, you know. Sam thinks finding out they're brother and sister will more than make up for the loss of a father neither of them ever really had."

I nodded. That made sense, especially since Sam considered that his strength as a director lay more in bittersweet comedies than tragedies.

I got up. Mrs. Donnelly got up too. She came over and stood by me and put her arm around me. "You have to do your duty," she said. "I know that. But I'd rather you leave me here. There's no place for me to run to, you know."

"Taking you in would be a feather in my cap, remember?"

"But now I think I'd rather wait here for the city police to come with a warrant," she said. "I'll have time to call the family lawyer and to prepare Clay and Christian . . ." Her voice trailed off.

That sounded reasonable, but I didn't believe her. "I think you'd better come with me, Mrs. Donnelly," I said.

She smiled, the first good smile I'd seen from her since before the murder. "Oh, Peggy, why are you so suspicious of everything? I don't want to be put on display, hounded by the media to gratify people's need to—to *gawk* at other people's misery, and then have to go to prison on top of that! I'm asking you for mercy. Let me kill myself. I can do it painlessly—I have pills. Won't that satisfy your need for justice? And if you don't tell what you know, it'll spare Christian and Clay. They don't deserve to be punished for what I've done."

Who did? I wondered. And what exactly had she done? And who would ever know for sure?

I walked to the front window, pulled aside the drapes, and stared out. The sleet had turned to snow. I kept an eye on Mrs. Donnelly, reflected in the glass. Behind her I could see the little fire in the fireplace and the grandfather clock in the entryway. It reminded me of an old judge I'd once observed in action. Among the reflections, I could see my own face too.

Would her death satisfy my need for justice? Human beings are too small to dispense justice, Buck had told me the other day, we have to leave that to God. We have the law instead—and television, the newspapers, the tabloids. Maybe that's why we are so small, because we're so willing to settle for so little.

I turned back to the room. "Don't you want to see how the story ends, Mrs. Donnelly? I do. Will Christian get a pro contract? Will he win the Super Bowl and then come out, shocking the entire sports world? Will it do any good?"

"Yes, Peggy," she said, smiling through tears, "but not from a prison cell."

"You're not going to kill yourself," I told her, "and I'm not going to turn you in."

She gave me a suspicious look. "You're just going to leave it like this?"

"I'm going to let you keep it in the family—the way Sam wants it."

I wasn't sure she believed me. A door opened somewhere in the back of the house, shut, footsteps approached.

"I have one favor to ask," I went on quickly. "I don't want you to tell Sam I know."

That seemed to convince her and her face lit up. "I'm good at keeping secrets," she whispered as her husband came into the room.

Thirty-six

I played my role as a cop in "The Emperor's New Clothes" that night, and went on playing it for the rest of the run—two more weekends. I changed into the costume that Sam had designed for me the bright blue pantaloons with matching vest, the yellow ruffle at the throat, the blue cocked hat with a huge feather in it—and went onstage: a cop pretending not to see what's there playing a cop pretending to see what's not there. I think I got better with each performance.

I no longer believed in the fairy tale ending, in which a child speaks the truth without consequences. But, after all, Hans Christian Andersen hadn't shown what the consequences were either. It wouldn't have been a fairy tale if he had.

I avoided Sam as much as I could, to the point where I caught him looking at me strangely sometimes backstage, but he never tried to talk to me about it. Pia called once and asked me how come I hadn't been in to see her at the Andersen library. I said I'd been busy.

"We make you nervous, huh, Christian and me? Or is it Sam and Christian?"

"You know that's not it." I told her I'd stop in and see her when I had time.

"Okay." She sounded skeptical. "We're not finished with each other, you know. I'm sending you an invitation to my graduation."

I couldn't help smiling, and said I'd come.

I told her to congratulate Christian for me on the team's having made it into one of the post-season bowl games.

"The professional scouts are thick as flies around him," she said indignantly. "They want him to drop out of school and turn pro. I told him he'd better not—they're just desperate for quarterbacks because they get hurt so often! Christian's got one year to go before he graduates. I told him a B.A. might come in handy someday, especially if he's stuck in a wheelchair for the rest of his life."

On the Monday after I'd talked to Mrs. Donnelly, Captain DiPrima called me into his office. Bixler was there. Buck wasn't. I was glad of that.

Hazard and I summarized the results of our investigations for DiPrima. It didn't take long. Hazard didn't mention his brief interest in Christian Donnelly's personal life.

After he'd asked each of us a few more questions, DiPrima sat back in his chair and smiled at me over a pencil he twirled in his long fingers. "Well, Officer O'Neill, this time you don't seem to have done any better than the city police."

Bixler had a grin on his face that an offal-eating bird might have found alluring. "Nada," he said, sneering. The man was a linguistic prodigy.

"However," DiPrima went on, ignoring the oaf, "I did promise you that if you assisted Lieutenant Hansen with this case, regardless of the outcome, we'd reclassify you as a detective at the first opportunity. You've kept your end of the bargain, so I'll keep mine."

For once it gave me no pleasure to see Hazard's already slack face fall. I didn't want to be a detective now, I wanted to get back out on patrol, alone and in the night where I think I see things clearly and feel at home. But if I turned down DiPrima's offer, it might get back to Buck, and he'd wonder why. And that might lead him to take a closer look at the people I'd grown attached to who were involved with Lindemann. Buck knows me all too well.

DiPrima misunderstood my hesitation. "You don't need

to take your failure on this case too hard, Officer O'Neill," he said. "We win some, lose some, all of us. Even your Lieutenant Hansen. With all his manpower and technology, he hasn't done any better than you."

His voice rising with conviction, he went on: "Whoever's responsible for Lindemann's murder has to live with the knowledge that he has an innocent man's blood on his hands—for I believe, after considering all the evidence, that the letters were the target, not Jens Aage Lindemann. Every time the killer looks at those letters, he'll remember their cost. Old-fashioned remorse, Officer O'Neill, may yet succeed in bringing a killer to justice where our modern police methods have failed."

He looked at me expectantly, as if wanting a response. I nodded and said, as I'd been taught to say it, "I see."

Author's Note

The letters Pia Austin is translating for her *summa* thesis in this novel are collected in *H.C. Andersen og Henriette Wulff, en Brevveksling* (*Hans Christian Andersen and Henriette Wulff, a Correspondence*), edited by H. Topsöe-Jensen (Odense: Denmark, 1959). The first volume of this work contains a biography of Jette Wulff by Topsöe-Jensen, to which I'm indebted for the facts surrounding her life and death.